# SHELBY

USA TODAY BESTSELLING AUTHOR

## MANDY HARBIN

"Are you ordering me to sleep with him?" Shelby Landry asked her smug boss as she stared across the conference room table at him. She loved her job as an FBI agent. It was a lot less messy than working in the garage back home. But in the three years she'd worked for the bureau, she'd never gone undercover alone. And even when she did work on assignment, she'd *never* been told she had to have sex with a man she didn't know. What kind of woman did he think she was?

"I'm not saying that," Rick, Mr. Smug himself, hedged. "The SEC has been cracking down on Ponzi Schemes ever since the Madoff embarrassment. The enforcement division had been investigating Feldstein and Baxter Investments for two years before even asking for FBI support. This is an inter-agency task now, and we're going to do what we can to help."

Shelby didn't like the sound of that. At. All.

"Mason Showalter is the newest partner at the brokerage firm. His connection with Blade Young of the Bang Shift didn't pan out," Rick said, practically sneering. It was no secret he didn't like those guys, not that she fully understood why. He'd been in the bureau a long time, though, so Shelby figured the reasons ran deep. Not that it made it right.

"He's on the level," Shelby said, cutting off her boss from whatever he was about to say about Blade. Not only was he a decent man, he was engaged to Anna Sue now, their former teammate who was still an FBI agent.

"I wouldn't go that far," Rick said but not elaborating. "We need to kick this investigation up a notch."

"So because the SEC has identified Showalter as a Dom, you want her to go undercover as a sexual submissive? I might lead a pretty vanilla sex life, boss, but even I can guess what happens at a *sex* club," Darrell said as he leaned back in his chair and folded his arms. Shelby could always count on Darrell to have her back. He'd mentored her from day one since joining the bureau.

Rick took a sip of the thick, black coffee he always drank and placed the Styrofoam cup next to his notepad. "Her objective is to gain his trust and see what intel she can garner. We don't know if he's privy to the illegal behavior at his firm. If he is, we can't tap his house or office without enough evidence against him. If he isn't, then maybe he can become an asset to us by getting information from the inside."

"Because someone going in to get info has already worked so well," Carson said, referencing Anna's last role as part of their unit.

Without acknowledging Carson's comment, Rick turned toward Shelby. "You're to obtain just enough to get a warrant. The SEC will do the rest. This is still their operation. We'll do our part to make the directors happy and then get out. We've been working on this too long already. We have other stuff to do."

"Bet you're glad you are a blonde, eh Viola?" Carson muttered. Carson Childers and Viola Lane rounded out the FBI investigative team Shelby worked on. Lucky for her, the enforcement division hadn't only discovered Mason's need for sexual domination, but also that he had a penchant for brunettes.

With long, flowing locks of the stuff, it was easy for Shelby to understand why she'd been chosen for this task. She'd been singled out for this particular assignment from the beginning. And not because of her mental assets. Hell, her specialty was linguistics. Under normal circumstances, she wouldn't have been considered unless the investment firm under the microscope had documents in Mandarin Chinese the F.B.I. needed her to translate. That, or they could use her mechanical skills like they had when they sent her to work at the Bang Shift Garage.

"Yeah, that, and I'm married. My husband was all kinds of pissed when I participated in that massage parlor sting op. How would I explain to him that I have to get nasty with a suspect?" Viola shivered.

God, Shelby didn't know if she could do this. She wasn't a virgin, and was definitely used to hearing and telling all kinds of dirty jokes, but she was also the type of person who had no qualms with the basic missionary position. What had Darrell called his sex life? Vanilla? Yes, she was a big ol' bowl of vanilla. Not even with sprinkles.

Rick sighed. "Let's keep this professional, Lane."

"There's a word for a sex professional, sir," Shelby finally said. "And prostitutes make a hell of a lot more money than me. Jeez, what if he wants to do this all in public?" It wasn't really a question she expected an answer to, more of a fear she hadn't known she'd had until right this second.

"I know this will be uncomfortable for you, but you don't *have* to have sex with Showalter. Would it make things easier? Maybe. But he and some of the other Doms help with sexual awakening when a woman thinks she might be a submissive. They have been known to engage in activities that do not involve intercourse. This is the angle we are playing."

"That's a big gray area," Darrell said as he glared at Rick.

"I know. But this is our best shot. She can't go in one evening with a wire and hope to get what we need. The man is very private, and it will take time to find out what he knows. If he knows anything, and that's a seriously big *if*."

"So she wears a wire, has some meetings with the man, and we analyze everything first before she gets too involved," Viola said, shrugging. "No need to go in guns blazing yet."

"Won't work," Carson said, frowning. "What if he wants to see her naked? We don't know how he decides to work with a submissive. It's the same reason why she can't wear a wire at all. At anytime she could be asked to strip. We have some very high-tech, inconspicuous devices, but they're not foolproof. Hell, for all we know, he could have some top-notch security measures in place to scramble the frequency, and that's if she doesn't get caught with one on her. The only way I see this working is going in undercover. She'd have to be the eyes and ears for us. Sorry," he added, looking at Shelby sheepishly.

"Agreed," Rick said. "We need Shelby to gain his trust so he'll let her get close to him and maybe even the more personal areas of his life. We only need enough to decide to bring him in to help us out or if we have to play hardball with him."

But the phrase *personal areas of his life* lingered in her mind. "How personal are we talking here?" she asked, gaping at her boss. Sure Carson had just teased about sex, but as the conversation went on, she got the sinking feeling her boss expected more from her than just showing up at the club.

He shrugged. "If you could get a date out of him, get him to take you someplace public, away from the club and any security measures it possesses, that would be a good start. We can record any conversation he has with you without needing a warrant. If you're someplace public, you could be wired without the fear of getting caught. That's just an idea, an option we'd have if it comes to that." He took another sip of his coffee. "The closer you get to him, the better our chances are of getting intel directly from the source."

"So I can't just come right out and ask him if he's involved or if he wants to help," she said with an edge of sarcasm, though it'd be a heck of a lot easier on her if she could do just that.

Rick slammed his fist on the conference table, startling her. "Use your head. That's what someone undercover does, Landry! You play along and get what you need through any means necessary." She'd thought of Anna and the hell the last assignment put her through, lying to the man she loved in the name of justice.

How many lives would this case try to ruin?

She knew the answer to that. One. One life. *Hers.*

At least Rick had finally answered her question.

Shelby was going undercover in a sex club and would have to sleep with a man who had connections with the company they were investigating. She could fight this assignment and be relegated to a desk job for the indefinite future. Or be transferred out of state like they'd done to Anna and be forced to start over with a new team.

Or she could suck it up and do what she needed to see an end to this case. There was really only one answer, assuming she honestly had a choice. Prostitution was supposed to be illegal, but apparently not if one's pimp was the federal government.

"Fine. I'll do it."

# CHAPTER ONE

MASON SAT AT THE BAR, looking through the dimly lit room. He wasn't staring at all the half-naked women—or fully naked in the case of Emory's sub for the night. He was just watching, monitoring the level of energy in the atmosphere. Some nights, the feeling was subdued, but others, it arced through the air, electrifying his sexual desires. But tonight, as was the case for many weeks now, it was almost dull. He hadn't lost his sense of need, but for some reason, he hadn't been able to latch onto an honest opportunity to feed his primal hunger either.

Oh, there'd been offers. Mason was one of the four Master Doms who owned the club they'd deftly named Scene, although Rafe was the one who managed it. Jedrek and Emory dealt mainly with ordering supplies, and Mason's finance background awarded him the dubious honor of handling the books. He'd tried to explain the difference between accounting and investment financing, but it had fallen on deaf ears. It was known throughout the club that all four of them were the owners, the Masters. And every sub in the place who wasn't attached to a Dom vied for their attention. Yeah, there'd definitely been propositions.

Problem was, Mason was bored. His friends and colleagues would laugh at him if he'd ever verbalized that. Besides owning the club, he was a new executive at one of the largest investment firms in the U.S. To those on the outside, he was already spread thin, but his professional aspirations far exceeded the average man's. He had every intention of rising up the ranks, getting as close to the top as he could without being blood related to the family who'd founded the company. And he would do just that. He sneered thinking about his new boss. That man was only there because he was in the family, but if Mason had his way, that prick wouldn't be his boss for long. He aspired for greatness and reporting to the runt of the litter was unacceptable. Mason had worked hard to get where he was today. Nobody handed him anything.

But business was second-nature to him. He'd even taken steps to achieve his latest professional goal at the firm.

He needed a real challenge now, one that he could only find in the company of a woman. He'd thought he'd found one when he'd met Cassie. They'd had a fun night together, but she'd been more into light play. Mason was a hardcore Dom. He demanded and deserved sexual obedience from his partners. If the women weren't willing to give themselves up to him completely, he just wasn't interested in anything beyond one night. Some may think of him as controlling, and well, he was in a way. But to him, there wasn't anything more beautiful than a woman letting herself go and entrusting herself with him. To be submissive required a truly strong person. The real power lay within his sexual counterpart, he merely the maestro to a woman's sexual orchestra.

"Well, what do we have here?" Jedrek said as he took the stool next to Mason.

Mason looked at him, surprised the man had made it that close without him knowing before now. He must've been really deep in thought. "What?"

"By the door. Ten o'clock." Jedrek pointed, and Mason followed the line of sight.

A woman wearing a leather skirt, stilettos, and a black lace top was talking to the bouncer. She had her hair pulled up, exposing her neck. Her collarless neck. For that to be so brazenly displayed, she was either screaming to every Dom in the room that she was up for grabs...or so new to the scene she was clueless. When she turned, Mason clenched his teeth as he saw her completely.

She was fucking beautiful. He appreciated the beauty in all women, but this one tipped the scales for him. He couldn't put his finger on what quality it was that made her stand out to him at a distance. Maybe if he got closer to her, he'd figure it out. One thing was for sure. She was someone he'd never seen before. He would've damn well remembered her.

"Want me to—"

"I've got this," Mason said, cutting off his partner as he stood. Since he didn't know her, she wasn't a member of the club, and tonight was closed to outsiders.

Jedrek chuckled...as much as the usually stoic man could. "Uh-huh, man, I'm sure you do. But you better get over there before one of the other Doms shows interest."

Mason grunted as he moved, heading straight toward the woman with dark brown hair. As he stepped up behind her, the bouncer grabbed her arm, and he heard her gasp. Mason gripped her hips and pulled her against his body, his dominant side roaring to life.

"What's the problem?" Mason barked, agitated that the other man would snatch her like that.

"Um, she's not a member, Mr. Showalter. I was just trying to explain to her that we're only open to the public on Tuesday nights." The man wisely released the beauty and took a few steps back.

The woman tensed against Mason. He lessened his hold on her, but didn't let go. "I'll speak with her. You can go."

"Yes, Sir."

Mason lowered his head and sniffed her hair. Even in her high heels, she was a couple inches shorter than his six-three. God, she smelled just as wonderful as she looked. "What is your name?"

"Shelby."

She trembled in his arms, and his dick stirred. He tightened his hold on her once again and stepped up against her, letting her feel what she was doing to his body.

"Why are you here, pet?"

"I-I didn't know this club was members only. I didn't mean to intrude. I can come back."

Mason wasn't sure if her stammering was because he was making her uncomfortable or because she was truly sorry for coming on a night she wasn't allowed.

"You didn't answer my question. Why are you here?"

"I, um." Her shoulders slumped. "I just need...I mean, I want to try something different."

At that, Mason turned her slowly to face him. Her big green eyes watched him as he studied her. Her skin looked flawless under all that makeup. She had a ton of it on. He'd have to fix that. The milky complexion of her cleavage revealed her true tone. But then he took what she actually had on and internally recoiled.

"You're dressed like a Domme." Why hadn't he considered she might be into domination before now? He cursed his body for responding to her as quickly as it had. If she wasn't submissive, she would be off-limits. Mason didn't switch. She immediately looked to the floor, her cheeks turning pink. His heart pounded at her reaction. Her body's instinctual reply reassured him she wasn't a Domme. "But you respond like a sub. Tell me, what is it you want to try?"

"I want to try submission, Sir, but I'm not sure how far I want to go."

Only one word came to mind at her confession—*perfect*. If any woman showed up at the club with the desire to try out the lifestyle, it was up to one of the partners, the Master Doms, to decide how to proceed. The situation hadn't happened before. The only inquires they'd gotten were some emails via their website with visits prearranged, so no woman had just shown up out of the blue. Until now. If she wanted to learn, he'd teach her. He didn't have a sub and hadn't felt like playing with any unattached subs lately, but for some reason, she ignited that desire, and he learned long ago to follow his instincts. Oh yeah, he'd teach her all right, starting with correcting her good-intended but wrong address. "Master."

Her head popped up.

"Call me Master," he said softly as he stroked her cheek. "And for the rest of the night, I will call you pet." When she didn't say anything, he continued. "Normally, a sub in this establishment addresses her Dom with the title of Master, as he has earned that right, and will call other Doms *Sir* unless, of course, her Master requires it or she feels comfortable addressing another Dom as such. But as you will learn, BDSM is filled with caveats all depending on where you play, who you play with, and many other exceptions. In this club, there is an exception to that *Sir* rule. All subs address me as Master Mason. Master Rafe, Master Jedrek, and Master Emory also have the distinction. Most subs are called pet. It's an endearment. I just told you a lot, but do you understand what I've told you?"

She nodded.

He frowned at her, giving this beauty an easy test.

"Yes...Master?"

He smiled. "Very good. Come with me." He wrapped his arm around her waist and guided her toward one of the couches disbursed throughout the first floor. He wanted a quiet place for them to talk. If she was interested in submission, he was going to be the one to help her, and communication was the key to that. He tried telling himself she was probably no different from the others in his past, but for some reason, he felt drawn to her. He wanted her to be a good fit for him...even if just for a little while. Maybe it'd help him get out of his slump and, at the very least, embrace new opportunities to dominate women who challenged him. He knew better than to hope for more.

Once they were seated, Shelby crossed her legs and placed her clasped hands on her lap. She was still tense, so he needed to navigate these waters carefully.

"Communication is very important, pet. For a man to fulfill your sexual desires, you must be open and honest with him at every step. Now, I'm going to ask you some questions. I want you to be completely honest with me."

"Yes, Master," Shelby said, whispering his title.

Mason smiled and rubbed her hands. Then he gently pried them apart and held one between his.

"I see no wedding ring on your finger. Are you married?"

She shook her head. He didn't correct her. She was very new to this.

"Are you in a relationship of any kind?"

"Nope, er, Master."

"Good. So you've never done anything like this before. Why'd you choose this club as your maiden voyage, so to speak?"

She cleared her throat and sat up a little straighter, her chin jutting out a little as she seemed to be gathering her nerve.

"I came here for you."

Mason gaped at her. What kind of answer was that? He'd never seen her before. He was absolutely sure of that. He would've remembered the auburn hues of her hair or the deep emerald of her eyes. Mason pinned her with his gaze. He also didn't flaunt his lifestyle. Nor did he like setups or women throwing themselves at him because of his money. Now he felt as if he was being played, which cooled any ardor he'd felt.

He was a man of control, but at this moment, he knew he had none. That fucking pissed him off, but he pushed down the need to toss her out without another word. He wanted an explanation, and he was going to damn well get it.

Instead of asking questions about her sexual experience, he'd switch gears completely and try to figure out just what the hell this woman was up to. His instincts about her must be way off, and that was something else he didn't like. He'd always been able to trust his instincts in both his personal and professional life. His jaw locked just thinking about both extremes. If on a personal mission, she would be sorely disappointed if she thought she could land him by pretending to be something she wasn't.

But she could also be tied up in something regarding his business, and that was another matter entirely.

Either way, he didn't take kindly to liars, especially those who did it out of disrespect for his lifestyle.

No, he didn't like that shit at all.

———

SHELBY WAS ABOUT TO BOLT. She couldn't do this. The man was very intimidating, much more so than his sexy photos had hinted.

Sexy didn't even cover it. The amount of confidence he oozed would make even an average-looking man sexy, and Mason was so far beyond that category the word *average* probably wasn't in his vocabulary. Even his hair was perfect, and his eyes? God, they were a beautiful liquid brown. Like smooth whiskey. He was tall, and his body had been very hard when he'd stood behind her. She felt her face flame at the memory. Yes, he had the entire package, and he'd been willing to help her just as she'd hoped—with the case, of course.

But now he looked mad. Strike that. He looked furious.

*Great, you just managed to piss off a tall, muscular Dom who might also be a criminal. Good job, Shelby.*

She needed to get herself together and stick to the story. She'd come prepared. Even showing up on a night she knew wasn't open to the general public had been part of the plan. She just had to play it cool. *Right.* Only that was easier said than done.

"I-I have a cousin who works in information technology," Shelby quickly began. "She recently transferred to California. Anyway, I went out to visit her a couple of weeks ago, and we started talking about sexual fantasies. I told her I'd never been truly satisfied by a man—um, I mean, the sex is usually okay, just not amazing—and that I'd often thought about what it would feel like to let go of any responsibilities in the bedroom. Um, I mean, I'd like to know what it would feel like for a man to take control. She encouraged me to try, but when I told her I was too scared because I didn't even know where to start, she mentioned I should look you up." God, had she gotten it all out without messing up? She was trembling too hard to think clearly.

"Why me?" he asked without so much as a pause.

"Um, Sasha said her best friend had tried submission with you once. My understanding is the lady seemed to trust you enough to try and that she really enjoyed it, but she was more into occasional play, so you two went your separate ways."

"Her name?"

Shelby licked her lips and tried to take a calming breath. "Um, Cassie Cope, but she's married now. I-I don't remember her maiden name, but I can call Sasha and ask."

Thankfully, the name seemed to click with Mason. His shoulders relaxed, and he nodded slowly. Shelby was able to find the air in the room and fill her burning lungs. This story was key to getting close to Mason. At first, they'd considered making a connection to Blade's family, but they needed a link Mason couldn't easily check out, and they figured tying in to his lifestyle would be the better option. The higher-ups somehow secured Sasha's help, providing Shelby a viable connection to a woman she'd never met and the man before her. It was a close enough link to Mason's personal life to be of use, but not so close that he'd easily find the holes in the story.

Going this route was the best chance they had to ensure Mason was the one who helped Shelby with her supposed sexual rediscovery. She hadn't expected him to walk right up to her, though.

"I'd heard Cassie got married," he finally said.

"When you came up behind me and that security guard called you by your name, I sorta panicked. I thought I'd have some time to work up the nerve to find you. Then you'd found me, and I started second-guessing myself." She laughed nervously because that much was true. She'd been ready to leave this place and never come back. Field work be damned...*hello desk job*.

"I see. Well, I apologize if I came off a little harsh. I'm a very private person—"

"Oh me too," Shelby blurted. "I don't think I want anybody knowing about this. I mean, it's no one's business what I'm into. I mean, what I might be into."

"Relax." Mason grabbed both her hands and put them in his lap, causing the butterflies in her stomach to practically riot. "I understand you're nervous. That's why we need to talk."

Shelby nodded, not sure she'd be able to find her voice.

"Since you brought up Cassie, you should know more about why we didn't work out—because it wasn't an isolated incident—so you'll understand what *I* want, and how I go about things. It might not be relevant tonight, but if we continue, I don't want there to be any surprises."

Oh shit, it was really happening. She tried not to flinch or make any sudden moves while mentally ordering her body to relax.

"I want complete submission in the bedroom. I'm not one to demand it outside of sexual encounters. Having a slave is, frankly, too much work, and my life is already demanding enough as it is. But in the bedroom, I will call the shots."

She nodded, absorbing it all. That s-word had her feeling anxious since it wasn't something she'd considered, but thankfully, it didn't seem to be an issue anyway.

"I understand trust is something earned, and will take time, but from the very beginning, I have to believe you are doing your very best to embrace your submissive side, giving yourself over to me. It won't be easy, and I'm not one to go lightly. Do you understand?"

"Yes, Master."

He flashed his smile at her, and she felt a tingle of happiness that he'd approved.

Then she frowned. She shouldn't be happy about that. This was a work assignment. She wasn't here for herself. She was here for the sake of the case she was on.

"I just lost you."

Her gaze darted to his, and he was searching her eyes. "Sorry. This is a lot to take in."

"I know, but if this is something you truly want, Shelby, you will experience pleasure like you've never known before."

But this wasn't something she really wanted. She was undercover. *No.* She buried that thought deep down to keep it from surfacing again. From here on out, she would not think about this as an assignment. She would make it as real for her as she could, so it would be as believable as possible. She had no other choice.

"Have you tried anything kinky before, even minor things like being spanked during sex?"

Shelby felt her face get hot, and she shook her head quickly. She might be willing to embrace this experience, but she wanted this conversation over like yesterday.

"All right. There's a process I like to follow when

training a new sub. If you can accept my terms, I'll agree to help you."

His gaze told her there'd be no negotiation on the matter. If she wanted to do this, she'd have to be on board with whatever he was going to say. This was it. Would she be able to do this? Get close to Mason Showalter and get the intel needed to crack this case? She was frozen in her seat as he continued.

"It involves putting you through four scenes. One each week. Normally, I'd want to start immediately if you're willing. You're new and a bit skittish, though, so I think you need a little time to adjust to the idea before we begin. You have to be absolutely sure this is what you want. Do you want this, pet?"

"Yes," she whispered. Jeez, was he not even going to tell her what kind of stuff these four scenes consisted of? Would they be public? *Please, baby Jesus, don't be public.*

"Are you free on Friday?"

Shelby nodded, unable to say anything.

"Good. We'll meet here, but I'll give you my number in case you change your mind." He stroked her sweaty hand. "This process will help you not only discover if this is the lifestyle you truly want, but also what you do and don't like sexually. Keep in mind, a submissive wants to please her Master, just as a Master wants to please his submissive. Sometimes one does things only for the benefit of the other because he or she knows it's what they want. This won't be easy, but hopefully, you'll reach a point where you embrace your submissive side, realizing submission is what you truly crave." He shrugged. "And if not, then you'll know for sure because what I put you through in these four scenes will give you a taste of what this life is about."

Her brain was swimming. Four scenes. She knew from

her research that meant he was going to do four BDSM activities with her, which may or may not include sex. She knew this was going to happen, and she felt her resolve settle in. She could do four. Putting a number on it seemed to make it more manageable. And one a week wouldn't be bad. It'd give her time to prepare for the scene and to decompress after it was over before another would start. Plus, it'd give her time to maybe work in some visits outside the club and get him recorded, maybe stopping her from doing all of them anyway.

"So what scenes will we be doing, Master?" It was slowly getting easier to call him that. Still felt weird, though.

He smiled at her. "I normally don't tell my subs the answer to that question, pet. The element of surprise plays a factor in building trust. But this is all new to you, and since this visit wasn't prearranged, you do need to know what you're getting into." He watched her closely before continuing. "First, we'll try spanking. It'll give you a taste of pain and help me test your tolerance. Next we will do bondage, then whipping, and finally, fire play."

Fire? Her mouth dropped. What the heck did he mean by fire?

"Uh-uh. I won't go into it any more than that. I don't want you focusing on the details while we are in the moment. Besides, we might not get to all of them if things don't work out."

"Work out?"

"Yes, pet. Depending on how you do one week will determine if we continue on to the next week."

"So if I'm not ready then we will wait?" She frowned at him. Why wait? He wasn't making sense.

"That's not what I mean. If you don't give me your absolute best while we are playing, then we will stop. We might stop during the scene, or we might finish it, but if I feel you aren't trying, or you're not as into it as you should be then our association will be over. I don't dominate women just because I like to order you around. I do it because I thrive off the response I get. If I'm not getting what I need, I can't give you what you need. It may seem mean to you, but that give and take is how it works. For me, anyway."

So not only did she have these scenes to do, but they would be like tests in a way. If she didn't pass, her opportunity to investigate him would stop. Period. She was taking a big risk for herself and for this case. Exposing herself like this could get them nowhere in the investigation, yet could totally change her on some level. She wondered again why she'd agreed to do this assignment, but then an even bigger question suddenly came to her, and she blurted it out before thinking better of it.

"Why are you agreeing to this? I mean, you don't know me." She knew why she'd sought him out, but she didn't understand why he'd agreed to it so quickly. It was wrong to question him because, at any time, he could reject her and she'd have to report back the failure, but on some level, she needed to know his reasoning.

"Because, pet, you came right when I needed a new challenge." He leaned in and gently brushed his lips across hers. Shelby gasped, and he retreated with a smile. "And I'm very much looking forward to it."

# CHAPTER TWO

M ASON STOOD inside his plush new office and grabbed his tablet off his custom walnut desk. The leather of his executive chair still had that new luxurious smell, one he would never tire of. When he'd been promoted to senior vice president of capital management a couple of weeks ago, he knew all his hard work over the years had finally paid off. Being in his mid-thirties, Mason was the youngest VP at the company, but he was also the only one who didn't have a wife and children at home who demanded some of his time. He'd climbed each rung of the corporate ladder with eighty-hour workweeks, new clients, and the appropriate amount of ass-kissing—though he loathed to look at it that way. He knew when to stand strong and when to schmooze. It was the nature of the business. He didn't make the rules, but he knew how to play by them.

Especially when they got him something he wanted.

He deserved to be where he was at today. He'd earned his position the blood-sweat-and-tears way, unlike his boss, who could only claim blood as his method. Not because he'd spilled any of his own. William Baxter was one of the founding members' great-nephew. He'd coasted into his position simply because of what coursed through his veins. The man was senior executive director of private clients and managed the funds of some of the wealthiest people in the world—a position Mason would do anything to get.

He would probably never become the CEO of Fieldstein and Baxter since he hadn't been born into the family like William, but Mason was content with his track to one day take over his new boss's position. Even if that meant he'd have to ruin the man's career in the process. It wasn't personal. Mason would never indulge in something as weak as emotion in his career. It was business, plain and simple.

He took the elevator up to the floor where the executive staff primarily worked since he was scheduled to meet with his new direct boss in five minutes for a conference call with some brokers. He knew how to play the game—come too early and William would think he wasn't busy enough, but come too late and William would be insulted by Mason wasting his precious time. It was a tune he'd danced to way too many times, and he never missed a step.

He was a shark when it came to business and knew the game so well he could go through the motions of his job, saying all the right things without even really having to think much about it. But that also afforded him the opportunity to be someplace else mentally...whether it was intentional or not.

As he walked into William's office, took the seat offered, and began to listen in on the call, his mind strayed to the place it had often sought since meeting the beautiful Shelby. On the outside, he listened to the execution of securities transactions, but in his mind, he was undressing Shelby, touching every inch of her body, kissing every exposed part of her, and bringing her to orgasm over and over while the voices of his colleagues droned on in the background. He'd envisioned paddling her bottom until it was rosy and hot to the touch, hearing her cry out as the confusion of pain as pleasure set in, and picturing her reaching subspace as euphoria took over her body and mind.

"That's an interesting point, Carl, but not why we're meeting. Mason will look into the hedge fund issue," William said toward the speakerphone.

"Sure thing," Mason replied easily. This wasn't the first time he'd mentally played out the scenes he'd planned for Shelby, but that didn't mean he liked her controlling his thoughts. He'd fantasized to the point of obsession, and that bothered him. He was a master at domination, yet could easily detach himself emotionally when it came to harmless play. For some reason, this one woman had perplexed him. He didn't know her, had never met her before that night, but he was already attached to her on a primal level. He'd found himself dreaming about her at night, moaning her name when he took himself in hand in the mornings, and getting lost in the pools of emeralds that graced her lovely face whenever he blinked longer than a second.

And he hadn't even seen her naked, had only held her and very briefly kissed her. That was all. And apparently, that was all it had taken to hook him.

He'd told himself it was just because he'd been bored lately and she was a new distraction, but even that felt false. He couldn't explain his reaction to her, but one thing was becoming painfully clear—he needed to get a handle on this sudden fascination. He didn't like it when he wasn't in control of anything, and that included his own emotions. He preferred things tightly tethered in all matters of his life, and when he thought of that woman, he felt frayed at the ends.

No, he didn't like that at all.

She'd come to him for guidance, and his sense of duty had swelled. With any sub he'd have had a hard time rejecting such a request, but with Shelby, he could not have turned her away even if he tried. It was that connection he did not understand but couldn't deny.

As a Dom, he'd easily put her needs before his. There was no doubt about that. However, as the man he was, he needed a dose of self-preservation. Hell, he'd wanted her to wait to be sure she was ready to submit, but instead, he was giving himself the time he apparently needed to control whatever connection he'd felt toward her. He could not let normal male weaknesses deter him.

As a powerful businessman, however, he really didn't need the distraction of Shelby right now. His plan for William had already been put into play, things already in motion, and he couldn't stop the momentum even if he wanted, which he didn't. He'd worked too fucking hard on his plan. It wasn't a good time to get involved with a woman on any emotional level. He glanced over at William and watched as the man continued with the meeting. *Yes, bad fucking timing.*

Something was going to have to change.

He clenched his jaw. He'd made an agreement with Shelby, so he couldn't back out. It wasn't that he was a man of his word. It was his role within the community that solidified his resolve to help once he'd agreed to. Only now, he'd have to switch gears. He would still guide her on her discovery as he'd promised, but there really was only one option for him now.

And he couldn't fucking stand the idea that had formed.

It did not sit will with him. At. All. But he saw no other choice.

Mason would be in control, but he was going to have to let another Dom experience what he'd been dreaming about for almost a week. It wasn't something he and Shelby had talked about specifically, but he couldn't see this working out any other way. If she wanted him as her Dom, even temporarily, she'd do as he instructed. This would be her first lesson—and a test for himself he hadn't expected. He'd never let another Dom top his sub before he got the privilege of doing so himself. He would have to watch as another man showed her the pleasure of the lifestyle.

That thought sickened him, which only strengthened his resolve. He could not, would not, allow himself to become attached to Shelby any more than he'd already become. This sudden bond wasn't healthy, and he was too powerful of a man to fall victim to it. Shelby was just another woman who wanted to experience submission. Period.

He was taking control of this situation, so it would not get out of hand. As soon as the meeting was over, he'd call Rafe before he had a chance to change his mind, not that he would. He knew what he had to do, and he was going to do it.

There really was no other option.

———

"WE HAVE new information from a source within Fieldstein and Baxter," Rick announced in the impromptu meeting scheduled late Friday afternoon.

Shelby was too nervous to focus on facts that were peripheral to the night's upcoming events. She'd entered

Mason's phone number into her cell a hundred different times since she'd met him with the intention of canceling their plans. No way could she do that. She'd be in serious trouble if she did anything to jeopardize this assignment. She was a nervous wreck who knew the score. She had to find a way to remain focused on her task and work her mark for information...somehow. One step at a time. If she concentrated on the immediate responsibility of the night, then maybe she'd be able to get through it. This was, after all, her mission.

And her job was important, even if she was picked for this assignment because of her looks. She had to be successful, so next time she'd be chosen because of her track record, not her bra size. Shelby had a lot to prove if she wanted to come out from under the protective shadow of her mentor, Darrell, and make a name for herself.

"Who's the source?" Darrell asked as he folded his arms and stared at their boss. "I hope the SEC isn't running around shouting to all the employees of F and B that they're looking for info. Kinda makes our job to help not necessary, don't cha think?"

Carson chuckled. "Yeah, not to mention flashing neon signs for the executives. If they get wind of this investigation, they'd lock themselves up tighter than a hooker with a poor man."

"You're such a sleaze," Viola said.

"Tighter than Fort Knox. Is that better?" he asked with a wink.

"Too little too late." Viola rolled her eyes at Carson. The man never missed an opportunity to flirt. "Anyway, his name is Carl O'Brian. He called his contact with the SEC to discuss some discrepancies he'd found within a hedge fund. He couldn't get the returns paid out to calculate based on the figures they were reporting. Since F and B is flagged in the computer, the contact reported this to our liaison, Jerome Parker, who then spent the last couple of days running the numbers. He couldn't make heads or tails on just how F and B reached the reported amounts either. Jerome called with the info a couple of hours ago."

"Viola then told me, which is why I called this meeting." Rick looked at Shelby, and she forced her knee to stop bouncing erratically under the table. "According to O'Brian, Mason has been assigned to work on the fund."

Shelby swallowed. "So Mason just went from someone who *might* know something to someone who *does* know something." Her heart pounded at this turn of events. She'd have to be extra careful. If it had been confirmed he was in on the crime, then being alone with him would make her extremely vulnerable. Under normal circumstances, she'd have major backup, but they already knew she couldn't wear a wire, and it wasn't open to the public tonight, which meant there would be no eyes inside the place besides hers.

"I think that's still iffy," Rick said, dragging Shelby out of her thoughts. "We only know he has a link to a fund that could be fraudulent. He might not even realize he knows anything yet."

It seemed too convenient to Shelby, though. She got the vibe he was very methodical, as if nothing got past him.

"What's the fund?" Carson asked as he clasped his hands on top of the table.

"It's the Culpeper Hedge Fund, named for founding member Edward Baxter's mother-in-law, Margaret Culpeper."

"That's one of the firm's elite funds. Mrs. Culpeper spent the last years of her life giving all kinds of money to charities. Society loved her, and F and B has been offering that fund in her honor for decades," Darrell said. "Always giving a percent of profits to her favorite charities."

"Correct. So the damage could go way back. When O'Brian made contact with Mason, our new mark was vague enough not to answer any questions outright while managing to sound as if O'Brian's concerns were overstated. According to O'Brian, Mason wasn't even fazed by the conflicts he'd found."

"He must be in on it," Carson said, sitting up. "He's trying to sweep the con under the rug."

Shelby agreed, but she kept her mouth shut. She knew that look in their boss's eyes. He wasn't going to make any assumptions. He would want concrete proof one way or the other before making an assessment. Normally, she'd concur with going that route, but *normally*, her ass wasn't the one on the line. An ass that might end up naked tonight.

"It's still too early to jump to that conclusion, Carson," Rick said, just as Shelby had predicted. Then he turned toward her. "But you're right. Before, Mason was just a possible way to get information since he was recently promoted, but now he's a link to busting this case wide open. We need to know what he knows. If he's innocent, we need to secure his help quickly. If he's guilty, we need to gather as much evidence on him and F and B as we can just as fast. There's going to be a lag time between the info you get and when we can analyze it. You'll have to make judgment calls as you learn things from him. Be smart about it."

As if there wasn't enough pressure already.

Shelby couldn't afford to be nervous about this anymore. She needed to pull up her big-girl panties and do her job. It wasn't as if she wasn't used to being in a testosterone-ridden room. She'd heard dirty jokes going up at her dad's car shop before she even understood them. She worked in a male-heavy career. Hell, her last assignment was working at the Bang Shift garage with mercenaries who had no clue why she'd really been put there. She could do this. She had to. This case meant F and B had swindled people out of hundreds of millions of dollars, but until now, she hadn't fully grasped how important it was for her to get Mason to talk. Shelby looked at her watch and stood. She was wasting precious time.

"I'll text Viola when I leave the club and report back on Monday. Right now, I have a date to get ready for."

She had every eye in the room on her. Some displayed hope while others sympathy, except for Darrell. He looked pissed, and if she didn't know the man was seriously dedicated to his career, she was pretty sure he would toss her over his shoulder and make a run for it to keep her from having to go through with this.

But none of that mattered. It was time for her to do the job she'd been selected for and see just what she could get out of Mason.

And hope Mason wouldn't take too much of her in return.

# CHAPTER THREE

Mason sipped his scotch slowly. He relished the burn, savoring the only drink he'd have for a while. He wouldn't allow his judgment to be hindered by alcohol. It had always been one drink before a scene to take the edge off and one drink after to help him relax.

But this time, he wouldn't be conducting the scene, not where it really counted. *Fuck.* He gulped the last of his drink and slammed the glass down. He'd made the right choice. Each time his body fought the decision, he knew it was right.

*Keep telling yourself that.*

The door of the club hadn't opened in seven minutes. Mason would know. He'd been watching it like a hawk, waiting for Shelby to arrive. He hadn't decided how he was going to break the news to her about the change in their arrangement, but he'd already brought Rafe up to speed. Mason had told his friend and business partner to give him some time alone with her before he came over to start. Rafe would be good for her...at least for introducing her to spankings. It was an area the other man excelled at.

When the main door finally opened and Shelby walked in, his heart raced as he stood. Jesus, she was a vision. She had on a pair of black jeans and a white blouse, nothing fancy, but the beauty was in its simplicity. Much better choice than leather. She signed in with the bouncer and looked around a little unsure of herself, but not as timid as she'd been the first night.

Her eyes met his, and he stood unmoving, waiting. He wanted to see how easily she came to him, and was immediately rewarded. She not only walked toward him, but with a sense of purpose in her stride. God, her will was an entity all its own. Beautiful.

Shelby stopped within a couple of feet from him, and her gaze dropped to the floor, an instinctual response that warmed him no matter the sub, but when she did it, his blood rushed in his veins. Instead of warmth, it was a raging fire.

"Hello, Master."

Mason reached for her. He couldn't help it. His arms were moving of their own accord, and his hands had clutched her as if they had the right. His. In this moment, she was his possession. It wasn't meant to last, but right now, he savored it.

"Hello, pet." He bent and kissed her cheek. "I take it you are ready to begin?"

"Yes, Master. I am."

"Good. Come. We have some things to talk about first."

Mason took her hand and guided her to one of the halls that housed playrooms. Some of the rooms were designed for scenes to be conducted with an audience, some had windows that allowed for viewing and intimacy, and a couple of them were completely private. He was taking her to one of the private rooms.

He opened the door, turned on the light, and motioned for her to enter while watching her reaction. Her eyes widened when her gaze landed on the riding crops on the wall, but that was her only response to the set up. She was resolved, really was ready to do this, to explore this side of her sexuality.

And he very much hated he wasn't going to be the one showing her.

Mason clasped his hand around hers again and drew her to the couch in the corner. A blanket was already there and tossed to the side for later. It helped with comforting after an intense scene and would come in handy. But now, they needed to talk, and it was a conversation he wasn't looking forward to.

"As a Dom, I must make decisions that I feel are best for you and me," he started, then took a resolved breath. "I have decided Rafe will be topping you tonight. His favorite play is spankings, and I trust him. He'll do an excellent job."

Shelby tried to yank her hand away, but he held onto it, refusing to let her go. He knew this was going to be hard for her—it was fucking brutal for him. He couldn't lose the connection of her touch right now. They both needed it.

"No. I want you. I only want you to do it," she said frantically. "This whole thing is hard for me. It's why I came to you."

"I know, pet. That's why I'll be right here with you, but this is for the best."

"Why?"

Why indeed? Because he knew himself better than anybody else, and if he started dominating this woman, he wouldn't want to stop until she became his for real. He couldn't explain it to himself as he'd never felt this strongly toward anyone this fast, so he knew there was no explaining it to her. But no matter the connection, there was no way he could encourage it. He had too much going on in his life right now, and anything that might develop with Shelby would get in his way. Any distraction beyond errant fantasies equaled a loss of control.

He would not allow that.

"Because you've asked me to dominate you, and as your Dom, I get to choose how we go about it. If you don't like the way I do things, then we can stop now." Jesus, part of him hoped she decided to quit and put an end to this insanity, but the other part demanded he do whatever she wanted if she just stayed. He had to stay strong, though. He would. To not be was failure.

After several long, agonizing moments, she finally said, "So Rafe will be doing the scenes and not you."

"No, pet. Rafe will be doing the scene tonight. He is best at spankings. Jedrek will do the binding scene, and Emory will do the whipping." There wasn't any chance in hell he'd let just one of them take over completely. He didn't want to risk her becoming attached to one of the other men. Besides, he'd assigned them scenes based on their specialties, so he knew she'd be in the best possible care.

"What about fire?" she asked softly.

Mason shut his eyes. There was only one person he trusted to do that scene, and there was no way around it. "I'll do that one, pet. I'm the only one who practices it enough for my liking, and it's too dangerous to let someone else do it."

Shelby nodded and then cleared her throat. "Do you expect me to have sex with them?"

He gritted his teeth. He'd shared many women with his business partners, but the few he'd been in relationships with he'd kept to himself. He wasn't in a relationship with

Shelby, but he didn't want any of the other men being that intimate with her...at least not before he could. But it wasn't his choice to make.

"That's up to you, pet. The club safe word is *red*, but since you are new, any indication that you want to stop, including saying *stop*, or *no*, or anything similar will be honored. Nothing will happen that you aren't completely comfortable with."

"We didn't really talk about sex before," Shelby said. It wasn't phrased as a question, but her eyes asked anyway.

"No, we didn't." He hesitated, thinking how best to continue. This was something else that would've been handled beforehand had her training been scheduled the proper way. "Scenes don't have to include penetration."

"I know," she said, almost too quickly.

"There are some who don't have sex at all, but there are others whose scenes are extremely sexually explicit. Depends on the individual. Personally, I don't like going into a scene with a lot of hard limits. I honor them, of course, might even entertain requests, but I want to be trusted to read my partner and for my partner to read me. In fact, I usually reject potential subs who are more focused on their limits than what they can learn." She frowned and looked around the room hesitantly. Mason realized he needed to be a little more open to help ease her concerns. "If you think about it, pet, the four scenes I use initially aren't directly sexual. There's a reason for that."

"But they can be very sexual."

He smiled softly. "Of course." Play *was* sexual, but it wasn't as if these particular scenes directly involved what she would consider sexual body parts. They could most definitely migrate to or end there, though.

She licked her lips, nodding slowly. Mason didn't think

it was because she agreed to his decision just yet. Rather, she was mulling it all over. "Um, can I request something now?"

"That depends," he hedged. When he'd said he might consider requests, he'd meant when a sub wanted him to do something specific. He got the feeling she was talking more about a limit.

"I-I'm not very experienced when it comes to men. I think I'd feel more comfortable—and therefore more open to this experience—if I knew going into this that...um...you'd be the only one touching me sexually. I mean, if it comes to something like that."

His dick twitched at the thought of touching her intimately, but if he did that, it'd defeat the whole purpose of letting other Doms conduct the scenes. He couldn't even think about the fire scene yet.

"I can't promise you that, pet, but if anything happens you don't want, you just have to say so, and it'll stop."

"But if we stop, then we won't go forward to the next scene."

Mason studied her. For a woman who really wanted to try, she seemed awfully concerned about the consequences of stopping. Maybe she was having a harder time since he wouldn't be the one topping her tonight. He'd try to be more understanding of her hesitation because he couldn't help with that. No matter how hard this was for her, it was damn near torture for him. "That's correct."

Shelby nodded without saying anything else.

It was settled then.

"Stand up."

Her gaze flew to his, and he waited patiently for her to comply. She slowly rose.

"Strip." He saw her throat working as she swallowed,

the rest of her frozen in place. "Shelby?" At this point, the discussion was over, and she was to do what she was ordered. Or stop.

She nodded infinitesimally and began to work the buttons of her blouse. One by one, she pushed them free, the pale lace of her bra peeking through until completely exposed. God, she was fucking exquisite.

Her shirt fell to the floor, and he allowed his gaze to focus on her luscious mounds before following the path of her hands to her belt. He spread his own legs to allow room for his growing cock. He wouldn't fight his body's reaction to her, nor would he hide it from her. She needed to understand what kind of effect her obedience had on a man like him if she was going to continue with this life after their time together.

She pushed her jeans with her panties down her legs and off her body before reaching for the clasp of her bra. Within seconds, she was completely naked before him.

"You're a very beautiful woman, Shelby. You're making it very difficult for me to let go of control tonight." She opened her mouth, and he shook his head. "You do not have permission to speak unless you are asked a question or want to stop the scene."

She shut her mouth and watched him. He nodded his approval.

"Just remember, pet, if you give yourself over to the pleasure, you may finally discover what you've longed for."

The door opened before he could say anything else, and her head whipped around to look. Rafe stood in the doorway, tall and as brooding as ever. It was no wonder that some of the subs shied away from him, but nowhere near as many as those who avoided Jedrek.

"Ready?" Rafe asked as he walked in and shut the door.

Shelby fisted her hands quickly before releasing them. Mason wanted to comfort her, but this was her battle. He had his own to wage tonight.

"Yes, Rafe."

"Come here, Shelby," Rafe said as he walked to the spanking bench.

Shelby looked at Mason, and he nodded at her. The fact that she deferred to him first made his growing dick rock hard. She was acting as if she was his sub. If only she understood what that did to a Dom. She walked toward Rafe. Mason stood and followed alongside her as if she was his to protect.

"I am Master Rafe. You can call me Master."

"*Sir*," Mason corrected suddenly. He knew he was overstepping because all four of Scene's business partners were called Master by any sub at the club. He didn't care. Mason was her only Master.

Rafe raised an eyebrow at him. "I see." Yeah, he just bet the other man was reading between the lines. Mason was asserting his leadership in the room, and Rafe would have to fall in line. This was new territory for them, but Rafe was a smart man. "Did you discuss the rules about safe words and stopping?"

"We've discussed everything. It's her wish that you not touch her in a sexual manner."

Rafe nodded at Mason and then turned to Shelby. "Sir will be fine. Please lay across the bench."

Shelby gave Mason one last glance before stepping over to do as she'd been told. She elegantly draped herself across the spanking horse, which left her ass canted upward for optimal access. Rafe walked up to her and bent. Without another word, he began strapping her to the piece of furniture in a quick, efficient manner. He knew his way around this piece of equipment so well he could work it in the dead of night without a hint of light. Once her arms and legs were secured, he stood once again and nodded at his handiwork.

"Your safe word is red, but you're permitted to use more conventional words to stop the scene. I would advise against using any of the sort unless you are absolutely sure you want the scene to stop for good because I do not take those commands lightly. If you are not sure or just think you need a breather, you may use the word yellow. I'll pause and decide if we're going to continue. Do you understand?"

"Yes, Sir."

"Very good."

Rafe walked over to the wall and selected a paddle. Mason braced himself. Once he let Rafe start, there'd be no going back.

———

SHELBY HEARD the sound of wood on metal right before heavy footfalls echoed in the room.

He was coming toward her.

This was so not what she'd planned. Jesus Christ, if her daddy knew his hard-earned classic restoration money was used to send her to college to learn five different languages so that her ass would be up in the air to be spanked, he'd have offered to do this shit for free. Well, minus the *tied up naked* part.

It'd taken her all week—all week—to work up just a semblance of a nerve to go through with this assignment, the meeting this afternoon sealing the deal. Mason could be a criminal. But he was also sexy. She'd be lying if that hadn't made it any easier to accept her fate. She'd decided she had a job to do and was going to do it regardless. As for the attraction she felt, she'd ignore it and focus on her job.

And then the prick changed the rules.

She'd been ready to flee when Mason announced this new little twist, but she also realized she didn't have a choice but to follow through. What the hell? Was this common practice? She didn't know if she should feel like a cheap piece of meat being so carelessly handed off to another man, or if she should feel honored that Mason was trying to make the best out of this experience for her by selecting specialized Doms for the individual scenes. The jury would probably stay out on that for a while. She kept her head down and waited, wondering when it was going to start. Having another man in the room would seriously hinder any questioning she tried—

Shelby suddenly flinched when a palm caressed her buttocks. *Shit, don't freak out!* She took a calming breath. Yeah, that so didn't work.

"You may scream."

That was the only warning she got before something hard landed on her rear. She gasped and looked up. She immediately found Mason watching her, his arms crossed over his chest, a look that rivaled anger etched on his face. She didn't understand why he was mad, but she'd seen him mad once before and this wasn't exactly the same. She didn't know him well enough to understand what emotion he was feeling.

Oddly enough, staring into his eyes seemed to help whatever *she* was feeling. Somehow, he grounded her without saying or doing anything.

When the next blow came, she squeaked a little sound, but was unable to catch her breath before Rafe smacked her again. Then again and again. Oh God, he wasn't stopping.

He kept striking her with something, the force making her breasts sway over the bench and her ass bloom in heat. It was too much too soon. She shut her eyes and dropped her head as the torrent of blows carried on.

"Look at me!" Mason ordered. Her head shot up, tears edging out of the corners of her eyes. She didn't know if she could keep doing this. This hurt. Who the hell got any pleasure from this?

The look he gave her brooked no argument, though. She stared at him while Rafe tortured her backside. The evil man pummeled both cheeks and the tops of her thighs with unrelenting finesse.

The heat in Mason's gaze startled her a little. He looked incredibly powerful and protective watching her. Undeniably sexy. And with the next blow, something in her changed, heated. She tried to squirm at the burn coming from within. What was happening? Was she getting turned on by this? Another hit, then another. Mason's gaze blazed. Oh God, she was getting turned on.

That wasn't right.

She didn't like this. She wasn't supposed to enjoy being beaten.

But she was. She didn't know why, but she liked it. God help her, she did.

When Rafe sped up, she finally screamed, releasing her anger and confusion in one long screech of relief. She sobbed in a breath when she stopped and noticed Mason had knelt before her. She hadn't shut her eyes, but she hadn't noticed him moving either.

"She's wet," Rafe said.

Shelby was too emotionally naked to be embarrassed by how turned on she'd gotten. Being strapped in this position left her exposed. Her legs were shaking. Oh yeah, she was wet. She ached to be touched. If she wasn't so turned on, she'd go from questioning it to being pissed about it, but right now all was lost to her except the need she felt.

"Move on," Mason said through gritted teeth.

Rafe grunted, and then Shelby heard him walk away. Was he leaving? Were they done? She didn't know how she felt about that. Something inside her screamed she wasn't ready to stop, but she didn't dare voice that.

Another soft sound in the background lit her ears and then Rafe's heavy, booted steps came toward her again.

She screamed when something long and thin stung her just below her bottom. He rapped it over and over along her upper thighs and lower cheeks while she wailed. The pain burned past the point of tolerance and soared into something numbing, almost pleasurable. What was happening to her? Her core flooded with need, and she unsuccessfully tried to wiggle her bottom. The restraints stopped her from moving an inch, but she wanted, needed him to touch her. Touch her where she needed it most.

"Oh God," she moaned. So confused. So turned on. So desperate to feel.

"She's ready, Mason," Rafe said, and then Shelby heard him walking away again.

Mason looked at her. The indecision warring in his eyes would've confused her even more if she cared to think about it at the moment. What did he have to be confused about? He wasn't the one aching for release.

"Pet," he whispered as he stroked her sweat-soaked hair. "You are doing wonderfully. Tell me what you need. I have to hear it."

"I-I." She didn't know what she needed, but she was burning for it.

"You can stop at any time, sweetness, and not be

punished. We can stop now and resume next week with the following scene, or we can continue right now with this one. I'm giving you the choice. If we move on, I'm going to take what I want. Do you understand me?" The look in his eyes burned with desire so strong that her knees would've given out if she'd been standing.

Her body shook. She could stop now and be free to come back next week or she could continue on and satisfy the aching void that had suddenly filled her, consumed her. Rafe's loud boots announced he'd returned to stand behind her, but he waited for her to reply.

There was only one answer. She knew logically she should fight it, but she didn't want to. It was the only answer to give.

"Please don't stop," she whispered while looking into Mason's eyes. Then something new landed so hard on her bottom that the air locked in her lungs.

# CHAPTER FOUR

Mason had to fight every urge in his body to take the flogger away from Rafe and fuck Shelby right here on the bench. She was the strongest submissive he'd witnessed in a long while, and his dick was so hard it could drive nails. But it wasn't only sexual desire for the woman that he felt. It'd been three years since a sub made it this far with Rafe, and a sense of pride also washed over him that it was Shelby who'd accomplished that feat.

Squatting in front of her forced her not to look away from him, but it also made it terribly uncomfortable for his erection, which was trapped in his leathers. He'd tolerated it as long as he could, but now that she'd given the go-ahead not to stop, he wasn't going to protect her from her effects any longer. He unzipped his pants and pulled out his cock. She looked down as he wrapped one hand around it, so he took his other hand and pulled her head back up by her hair. Just because he couldn't take her didn't mean he wouldn't be able to fully enjoy the display of her.

"You're so amazing, Shelby," he breathed.

She whimpered, and he knew she was just as turned on as he was. He smelled her arousal, her glistening inner thigh taunting him with what he couldn't have.

Then Rafe altered the angle of the next blow, lightly tapping her. She screamed and bucked.

"Oh God, oh God, oh God. Please!"

Rafe had let the crop land gently on her pussy, and Mason knew how fast that'd throw a woman over the edge. He wasn't ready for her to come. Not yet. And she hadn't wanted another man touching her. Granted, it wasn't Rafe's hand, but for Mason it was too much. He wasn't ready to give that power to another man. She was his possession, no one else's.

"No," Mason growled as he stood slightly and leaned over Shelby's back to snatch the crop from Rafe, but his dick brushed against the side of Shelby's head in the process, and something warm encased it.

Mason groaned, tossed the crop across the floor, and grabbed Shelby's hair with both hands to pull her heavenly mouth off his cock.

"Baby, you don't have to do that." He should chastise her for doing something without being told, but Jesus, he didn't want her to stop. He had to force himself to be reasonable.

"Please, Master."

Oh shit. She needed, and he'd give it to her. He was powerless to stop, his own aching body demanding nothing less.

He looked at Rafe. "You're done here." Mason didn't watch Rafe leave. Instead, he turned his gaze to Shelby, whose pleading eyes trapped him. The sound of the door opening and closing was the only indication his business partner had complied.

Mason moaned as he leaned forward, knowing he wouldn't be able to end this until he'd become an expert of every inch of her body. She opened without having to be prompted, and he sunk into her wet heat.

"Ahh, baby. That feels so good." He held her head still while he slowly fucked her mouth. She tried sucking, taking control, but he fisted his hands tighter in warning without ever stopping. This woman might be bringing him to his knees, but he'd always be in control of their sex.

She moaned around his dick and tried wiggling on the bench. He released one of his hands from her hair and massaged the bright red marks on her ass. She whimpered and tried sucking him faster. He clenched her hair to halt her and slid a finger between her ass cheeks. He kept moving until he was partially bent over her and his finger was poised at her entrance. When he gently traced her opening, her whole body began to shake. She was so close. Mason grabbed her hair and fucked her mouth forcefully while he stabbed two fingers inside her. She squealed around his cock, but he didn't stop. He kept thrusting into her in both places.

"You can't come yet."

She groaned loudly and he removed his fingers because she was too close to chance it. He grabbed her hair and held her still on his dick. "Suck it."

She sucked him hard, and he was about to blow. He needed this so he could continue. His aching dick was a distraction he didn't need right now.

"You're gonna make me come down your throat, baby. Do you want it?"

She nodded while she continued to suck, and then he began to thrust into her mouth again. The combination of her sucking and him hammering into her mouth set him off.

He roared out his release and kept coming as if he hadn't felt this ecstasy in months. Truth was, he might not have gotten off with a sexual partner in months, but he'd never felt anything like this before.

With the last of the twitches subsiding, he pulled out and moved behind her, not wanting to wait another second to taste her. He dropped to his knees and licked one of the trails of her natural juices up the inside of her thigh. God, she tasted so sweet, and her scent was driving him wild. His dick was trying to get hard again already. At this rate, it would succeed with that feat, breaking any previous recovery time his body had needed.

"Please, please, please," his impatient little sub chanted.

"Pet, I didn't give you permission to speak."

She huffed out a moan as her head dropped, but he really didn't have it in him to make her wait. He wanted to give her exactly what she'd craved. Mason inhaled deeply, drawing her essence into every part of his body, before he lowered and licked her slowly from clit to ass. She gasped and he did it again. Harder. Faster.

And then he was devouring her. He sucked on her supple folds, drove into her crease, stabbed into her opening, and made her experience a torment other than the one Rafe had dealt her. The spanking might've heightened her awareness of pain, but squeezing her ass while Mason consumed her would push her over the brink.

It took her a while, the torment of pain and pleasure, drawing her orgasm from deep within her core. It'd be strong when she reached it. He knew it with every fiber of his being. When her body tightened and her cries bounced off the walls in the room, his erection was back with a vengeance.

He couldn't stop what was happening now. The line had been crossed. Line? He'd been a fool to think there could be one of those with this woman.

He gripped one of her thighs to stabilize himself, puckered his lips around her clit, and spanked her ass in quick, hard slaps with his other hand while he sucked.

Mason knew the moment she came because the tenor of her cries changed into a shocked scream as her body quaked, a siren to his raging cock. He needed, and he wouldn't be denying that need. He pulled away and grabbed one of the many condoms in the room. He had it on so quickly that he was behind her, ready, before she'd come completely down.

"Didn't I say you couldn't come yet?"

Her body lay limp below him in apparent exhaustion, but her thighs were shaking with both the force of her orgasm and the need for more.

"Answer me." He knew he was pushing her now. But it was only because she was pushing him. She just didn't know it or understand it. Hell, he didn't understand it himself. So he used what he could to hold on to his control. He knew he'd made her come before, but he hadn't told her she could. It was a fine line between controlling her body's reactions and her realizing he could wield that kind of power.

"Yes, Master."

"Do you want me to fuck you, Shelby?" God, he didn't know if he could stop now if she demanded it. He'd have to tease her into accepting the inevitable.

"Yes, Master," she whispered.

"Say it like you mean it," he ordered as he put the head of his dick at her entrance.

"I want you to fuck me!" she yelled, and strained against her restraints.

Mason rubbed his cock up to clit, let the head rub it before positioning it back at her core. "Beg." He spanked the side of her ass. Pushing her, testing her.

She moaned and shook her head in denial, but she wiggled her ass as much as she could against his dick.

He swatted her again and again. "Beg for it, damn you!" He continued his punishment—punishing her for not obeying and punishing himself for needing it so badly, for waiting even a second longer than necessary to take her. His hand burned from his assault on her ass until she screamed.

"Fuck me, please. Please! Do it!"

Mason shoved into her hard and fast as he came over her, his chest against her back, his mouth at her ear as he grunted with the force of his thrusts.

"God, you feel so fucking good. Is this what you wanted?"

"Yes," she moaned, trying to push back into his thrusts. She would have to learn to give control over to him completely, but he'd save that battle for another time.

She was squeezing the life out of him as he fucked her, her pussy the tightest little heaven he'd ever experienced. Perfect.

"Ahhh, I'm gonna come," she warned. He knew with the first one out of the way, her subsequent ones would come fast and furious. She hadn't really asked if she could. They'd work on that later, too.

"Come for me, baby. Come all over my hard cock."

He reared up, grabbed her hips, and slammed into her forcefully one, two, three times, and then she started screaming again. Only, this time, he'd felt the telltale clenches right before she exploded.

Like a madman, he kept thrusting into her, lost in her heat, out of his mind with need. Within moments, she was coming again. She'd muttered out a similar warning, but this time, it was too much for him.

Mason bellowed as he came deep inside her while she crashed over again, the feeling of something being ripped from his soul almost too much to bear. He kept pumping until he'd emptied all he had to give into the condom and then collapsed over her, panting, drained of more than just the physical evidence of his release.

He kissed her shoulder and noticed the glaze in her eyes. He didn't have time to rest just yet, the sense of duty washing over any feelings of exhaustion. He quickly pulled out and took care of the condom, unlatched her restraints, and scooped her up into his arms. He walked over to the couch and snagged the blanket before sitting. He wrapped it around her as best he could and held her to him as he gently stroked her sweat-soaked hair. She was completely limp as she stared off into the room, not seeing.

Her first time playing, and she'd reached subspace, the epitome of submission, and she'd achieved it. Because of him.

This hadn't gone as he'd planned. He wasn't going to touch her, so there hadn't been a possibility of them having sex. At the moment, he couldn't bring himself to care, though. Oh, he'd berate himself later for not being stronger. Right now, he needed to tend to Shelby. He held her to him and murmured soft words of praise until she finally looked up at him, so open, vulnerable. In this moment, she was true perfection, and his chest tightened almost to the point of pain as he gazed at her.

It was a reaction he quickly ignored.

———

SOMEONE WAS SCREAMING.

Shelby was flying, soaring into the clouds as fireworks exploded in the distance. But the screaming was still there. She didn't care. She was airborne, the air whistling around her as she reached new heights, peaks she hadn't even dreamed of discovering before this very moment.

Then quiet filled the space around her. She was shifting, the world tilting around her.

Warmth. She was wrapped in a layer of something soft, pillowing around her while hot air fanned her, blanketing her in comfortable heat. The air was moist with a hint of masculinity. Breath? Was something breathing on her? She blinked and looked to the side. She was in a room that wasn't unfamiliar. She looked to the other side and saw eyes peering down at her.

"Welcome back, pet."

Master.

No. *Mason*. Mason Showalter. The man she was investigating. She looked down and noticed the red blanket wrapped around her as if she was a swaddled baby. She shivered as she tried to move.

"No, Shelby. Just relax. You've experienced something powerful. Just breathe for me." He gently nudged her head back to his chest. "Breathe," he whispered.

She did because she didn't know what else to do. She felt confused...but at peace. She also felt something else when she shifted. Her rear end was on fire. That really big man had used various implements to spank her. At first, she'd tried detaching herself so she could just get through the night. She'd told herself she wouldn't do that, that she would fully immerse herself in this experience, but that had been when she thought Mason would be the one dealing out the sexual torture. The game had changed. But even her newly found determination to distance herself from the other man hadn't lasted long. She quickly found herself sinking into the abyss with the onslaught of his ministrations. She looked around again, but didn't see him.

"Where's Master Rafe?" she muttered, mostly to herself.

"He left a while ago, Shelby."

She nodded as her brain fast-forwarded to that moment, and then she gasped, her head whipping in Mason's direction. She stared at him as the final pieces clicked into place. They'd had sex. Oh God. She'd sucked his dick. Then he'd...then they'd... Oh. God. Her face was now burning almost as much as her ass.

He tsked and shook his head. "You have no reason to be embarrassed, pet. It's not uncommon for a sub to experience subspace. It doesn't happen all the time, and I honestly didn't expect you to experience it on your first night, but it's totally natural. I hear it's very euphoric."

Sub-*what?* What was he talking about? Whatever it was, he seemed to think her flaming face was due to her momentary memory loss. He couldn't be farther from the truth. She had to get away from him. She hadn't wanted to have sex with him.

*Oh really? Then why did you beg for it?*

She slammed the door shut on that thought. She had a job to do. That's why. It was because of her job. And it was because of her mission that she needed to get away now. She'd accomplished getting close, but that was all she could do tonight. No way was she in the right mindset to get information out of him right now. She was already feeling something she couldn't put her finger on. Trapped? Maybe, but not quite. Whatever it was, it was uncomfortable, unnatural...yet not.

"I have to go."

Mason narrowed his eyes. "Why?"

"I, er, I'm supposed to meet someone." That was partially true.

"You set up a date after our scene?" The incredulity in his tone almost made her wince. The angry glint in his eyes made her want to explain.

"No. I have a friend. Viola. She knows I'm here. It's a safety thing." The tick in his jaw had her scrambling to finish. "I-I wasn't sure what all would happen tonight, and she was worried about me. She insisted I meet up with her afterward, or she told me she'd have the cops bust down the door and come searching for me." Again, partially true, but true enough.

Mason took a deep breath. "I see. But here's another lesson for you. Recovery time isn't just for the sub. You need to be held and comforted just as much as I need to do those things for you. It's part of building that trust between us."

She swallowed as she looked up at him. Did he expect them to bond over this? He'd let another man beat her ass, and then he'd fucked her while she was strapped to a bench. She might've wanted it at the time, but now that the haze of lust had lifted, she was able to think a little clearer. She refused to think about how much she'd wanted him earlier, or how sexy he was, or how being in his arms made her feel. Right now, she just wanted to leave.

He sighed. "Okay, pet. This is enough for one night. Next time, don't make plans afterward. I don't like being rushed, but I applaud your friend's safety instincts."

"Um, she'll want a timeline," Shelby quickly said. She couldn't just give this man an indefinite amount of time.

She might be new to this BDSM stuff, but the next scene was supposed to be bondage, which implied being tied up. No way was she going to let him tie her up for hours on end with no fallback plan.

*You were just bound to a spanking bench for lord knows how long.* Again with the voice in her head. She shut it out too. Thinking about that stuff would make her actually accept what had happened. It was better to ignore it. At least until she got out of this man's arms.

"Too bad, Shelby. You'll have to trust me to protect you. If you don't want to try, then we'll call an end to this right now." He licked his lips and lowered his head. "Is that what you want?"

She shivered. What was this man doing to her? No, she was *not* going there right now. She'd do nothing but think—obsess, really—once she left. But maybe she could get a little something out of him, a nugget of information at least, so she could focus on *that* rather than the events that had happened. Doubtful, but she was desperate.

"No," she answered. "But are you going to tell me anything about you, or is that something that's off limits?" She heard the sarcastic edge to her voice, but right now, she couldn't control her conflicting emotions. She'd just had sex with a man she hardly knew. In a sex club, tied to a bench, while being spanked. With a possible criminal. And she'd wanted it. *Begged* for it. She shuddered. No matter how hard she tried not to contemplate what had happened, her mind—and body—were demanding it. She was losing the battle very quickly, and that was assuming she had a fighting chance to begin with.

God, she should've just left without opening her mouth. Apparently, her obsessive thoughts weren't going to wait for their assault on her psyche.

He smiled. And what a sexy-ass smile it was. "What would you like to know, Shelby?"

Damn him for being so attractive.

"Um, well, any man I've dated—not that we're dating," she added quickly. "Just any man I've seen in a romantic capacity at all, I've at least known what he does for a living." She shrugged, hoping she sounded nonchalant.

"Fair enough. I'm an investment broker."

Okay. This she could do. Focus on the conversation. She wrinkled her nose. "That sounds positively boring."

He laughed, a genuine sound she hadn't heard from him before. "You think that's bad? I also do the accounting for this club. My partners seem to think investment and accounting go hand-in-hand."

She smiled as she digested the information. He did the accounting for the club. That was very interesting. "What do you mean by partners?" Although she knew the answer to that based on the investigation file on him, and could find just about anything on him with a few computer searches, but small talk could lead to helpful information.

"The other Master Doms I told you about and I own this club. Rafe and Emory go way back. They'd frequented many of the sex clubs in the area, but were never happy with what they'd found. We've been friends for about ten years, and about four years ago, we partnered with Jedrek Carter to open Scene. It's more a labor of love than of money, though we stay afloat." He smiled back at her. "Anything else you'd like to know?"

"You asked me before if I was married. Have you ever been married?"

"Nope. Never."

"Good," she breathed, then slightly shook her head at

that immediate reaction. It didn't matter that he'd never been married. She wasn't here for personal attachments.

*So sex wasn't personal?* She wanted to groan, but somehow refrained.

"What do you do for a living, Shelby?"

She looked at him through the corner of her eye. "I'm not sure I want to say. It might taint your perception of me."

He chuckled. "Well then, now you *have* to tell me."

She smiled and gave the answer she'd prepared to give when her profession was addressed. "I'm a massage therapist."

"Now why would that taint my perception of you?" he asked as he playfully tapped the tip of her nose.

"Well, for one, I help people cope with pain, yet you dish it out. Sorta makes me look like a woman who doesn't know what she wants." Shelby shrugged. "And two, if I had a nickel for every time a male customer asked me if I gave 'happy endings,' it'd be the only currency I'd ever have to use." He chuckled, but she continued, "You might think I was the type of person who did that for strangers since I sought you out for my own sexual experience."

Mason frowned at her then. She didn't like it when he did that. It was as if she'd disappointed him somehow. But that shouldn't matter. *He* shouldn't matter. Not beyond this case.

"Shelby, your profession doesn't define who you are. You'll learn there are all walks of life that dabble in this life. Police officers, doctors, those who stitch up wounds by day, may do bloodletting play at night. You can certainly help clients with their pain, but enjoy being spanked. Hell, experiencing various levels of pain could actually help you in treating your clients."

Shelby gaped at him. She knew Mason was talking

about her cover job, not her role with the FBI, but she couldn't help but apply it to her real life. She'd always felt the FBI did define her. Hell, the bureau had basically ordered her to have sex with this person of interest. And she'd complied with little question.

*And you liked it.*

Definitely time to go.

"As for the 'happy endings' comment, I really can't blame them for trying." She blinked at him, trying to clear her thoughts as he pulled her back into the conversation.

"Yeah, well, it's illegal."

"Sometimes legality is just a frame of mind. There's too much gray area for there to always be right and wrong."

*Spoken like a criminal.* She shifted and stood. This time, Mason not only let her, but he guided her and stood with her.

"I'll be here next week."

He lifted his hands and gently stroked her cheeks. Then he ran his fingers into her hair and tilted her head back. She gasped at the sudden power he emanated. He should scare her.

He did...but not for reasons she could prepare for.

"I'll be looking forward to it," he murmured as he lowered his head. He brushed his lips across hers, then took her top lip between his two lips. His mouth was soft and hot as he tasted her. She moaned softly, body tingling all over still from his earlier attention. His mouth covered hers completely, and he kissed her fully for the first time. She'd never had sex with a man before the first *real* kiss. But this right here felt more intimate than what they'd gone through tonight. Heat flooded her, and she did her best not to grab him and kiss him harder. He controlled it anyway, took what he wanted, and she was way too eager giving it.

As he devoured her mouth, she knew right then no matter how much she tried to remain detached on this mission, she wouldn't be able to deny this man anything.

She liked everything he did to her.

Every single bit of it.

## CHAPTER FIVE

Shelby sat across from Viola at lunch on Monday, barely eating her sandwich and fries. She was both mentally and physically exhausted after giving her *very uncomfortable* report on Friday night's events to her team members. It had taken nearly two hours this morning for her to divulge almost everything. Almost.

She'd omitted the part where she actually had intercourse with a possible criminal. She hadn't been asked pointblank, but her description had been very detailed otherwise, so Shelby figured her boss hadn't had a reason to suspect there'd been more. She wasn't ready to admit that. She didn't know if she ever would be. Regardless, if Rick ever found out she'd left that one tiny detail out of her official investigation, there'd be hell to pay. There was no going back now.

True on so many levels.

"So, does it hurt to sit down?" Viola asked with a sympathetic wince.

Boy, did it ever. "I was still numb most of Saturday.

Yesterday, I started hurting, and today, I feel like I've been through a really tough workout. I should be back to normal in a couple of days." Though, she couldn't deny the memories that flooded her every time she moved.

"Which means you'll be ready for the next event."

"Scene," Shelby corrected, not wanting to think about it just yet.

"Right," Viola said as she dug into her salad. "Do you really think he believed the massage therapist cover?"

Shelby nodded. "It was a good idea. Since we went through training for that op last year, I wouldn't have any problem doing it if it came to that. Easy profession to be self-employed in, too, which helps me out if he does any digging."

"You're welcome," Viola said, smiling. She'd been the one to suggest it to the team. "It's hard to trace a job like that. Some states don't even regulate that profession." She chuckled. "Which is why we were called in last year."

Shelby picked up a French fry and nibbled on it, contemplating if she could confide in Viola. Work was her life. She didn't have time for friends not connected to the bureau, but she did consider Viola a friend. Of course, she was closest to Darrell on the team, but no way would she tell her mentor she'd gone all the way with their mark. He already didn't like the idea of her working the case. More importantly, he was a by-the-books kind of man. If she told him details she'd left out in the meeting, he'd scold her for such a rookie move and demand she immediately bring Rick up to speed. He was definitely out.

She was friends with Anna Sue, too, but she was back in Arkansas. Shelby had been put on assignment there and hung out with Xan and Roxie some off the clock. Even visited with Maya and Heather. But Shelby didn't know those ladies well enough to reach out about something personal. In fact, except for Anna Sue, she was closer to the Bang Shift men than she was the women in that town. It wasn't surprising considering her upbringing, not that it did her any good with this predicament.

All that was left was her family. Her male family. Her dad, an old-school grease monkey. *No.* Her brother, Axle, a badass Navy SEAL. *Hell no.* Shelby couldn't even think about talking to them about this assignment. No freaking way.

If she was going to tiptoe into this subject with anyone, she'd rather talk to another woman anyway. And that conversation would be much better to have face-to-face, an opportunity she was currently in.

Shelby had spent a lot of time with Viola on assignments and hanging out during down time. The woman was a heck of an agent and a good friend. Plus, she was also a woman. She couldn't tell her everything. No way would Shelby even think of testing the female bonds of friendship by putting her colleague in an awkward position of having to report her. But maybe she could touch on some stuff without going into too much detail, talk about things she couldn't really bring up in the middle of a status meeting in front of a bunch of men.

"Have you ever experienced anything, um, sexual of this magnitude?" Shelby finally asked. If she could somehow get a handle on her conflicted emotions, maybe it'd be easier for her to compartmentalize what was happening.

"No. Well, Dave once used my handcuffs on me while we were having sex. Big mistake. You know they pad the toy ones for a reason. My wrists got abraded, and we had to stop. It ended up killing the mood."

No bureau issued handcuffs. *Check.*

"Why do you ask?" Viola frowned at her and put her fork down. Shelby didn't like that look of concern crossing her colleague's face. "Honey, if you need to talk to someone, you should go see the counselor. He's trained to deal with law enforcement stressors."

Shelby did *not* want a psych eval over this. "It's okay. I'm just new to the lifestyle. A little curious how common it is."

Viola arched a perfectly manicured eyebrow. "You're not new to the lifestyle, honey. You're investigating a person of interest."

Shelby swallowed. "Right. Of course. I know that. I'm just trying to fully submerse myself into the case."

Viola nodded and picked up her fork again. "Makes sense, I guess." She stabbed at her salad.

Really? Because nothing made sense to Shelby. She was floundering in the sea of the unknown and didn't know how she could wrap her head around everything.

As soon as she'd arrived home Friday night, she'd stripped out of her clothes and examined her backside. It had been covered in welts and various red marks. Her body tingled in ways she'd never felt before. She'd been spanked to the point of being turned on. Not only that, Mason ordering her around sexually had aroused her so quickly she'd been stunned by her immediate reaction. She'd never let a man tell her what to do, inside or outside the bedroom. But letting Mason take control had felt liberating. Yeah, that had been the word she couldn't identify that night. Not *uncomfortable* like her report had been this morning, not *unnatural* like she'd assumed it would be. Liberating.

How was it even possible that giving a man that kind of control could be freeing? She thought of her upbringing, of all the men who worked at her dad's garage, of all the boys she grew up with, and she couldn't imagine letting a single one do anything like that to her. None of her past boyfriends either. Or fellow agents. Hell, not even any of the Bang Shift guys, and they were all big and cocky. It was as if Mason was the only one she could even picture in that role. And she didn't have to imagine it. The man had truly mastered her. Body and soul. Rafe was just an instrument. Mason Showalter was the *maestro*.

Had he awakened something inside of her? Or was it really just him? She honestly didn't know. It didn't help at all that she was attracted to the man. As in seriously, ridiculously attracted.

Yeah, that was a big problem. If she was smart, she'd confess this little tidbit to Rick and remove herself from the investigation. But that wasn't an option. This was her first major assignment, and she had to stay focused on getting the information the FBI needed on F and B.

What a mess.

"Sweetie, I think this case has to be screwing with your mind. If you don't want to talk to the psychiatrist, I'm all ears."

Shelby opened her mouth, closed it, opened it again. Viola was giving her the chance to relate everything as if she somehow knew Shelby needed to...what? Vent? That didn't feel adequate. Venting required a certain amount of ranting, which meant she would have to understand what was happening to her enough to be at a point to rant.

She wasn't. More than anything, she was confused. If she talked now, she'd open herself to a barrage of questions she couldn't answer. Not because she didn't want to, but because she was unable to, which was a big reason why she didn't bring it up in the meeting and why she had to be vague about it all now.

Didn't matter that talking about the specifics wasn't an option with Viola. Even if she had someone outside of work to talk to, she doubted she could even begin to articulate what was going on. She'd have to get a handle on this all by herself.

"I'll be okay." There was no other option. She'd either power through and deal with all this after the assignment was over. Or...or she could use her time on this case to dig a little into her sexuality—to see if this was something she wanted to pursue in life or if she was just making the best out of the situation. There was no reason she couldn't do both.

Viola's lips pressed together in obvious disbelief. Shelby couldn't blame her. The woman shouldn't believe she was okay. After staring at her for several seconds, her head jerked in a quick nod. "All right. But invitation still stands. I have a feeling as this investigation continues, you're going to need it."

"You and me both," Shelby muttered. "You and me both."

———

"CARL KEEPS RAMBLING on about the Culpeper Hedge Fund. Did you get it resolved?" William asked Mason as his boss sat across from him in his office Monday morning.

Friday night with Shelby had been damn near perfect, and he'd spent the rest of the weekend allowing himself to relive many of those precious moments in his head. If he had it to do over again, it would be to omit Rafe from the evening. But since he'd started Shelby's four-part learning experience and submission test with the help of his partners, he couldn't change the plan now. His colleagues would grow suspicious as to why he was suddenly acting like a dog guarding his favorite toy.

Which was exactly how he felt. He wasn't one to believe in an immediate attraction like this, but he couldn't explain his reaction to himself either. Shelby was a breathtakingly beautiful woman, one who wanted to experience something he lived for. When a Dom connected with a sub on that level, it was magical. Or so he'd always believed. He'd never felt like this with a new sub before. Or any woman prior to meeting Shelby. Feeling anything beyond the need to teach her the ways of the lifestyle wasn't part of the deal, so he needed to stick to the new plan. As much as he hated the idea even more so now, his partners must be included in her scenes.

Those guys being there with Mason might keep him from becoming too attached to her. He couldn't lose his control over his emotions. It was why he'd brought his partners in to assist. And yet...he couldn't wait until this Friday when he'd be able to see her again.

Yes, he was conflicted. He didn't like having a grasp on what was happening, but he'd taken measures to mitigate any damages. Now it was best to just put it aside and focus on work. No matter what, he was always the type of man that could shut down his personal side for business matters. And with Carl running around blabbing to anybody who'd listen, it was very important that Mason do just that. He squared his shoulders and looked at his boss. He'd dealt with Shelby as best he could, and now he must handle this issue. At least with business, he could be totally emotionless.

"There's nothing to resolve. He found some things he thought looked suspicious and started throwing around dangerous words like fraud and front-running. I told him that Fieldstein and Baxter did not engage in illegal activity." Mason stared at William. The silence stretched, thickening into something else. A challenge, he knew. But Mason refused to back down.

"Do you think he's a threat?" William finally asked.

Mason shrugged as he shuffled some papers on his desk. "Don't know. If he goes to the feds, it'd surely throw us into an audit. They protect whistleblowers and don't think too kindly of people who are allegedly stealing money."

"What do you propose we do? We can't just let him go around waving a bunch of red flags."

Mason crossed his arms and leaned back in his chair. "Don't worry, William. You asked me to handle this, and I'm on it."

William glared at him. "Just what the hell are you going to do about it?"

It was time to dangle the carrot in front of the jack-ass-rabbit. "It's best if you don't know. The fewer people who are in on this, the better. Trust me. I know the score." He leveled his stare, conveying with actions what words would not do.

The other man stood. "Don't get fucking caught. I'm not spending time in jail over *this* shit."

*Got you.* His response implied there were other shady dealings he deemed more worthy being involved in that could result in prison time. How the man lasted this long in business had Mason wondering just how far his treachery went. He readied himself for any clue William might drop.

"Sometimes, legality is just a frame of mind, William. There's too much gray area for there to always be right and wrong. Don't you agree?" He smiled as he remembered telling Shelby something similar the other night. It was interesting how many things didn't fit into one mold or another, regardless of the topic.

His boss left without responding, and Mason just sat there staring after him. Well, shit. He'd hoped the man would say something more, something Mason could use. He'd have to utilize something better than a carrot of information if he wanted to keep William within his clutches.

God, sometimes Mason really hated this job. He loved the power and the money, but could really do without the bullshit, which included working for a man who was seriously beneath his intellectual level. The sooner William was gone, the sooner Mason would be closer to his professional goal.

He stood, walked over to his door, and locked it. When he returned to his desk, he dug into his briefcase for the cell phone given to him, and called the untraceable number saved on it. It stopped ringing after the second time it sounded, but no one spoke on the other end.

"He knows something," Mason said in way of greeting. He didn't like that things had come to this, but failure was not an option for him.

"We know he does," the man he'd only met once replied. "Find out what."

"He's not talking." Mason sighed as he pinched the bridge of his nose. No, William wasn't talking yet, but he would. Mason was sure of it. "Did you take care of Carl?"

"Carl O'Brian is as good as dead."

"Not good enough."

"Don't worry. Carl O'Brian will be found at the bottom of a ravine. There will be no more interference by him."

At least one loose end had been severed. Maybe it had been a good idea to make a deal with the devil after all. "Good."

Mason ended the call and collapsed into his chair. Oh, yeah. Legality was definitely a frame of mind.

# CHAPTER SIX

Sex was a complicated thing. Or so Shelby had discovered the moment she let Mason take her, *seduce her*, Friday night. Before she'd ever heard his name, her sex life was practically nonexistent. Not that she enjoyed it being like that. But prior to Mason mastering her body, what little sex she had engaged in had been nice. It wasn't as if she had difficulty climaxing or that sex in general hadn't been pleasant on those few occasions. Shelby wrinkled her nose as she took a sip of her coffee, and it wasn't because of the brew. *Nice. Pleasant.* It was as if she'd been describing an evening with an okay book, not scratching a sexual itch. What woman her age thought of getting laid in those terms?

Obviously, one did. *Her*.

The only thing that had bothered Shelby about sex in her past was the frequency not the...what? Quality? She sighed. Thinking of it like that didn't seem fair either. Nor did it help her ire any.

Words like nice and pleasant could in no way be mixed into the erotic tidal wave that was Mason. He was all-consuming, every touch—both gentle and hard—had demanded a response from her, and her body wouldn't deny him. He'd taken what he wanted while giving her more than she'd ever gotten from a lover. He wasn't her lover, though. He was a person of interest in the case she and the rest of her FBI team was assisting the SEC on. She'd do well not to forget that.

Though forgetting wasn't the problem. Thoughts of Mason Showalter had consumed her to the point her body had hummed in remembrance of the heights of passion he'd shown her. Then reality would douse her like ice water being thrown in her face, and in its wake was guilt for not telling her boss and the rest of her team she'd actually had sex with Mason. The guilt would quickly vanish—after all Rick had all but ordered her to do the deed with Mason—leaving her swimming in her thoughts of that brown-haired, brown-eyed man. The cycle had been vicious, taunting her while she was at work, heating her in the middle of the night while sleep eluded her. She couldn't get away from images of him. She'd cursed him for being so sexy and herself for not trying harder to ignore the memories haunting her. And when he wasn't invading her thoughts while she was at home, she was looking up BDSM.

She'd learned a lot thanks to Google. Most just compounded her questions rather than answering them. Oh, she'd gained knowledge, but any extrapolation formed more uncertainty. One such example was *subspace,* as he'd called it. Now she understood what it was. She'd practically blacked out after reaching an amazing orgasm and had this almost surreal feeling of peace. Knowing what it was didn't help her. Being in that state made her too vulnerable, more so than at any other time, which was saying a lot. She had to do her best to make sure it didn't happen again. She couldn't afford any states of near unconsciousness in the future.

However, said opportunity was based on a rather large assumption at this point because she hadn't even spoken to him since she saw him on Friday.

Not. One. Word.

This past week she'd met with her team every day on the status of the investigation, though there hadn't been much in the way of progress. Jerome Parker and his SEC team were knee-deep in Fieldstein and Baxter financial reports. The focus had been on the Culpeper Hedge Fund, but they were looking at everything. As for her development with Mason, what else could she report? She hadn't had any opportunity to get intel from him. If she hadn't already sacrificed enough for this case, she'd feel as if she wasn't pulling her weight, but that didn't answer that lingering question. Why hadn't he contacted her? She wasn't sure how she felt about that. She should be happy. *Should.*

She wasn't. Was he not as affected by her as she was him? She already knew the answer to that. Why would he be? He was used to this lifestyle, had probably spanked, and screwed, hundreds of women over the years. She wasn't anything special to him, just another woman who wanted to explore her submissive side. The fact that Mason wasn't as consumed with her as Rick had suspected he would be didn't look good for her either. She had an objective to get in —earn Mason's trust, and find out what he knew. She couldn't do that if what little time they spent together was of the naked kind. So yeah, she wasn't happy about no contact. If her feelings were hurt, she ignored it and focused on the problems lack of contact caused her case.

She stopped staring blankly at her computer screen to glance at her phone again. She'd stopped counting the number of times she'd looked at it. It was Thursday. Tomorrow would be one week since the spanking scene. Why hadn't he called with details of the next scene yet? He hadn't said the scenes would all be on Fridays, just once a week. Now the week was nearing its end, and he still hadn't called. Sure, she'd told him she'd see him next week, but she assumed he'd call her with some details. Was she supposed to just show up and hope he was there? She was going to go crazy waiting to hear something from him. Hell, she was already halfway to Crazy-ville.

"Whatcha doing?" Viola asked, startling her.

She dropped her phone onto her desk and picked up her coffee. "Nothing."

"Don't let Rick hear you say that." Viola laughed. "He'll start spouting off crap about not paying you to sit around."

"But he pays me to get naked and spanked by strangers," Shelby said dryly.

Viola pulled up a chair and sat across from her. "True. Guess that does earn you some slacking off."

Shelby sighed. "I wasn't slacking. I was checking my phone. Mason still hasn't called."

"I see." Viola sipped her coffee, but Shelby could see the war of words in her eyes.

"What?"

"Just seems you're a little obsessed with that fact."

Shelby clenched her teeth. "This is an important case, and I'm in a precarious position."

"That you are." She smiled. "Because of Rick and Mr. Showalter...I mean *Mason*."

Shelby shook her head. "I'm going to give you so much hell the next time you draw the assignment short stick."

"Bring it on, sister. Though fooling around with a rich hottie like Mason Showalter is so much better than rubbing down old wrinkled men any day of the week and twice on Sunday."

"Hey, we both had to work that massage clinic op."

Viola shivered. "Don't remind me. You can't un-see old-man balls. That shit stays with you forever."

Shelby's laugh shocked her, but Viola jumped in and giggled with her. "Thanks, I needed that."

"Anytime. I should get back to work before the boss man catches me gossiping." Viola stood. "Just don't forget—"

Shelby's phone ringing cut her off. Both of their gazes shot to it. She looked at the display and her heart took off. "It's him," she barely said. Oh God, it was him. Calling her. This is what she'd wanted, wasn't it? For the case...and for other reasons that made her tummy tingle. Damn the man for having this effect on her.

"Pick it up," Viola whispered as if there was a risk of him overhearing her.

Shelby grabbed it and waved Viola away. She didn't need her overhearing. "Hello?"

"Hello, pet." His voice poured over her like her favorite wine.

She bit her lip. "Hi," she breathed. She warmed all over, unable to control her body's reaction to him even in this. She glanced up and saw Viola watching her curiously. Shelby narrowed her gaze and shooed her away again. Viola opened her mouth as if to speak, but Shelby waved her hand to stop her. Shelby had to focus, and having Viola gawking while trying to interject wouldn't help. After a brief standoff, her annoying coworker finally walked away. She took a deep breath. "I wondered if you were going to call," she said softly.

"Mmm, I'm both relieved you wanted to hear from me and irritated I caused the distress in your voice by not calling sooner. My lack of contact has nothing to do with you, I assure you, pet. Work has been...complicated this week.

Shelby squeezed her eyes shut. She had a damn job to do and said job did not include swooning over the suspect. She needed to get her shit together. Now was a perfect time to make progress on this case, and she damn well better. He'd mentioned work, and she needed to snatch up the opportunity. "I'm sorry your work has not gone well. Anything you'd like to talk about?" She thought it best not to come right out and ask for specifics.

He was quiet for several seconds, his breathing heavy. Finally, he said, "There are better things I'd rather talk about." His voice pitched lower. "I've missed you, and I'm not one to miss the absence of a woman." He hesitated, as if there were more words he was holding back. Her heart beat so hard she had to shut her eyes to will it to steady while she waited. "Why you?" He sounded puzzled, genuine.

She swallowed. Either he was playing her very well or he hadn't been as unaffected as she'd feared. He had no reason to play up to her, though. As far as he was concerned, she was just a woman at a sexual crossroads. Something that had turned out to be more truth and less cover for the assignment. This reality and his reaction to her complicated things. She had a job to do. She knew that. But this was also her life the FBI was playing with. For the good of the assignment and her own need to learn more about this newly discovered facet about her, she'd be as honest with him as she could be.

And go all in.

"I've wondered the same about you."

"Does that mean you've missed me, pet?" he asked, more confidence in his voice. Did she miss him, or was it just his dominant side she missed? When she didn't answer right away, he sighed. "I've worried about relapses in your training."

What had he meant by that? Had she done something to displease him? Something inside her kept the question from being vocalized. She was unbalanced, and she hated that. What did it matter if something she did or did not do pissed him off? It shouldn't matter.

It did.

"Are you not speaking at all?"

"Sorry," she mumbled, her head dropping. "I—" But nothing else came out.

He sighed. "I haven't given you the reinforcement you need. I can't explain why that is, but I'm sorry. It won't happen again. Are you free tonight?"

"Why?" Was he asking her out on a date?

"We have another scene to do, pet. If you pass this one, I promise not to leave you hanging after." He chuckled. "Pun not intended."

She didn't understand his comment, but it answered the question that these scenes wouldn't just be on Fridays. She licked her lips, the authority in his voice turning her on in ways it shouldn't. Yeah, she missed his power. Whether she'd crave the same domination from another man was yet to be determined. She had weeks before she'd be forced to analyze that. "I'm free."

"Good. Meet me at the club at seven. Oh, and Shelby? This time, you do not get to leave when you want to. If the scene goes well, I plan on keeping you all night long."

"Y-yes, Sir."

"Master," he corrected. "But we'll work on that more later. I look forward to seeing you, pet."

He disconnected without her replying, and she stared

blankly at her phone as his words clicked in... All. Night. Along. *Holy—*

"So what did he say? When are you seeing him again?" Viola asked, leaning in.

"That's none of your business," Shelby whispered heatedly.

One of Viola's eyebrows arched. "Actually, it is. It's bureau business."

Shelby squeezed her eyes shut. "I know that. Jeez. I'm still trying to process the conversation." That much was true, but this was still her job. That was the part that mattered here. She looked at her friend and sighed. "Tonight. He wants to see me tonight."

"At the club or at his house?"

Shelby glared at her. "That was the first time I've spoken to him since I saw him. I think you know the answer to that."

"Quit being so defensive. I'm in your corner here."

Shelby groaned and rubbed her face. "Sorry. Just feeling a little out of my element."

"I think you need a latte or a bitch slap. My treat either way." Shelby looked up and Viola snickered. "Though I'd be pissed if option number two ruins my mani." She glanced at her red French tips before winking at Shelby.

"I think I need something stronger than coffee," Shelby muttered.

"Right. Let me finish up some paperwork, and we can grab lunch. I won't tell Rick about having a margarita with my chips and salsa if you won't."

"Don't worry. My lips are sealed." Keeping things from her boss was becoming second nature.

## CHAPTER SEVEN

MASON ENDED the call with Shelby and stared at his phone. What the hell was he doing? He hadn't planned on seeing her tonight. Hell, he'd spent the last several days trying to ignore the fact that his thoughts trailed to her when he wasn't forcing himself to focus on work and this clusterfuck he was in. He hadn't lied to Shelby about being swamped—just not with his assigned duties. Even this morning, when he kept trying to prep for his meeting with William, he couldn't concentrate, and the fault lay with one dark-headed beauty.

He'd called her before he'd even realized he'd picked up his phone.

"Shit," he breathed as he searched for Jedrek's number and called his business partner.

"What?" Jedrek said in way of greeting him. He hadn't barked it. No, that would require more emotion than the solemn man was capable of. Jedrek was more machine on autopilot than the average person. Not that Mason considered himself average. But the only time he noticed life spark in Jedrek's eyes was whenever he conducted a scene. And even then that spark was tightly leashed. The guy had more secrets than Mason did, and that was saying something.

"Hey, man. You busy tonight?"

"Depends. Where've you been?"

"Had to take care of some stuff with F and B." That was an understatement, but he couldn't really go into any details at the moment. "I need you at the club tonight."

"This a date?"

"I'm working with a new sub. I want her bound and you to do it," he said, ignoring his friend's attempt at sarcasm.

"If you're training her, why aren't you doing it?"

He pinched the bridge of his nose. God, he wanted to be the one to tie her up, which was exactly why he wouldn't. "You're the best at it. Besides, I think it's a good idea to expose her to different Doms. She's new. I don't want her getting comfortable with me." *Liar.*

"Gotcha. All right, I'll do it. Does she have any hard no's?"

"You can't touch her sexually. She's agreed to work with various Doms, but only wants me to be the one to stimulate her should it come to that."

"Should it come to that? You're going to be there, too?"

"Yes."

There was silence before Jedrek continued. "Forget it. I'm not interested in being your bitch. Ask someone else."

"C'mon, man. You know how it is, and it's not like that. Rafe helped me with a spanking scene, and I'm going to ask Emory to help with whipping. Your knots are a work of art."

"I'm dominating for a reason, Mason. I don't like having other Doms tell me what I can and can't do to a sub."

"Just think of her as belonging to another Dom. You're always respectful of the rules in those relationships."

"Do you two have an arrangement?" he asked, almost

disinterested. "I didn't think you were interested in taking on a sub full-time."

"No. She came to me because of a mutual friend." He wasn't touching the comment about him taking on a sub.

He sighed. "Fine. I'll be there when I get off work."

Mason's door opened, and William walked in. What the hell? He looked at his watch as he replied to Jedrek. "Thanks. See you then." He hung up and looked at his boss. "I thought we were meeting in your office."

William glared at him as he walked toward his desk and slowly took a seat in one of the chairs in front of it. "I just got done meeting with Fieldstein, and his office is closer to yours than mine."

Really? No such meeting was on the company's online calendar. All meetings were kept on it, so no one would be overbooked. Was he lying or was the meeting impromptu? Knowing William's schedule came in handy, but Mason hated having his displayed for everyone to see. It felt too much like being micromanaged, but he didn't make the rules around here. Not yet anyway. For now, he'd comply, but use it and all the other resources he could get to expose William. "What about?"

"None of your damn business, Showalter." He jerked at the lapels of his jacket as he shifted in his seat. "What's the status on Carl?"

Mason gritted his teeth before responding. If he didn't, he'd verbally rip into his boss, and telling him just where he could go wouldn't help anything. "He's gone."

William stopped picking at his sleeve and glanced up at him without moving his head. "I can see that. He hasn't been in all week. When he started raising questions about the Culpeper Hedge Fund, you said you'd take care of it. Have you?"

Mason stared at him, wondering how much he should say. If he didn't say enough, William would question him, wonder too much. The last thing he needed was that jackass snooping around. He couldn't let the tables be turned. No way was he losing his upper hand. But it was too early to reveal the truth and lose everything he'd worked for. "I've spent the last four days scouring our financial reports, accounting summaries, investor statements, everything I could get my hands on. There are no discrepancies. When I tried contacting Carl to get his details, his assistant said he had a family emergency out of town." Mason smirked. "Imagine that," he said with false innocence.

"I'd heard about that. Seems awfully convenient he had to up and leave when he tried to throw us under the bus." He smiled, and it looked purely evil. "I'd wondered if you'd had him eliminated."

As in *killed*. Mason knew what he'd meant, but alluding to something and coming right out and asking were two different things. He needed to approach this carefully. William was a smart man. Mason just needed one little slip up to go in for the kill...the one he really wanted. He laughed. "Would've been a lot easier than weeding through all those damn documents to prove him wrong."

William chuckled. "True. So what do you think's going on?"

Mason forced a casual shrug. "I think he tried to screw over F and B, couldn't make it work, and made a run for it to figure out how to get out of the mess he caused himself."

"You think he's dirty."

"I'm saying the numbers all added up." He maintained eye contact, wanted to make sure he seemed confident as he continued down his path of treachery to lure William into a false sense of security. "Do you think he's capable of lying? You've worked with him longer than I have."

"I think everybody's capable of it if given the right opportunity."

Opportunity? Interesting choice of words. Most honest people wouldn't consider a chance to fuck people over for personal gain an opportunity...a *right* opportunity at that. Then again, most honest people wouldn't see the real meaning behind his reply either. Mason was nothing if not shrewd, which came with shadowed respectability. "Opportunity implies Carl hadn't set out to frame the company intentionally." He quirked an eyebrow as he stared at his boss. "You think something happened that made him do this?"

"Carl is a numbers man. If he wanted to harm the company, he'd have the means to do it and make it look real."

"But?" William wanted to say more. Mason could practically smell it.

"But he's not street-smart. Having the know-how to make the papers look real isn't enough motivation for him."

"So someone could've planted the idea in his head."

"Sure. For all we know, he was tipped off that questioning the Fund raised flags and he fixed everything before he left."

"Okay, but who'd be cunning enough to approach him without getting himself caught in the process?" Mason asked without skipping a beat.

William stood. "I don't know. But I want you to find out whoever that is and do to him whatever you did to Carl to make him disappear."

Mason's schooled expression was the product of years' worth of practiced restraint. He knew the drill and was fully prepared to do what was necessary...as long as those actions fell in line with achieving his own goals. "I don't know what you mean. Carl's out of town dealing with a family crisis."

"Of course he is." The way William said it proved he knew differently.

"What if there isn't anybody else? What if Carl was it?" he asked, rather than focusing on the specifics of Carl.

William's gaze was cold, but Mason refused to look away. "Then the matter is effectively dead, and everybody else moves on." He stepped out and shut the door behind him.

Mason glanced at his phone but pulled out his other cell. He didn't like making these calls from his office, but he needed to relay this information as soon as he got it. He pressed the only entry in the address book and waited for line to be connected.

"He knows Carl's gone," Mason said immediately.

"And? Carl *is* gone."

"He thinks someone else is involved and wants me to eliminate the threat."

"Oh, come now, he didn't say those exact words."

Mason gaped at the air before him. "How the hell do you know that?" But he knew. The reality slammed into him just as he asked.

"We have your office tapped."

"Fuck!" Mason's head was reeling. "Why all the secrecy then? Why give me a phone to update you when I learn something if you're just going to listen in on my conversations? And why is my office tapped when you can just plant bugs in his? You can go to the fucking source."

"It's all for your protection."

"Bullshit. You're not worried about me. You want

William almost as bad as I do." Mason growled as his thoughts turned back to the man in question. He was screwing over the company. Mason had no doubt about it. He just couldn't prove it. Yet. Once he was able to, he'd be sliding into William's job before he knew what happened. "The man practically ordered me to off someone. He has a God complex and needs to be dealt with. I don't have time for this shit. Take him the fuck out!" Mason whispered heatedly.

"God complex? That's a good way to describe you. I know you're only in this for personal reasons. Don't try to convince me otherwise. You were the one who came to us, remember?"

"Only because *you* came highly recommended, and *you* assured me you'd take care of him." Mason took a deep breath, trying to calm his ire. "Have you and your resources found anything out?"

"Yes. We believe the threat to the Culpeper Hedge Fund is real. We got our hands on Carl's reports before he was dealt with, and from what we can deduce, this has the makings of a major Ponzi scheme. We also believe William Baxter is correct in his assessment that someone else was the brainpower behind tampering with it. We believe that person *is* William Baxter."

Oh shit. Mason shut his eyes. "That's impossible."

"Why? You were the one who found possible erroneous expenses on a small open-ended fund he managed."

"That, and he was kiting. I thought he was trying to screw over F and B, not bilk investors." If William was stealing from clients, Mason was in much deeper than he'd realized. It went way beyond bogus expenses and delaying transactions. "I know he's dirty enough to skirt the law, but what you're suggesting is in another realm." If there was any truth to this and word got out, it would destroy the company. Hell, even if it wasn't true but suspicions came to light, it would be almost as damaging. All of Mason's work would be for nothing.

The man laughed. "So *murder* isn't a big stretch, but stealing millions is?"

Mason swallowed and tried to slow his frantic thoughts. "Okay. For the sake of argument, let's say this is true. That Carl was working something big, and William was the brainpower behind it. Why would he order me to kill the man working with Carl if he's that man?"

"I never said Carl was working on this. He's just a pawn in William's game. But if he has you believe Carl was involved and has you searching for someone else, it'll throw you off his trail. Not to mention, make you focus on something where his name isn't directly attached. He knows Carl is gone, and now he has you chasing a ghost." There was a pause, and Mason was momentarily speechless while he waited. "We need you to confirm this, of course. "

"Damn it! I didn't sign up for this." Oh no, this definitely changed things. A fucking lot. "How the hell am I going to get him to admit anything?" If William was even slightly smart, he'd have covered all his tracks.

"We'll leave that up to you. We can't take him out without knowing what he did or how involved he is."

"That doesn't help me."

"Sorry. You have a job to do, and so do I."

The phone went dead, and Mason threw it on his desk. How the hell did this get so big so fast? If he was being honest, he wasn't too surprised about William being involved in something bigger than tampering with a small hedge fund, but it sure as hell didn't make things easy for Mason.

When he'd found excessive billing on the fund William controlled, he'd thought he could dig up more wrongdoing and take it to the executives. He couldn't go with something that'd just get the man a slap on the wrist. William was Edward Baxter's son, for crying out loud. It'd take more than what he'd uncovered to push William out the door and leave his position free and clear for Mason. If William had orchestrated a major Ponzi scheme, losing his job would be the least of his worries. The man would be facing serious jail time.

Jesus, if William was stealing millions of dollars from investors and using one of the company's most prestigious funds to do it, Mason knew he'd stumbled upon something huge. William was going down, but Mason had to be careful not to let the jerk take the company down with him.

Problem was Mason didn't know how huge this scheme was, how deep it went...or who he'd be able to trust.

# CHAPTER EIGHT

THIS WAS all kinds of *fucked up*.

It'd taken Mason hours to wrap his head around the latest development, and it had been a bitter pill to swallow. Years building a name for himself at this company, fighting his way up the corporate ladder, could all be obliterated. It wasn't just the knowledge many people could be in on the wrongdoing, but that said illegal activity could bring down the entire fucking organization. If they were talking just a few million dollars and a few people, then Fieldstein and Baxter could pay investors back out of profits, even be able to pay fines while the key players were thrown in jail. But if this had been going on a while, the amount stolen could be astronomical. Not to mention what a scandal of this caliber would do to the company's image.

It would cease to exist.

Mason had big aspirations, always had. When he'd stumbled upon William's skimming money off the top of the fund he'd managed, Mason saw it as an opportunity knock out his competition and move up to the highest position he'd envisioned ever reaching at his firm. But he had no idea it could lead him down this path of professional destruction. Now everything he'd worked for could be gone, and if that wasn't bad enough, he would be the one wielding the wrecking ball to crush his dreams. It was career suicide, and he knew it.

"There he is," Rafe bellowed from across the empty club when Mason walked in. "Where've you been hiding?"

"Jesus, not you, too. Jedrek already chewed my ass out for being M.I.A." Mason lightly punched Rafe's shoulder when he reached him. Thank God he had the club. No matter how fucked up things got at the firm, he could seek solace here.

Rafe chuckled. "Doubt that, man. Jedrek doesn't know how to get riled up. He's the silent, brooding type." He reached behind the bar and grabbed a beer. "Wanna drink?"

Mason shook his head. "I'm doing a scene with Shelby again tonight."

Rafe's eyebrows shot up. "So she's coming back for more?" he asked as he popped open his beer. He took a swig while Mason watched and mentally gauged if he had enough time to drink one, too. He deserved one after the shitty day he'd had.

"Yeah," he sighed. "Mr. Brooding himself is going to assist me tonight."

Rafe's grumbling sound wasn't missed. "You gonna let him have some fun? I got cock blocked."

"Get me a beer," he muttered as he sat at the edge of the bar. Fuck it. He had time for one. Rafe grabbed a cold one, popped the top, and handed it to Mason. He stared before replying, "No. It's her rule, man, not mine." Though he was thrilled with her self-imposed guidelines. He took a long pull from his beer and relished the burn. If he didn't have the scene tonight, he'd be partaking in a lot more than just one.

"And as her practicing Dom, you get to decide what's best for her." It felt like a challenge, and Mason wasn't up for playing games. Not this kind of game anyway.

He glared at Rafe. "And as her Dom, I respect her boundaries, as I would with *any* sub. So would you. You know the drill, man. Quit trying to bait me."

Rafe swore under his breath before taking another drink. "Sorry. You're right. Been a helluva week. The alcohol shipment was short. On Tuesday, Nick knocked over a whole rack of beer mugs, breaking half of them, so I had to order more and get one of the other partners to sign since you weren't around to approve the expense. Plus, one of the bouncers got knocked out last night by a jealous ex. Thank God he's okay and not the suing type. I need a vacation."

Mason groaned. "Damn. I'm sorry. You should've called me. I'd have been here anyway if my boss hadn't put me on something that needed to be dealt with. But I'd have come running if you needed me."

"Don't sweat it. We all know that prick has been shitting on you." He leaned over and tapped his bottle against Mason's. "It's all good."

If only Rafe knew how wrong he was. Nothing was good, but Mason didn't have the time to dwell on it right now. Tonight, he had Shelby to focus on. Tomorrow, he could go back to accepting his impending doom. He stood and grabbed his bottle. "C'mon. I've got a couple of hours before Shelby will be here. You can fill me in on the mugs and everything else you've spent money on this week, so I can update the accounting system."

Rafe chuckled as he walked around the bar. "Told you

we didn't need to hire an accountant. You know just how an auditor thinks."

"How many times do I have to keep telling you it's not the same thing?" he asked incredulously.

"Quit your bitching and come use those Ivy League skills to balance our accounts."

Mason followed him toward the closed-off area where their offices were, all the while thinking it was good thing he paid attention to his accounting classes in college. After the debacle at Fieldstein and Baxter, he just might need those damn skills to fall back on after all.

*God, I hate accounting.*

———

*GOD, I hate accounting.* Shelby shoved the mouse away from her, rolled her chair away from her desk, and laced her fingers above her head as she exhaled slowly while staring at the computer screen. How any person in his right mind would seek out a career crunching numbers was beyond her. She did her best to remember not throwing away receipts, so she could give them to her tax preparer every year, and half the time failed miserably at that. At least she could print out her checking and credit card statements. If it wasn't for online banking she'd be totally screwed, and that was just dealing with personal finances. She'd rather stab her eyes out than look at business finances.

There was never an eye-poking-out device when she needed one.

Staring at F and B's quarterly and annual financial reports was seriously making her brain hurt. Generally Accepted Accounting Principles might as well be Greek. Strike that, it'd probably make more sense to her if it *was* in a different language. At least then she'd be in her own element. Business reporting was a beast in and of itself. A big scary, scaly beast with bloody fangs. She was a letters person, not numbers. Just one more example that her intellectual contribution hadn't been priority when selecting her for this assignment.

She released her hands and shook them, trying to release the tension from her fingers. She had to be missing something. She'd logged onto the SEC's website and pulled several years' worth of statements. From what she could see, everything seemed to be in order, but she was no expert. Heck, she wasn't even a novice. After she nudged back toward her desk, she picked up her phone and dialed Darrell's extension.

"Tobin," he answered.

"Hey, Darrell. It's me."

"I know," he said with a chuckle. Shelby heard papers rustling in the background. "Didn't know if you'd have me on speaker with an audience. Can't have the boss man hearing me call you 'little bit' now, can I?"

"True." She smiled despite herself. Darrell had always watched out for her and had a knack for improving her mood with just idle chatter. "So I've been looking over some F and B financial statements—"

"Damn, girl. That's no light reading."

"Tell me about it. Something's off. I know it is, but I can't put my finger on it."

"That's Jerome Parker's job. SEC has been scouring all those business filings—*shit*," he breathed.

"What?"

"Been through this file four times now and can't find the damn police report from when William Baxter got pulled over for speeding two years ago in Miami." He took a deep breath. "Sorry. You were saying?"

Shelby giggled. "Actually *you* were saying how it's Parker's job to analyze the financial reports, not mine."

"Oh, right, right. We were brought in to get info out of Showalter. Jerome and his team have been all over those reports. Hell, the SEC maintains that stuff. They know what they're looking for. They need us to investigate what they don't already have access to."

She groaned. "I know. I just think it wouldn't hurt if fresh eyes looked at them. Maybe they'd provide a clue for us that the SEC wouldn't pick up on. I mean, why are you looking for an old ticket of Baxter's when it doesn't have anything to do with the firm?"

Darrell harrumphed. "You tell me."

But she could tell from his tone that he already knew where she was going with this...and that was to prove her point. "Because you're looking for a clue, just like I am."

"Yeah. There's a judge in Miami-Dade that the IRS is investigating for tax evasion. I'm trying to see if there's a link between him and Baxter. If maybe he paid him off."

"Exactly. You're investigating this case just like I am."

"How did you get so good at this?" he asked, and she could clearly hear the smile in his voice.

"I learned from the best."

"Flattery will get you everywhere."

She chuckled. "Just being honest."

Darrell took a deep breath. "Call Carson. He may have a master's in system design from M.I.T., but he also majored in business at the undergrad level. He's a wiz at forensic accounting. If anybody on our team can help you, he can."

Shelby was glad she wasn't talking to Darrell in person because she was unable to suppress the twisted face she made at the mention of Carson's name. The man was a flirt, and she didn't like walking right into his advances. Carson was harmless, but she didn't have the energy to put up with him right now. "Okay. Thanks. Good luck fishing out that speeding ticket."

"Thanks, little bit."

After disconnecting the call, Shelby stared at the computer screen for several more minutes. If the numbers jumped off the monitor and started doing the Hokey Pokey, it still wouldn't be any more exciting. *Gah.* Energetic or not, she'd have to call her other teammate, and if she didn't do it soon, she'd have to call her hairdresser to fix the bald spots formed by ripping gobs of her hair out. Without giving it much more thought, she grabbed the receiver and hit Carson's extension.

"Well, hello there, Shelby." He obviously didn't care if she had her phone on speaker.

Rather than dragging this out, Shelby quickly ran through her spiel before asking, "So can you look at the reports?"

"What's in it for me?"

She rolled her eyes. "Don't be a dick. Are you going to help me or not?"

"Only because you said dick."

"One of these days, you're either going to be up to your eyeballs in sexual harassment suits or missing you balls altogether because you messed with the wrong woman." She picked up a pencil and tapped it on her desk.

"Give me forty-eight hours, and I'll let you know what I find," he said more seriously, and hung up.

She glanced at the clock. It was almost quitting time, but since she was working overtime tonight as a legal streetwalker, she was going to leave now. Taking a calming breath, she stood and gathered her things. She couldn't let Carson, or anybody else, get into her head. She needed it ready for what was to come.

Right now, she had to focus on making sure she found the perfect thing to wear to make herself presentable to Mason. On her way out, she briefly considered stopping and visiting with Viola, but she was chatting with Rick. Shelby had already brought her team up to speed on tonight, so she had no desire to get into another conversation with her boss. She slipped out of the building and got into her car. The radio blared a sexy song, and she quickly turned it off before merging onto the road. She didn't need external forces affecting her mood. No, Shelby needed her head in the game.

*Yeah, because letting a possible criminal have his way with your body is just fun and games.*

Her thoughts trailed back and forth on the drive home. Tonight, Mason was going to tie her up somehow. She didn't understand the necessity of it since she'd technically been restrained last week, but he was the master here. Literally.

By the time she got home, she'd scolded herself half a dozen times through her wayward thoughts. It didn't matter why Mason chose the scenes he'd picked out. What mattered was gaining information from him on F and B and determining how guilty he was in tampering with the Culpeper Hedge Fund. She had to focus on her mission.

With renewed energy, she headed straight for the bathroom to shower. When she opened the cabinet to get a towel, she froze at the sight before her.

*Massage oils.* One thing she'd learned from that previous assignment was some people liked to talk when getting their bodies rubbed down. She smiled as she stared at the bag of FBI issued essential oils. She'd loved learning the art of Chinese massage as it related to Traditional Chinese Medicine. She'd been good at it, too.

Mason believed her story, and no one said it couldn't be used as more than just a cover for this mission. She smiled, thinking of practicing her skills on him. There was no reason why she couldn't bring her supplies with her tonight and try her talent out on the big, bad Dom. Maybe his tongue would loosen as fast as his muscles did.

She pulled it out to see if she still had all of the supplies and a tiny scrap of material fell to the floor.

The ridiculously tiny uniform from the parlor.

God, she'd hated wearing that thing on the assignment. It had felt both slutty and culturally insensitive, but it was what all the workers—regardless of nationality—had worn if they'd been assigned to provide extra services for men. She picked it up and caressed it as she contemplating donning it again, and the thought of wearing this for *Mason* caused a nervous thrill to course through her, her body humming with possibilities. It wasn't as if she hadn't worn this in front of strangers. He'd already seen her in much less. She never thought she'd have to wear this again for work, but here she was, practically giggling at the irony as she jumped into the shower.

This would either go well or smack her in the face. Only one way to find out.

CHAPTER NINE

———

WHEN SHELBY REACHED the front door of Scene, she paused as she heard the muffled music filtering through the walls of the club. Her nerves kicked up a notch at actually going through with this. Not just the scene with Mason, but with her clothes. She hoisted the shoulder strap of her bag, looked down at her dress, and tugged at the hem before pushing in.

She could do this. She would. Whatever it took to get this assignment rolling.

No longer hindered by walls, the music thumped as unabashed as some of the subs who were dancing to it. God, didn't these people have jobs? She couldn't remember the last time she'd ever gone to a club in the middle of the week. No way would she be able to party all night and be able to focus first thing in the morning. She couldn't even give them the excuse of youth...she was only in her mid-twenties. Plenty young enough by society's standards to be sowing her wild oats.

Maybe she *was* in a way.

She bit her lip but then immediately stopped, remembering the cherry-red lip color. Oh yeah, she'd gone all out all right. Not only was she in a short-as-sin dress, but she had her hair twisted up in sticks. Her red lips accentuated her heavy eyeliner. But her legs? She'd left them uncovered. In fact, she bent over, kicked off her slippers, and stored them in her bag. Tonight, she was going barefoot.

When she'd researched BDSM, some sites had commented how subs would remain nude, including going without shoes, while in the presence of their Doms. Mason wasn't really hers, but as far as this mission—and the scenes he was training her on—he was close enough. She needed him to talk tonight and hoped the token of her submission would soften him to the possibility.

He'd commented before how she'd dressed like a Domme. Hopefully, her appearance was less harsh than before. The lack of shoes...and panties...would hopefully pass his appraisal.

"Hello, Ms. Landry."

She jumped and turned to the side where the bouncer from the first night she'd shown up here was standing.

"Hi," she squeaked, then cleared her throat. "I'm supposed to be here. I'm meeting—"

"I know. Mr. Showalter said to have you meet him upstairs in the room you were in last week. Do you remember where it is?"

"Yes."

He raised an eyebrow and studied her. She straightened her shoulders and leveled her glare on him. Just because she was on assignment didn't mean she'd let just any man do or say whatever he wanted. She knew how to take down guys this size. She wouldn't come away unscathed, but at least he'd be worse off than she.

The brute chuckled. "Head straight back. Don't talk to

anyone. If a Dom stops you, say, 'My Master awaits.' Any Dom at this club knows that's code for 'leave me the fuck alone'. It's like using your safe word in a scene. Understood?"

"Understood," she repeated before grabbing the strap of her bag to ensure it wouldn't slip off as she waded through the crowd.

*My Master awaits?* Had she traveled back in time to some English manor where her duties included milking Betsy and stuffing her lord's straw bed with this morning's clippings? *My Master awaits?* In his damn dreams. It was one thing to play in the bedroom, but no way was she comfortable taking any of this BDSM stuff outside into the world. Hell no.

Laughter drifted out of the room as she neared, taking her ire with it. She knew the person behind the joyful voice, but the laughter felt foreign. Mason had been so serious on the two occasions they'd been together, and their phone conversations hadn't netted a reaction like this. She liked that he felt at ease with the other man in the room.

Dread punched in her gut. She'd forgotten they wouldn't be alone. Her steps faltered as she gazed down at her dress. Insecurity swamped her again, but the jovial sound coming from room reassured her the man at least had a sense of humor. She pushed through the door and the joyful camaraderie that had been shared seconds before died.

She stared at Mason, who gaped at her wordlessly. Her nervous smile shook in its place to the point she had to draw her lips in and bit them both to still the quaking.

"Damn," the other man in the room muttered. He blinked at Mason. "You didn't say anything about role playing. You know I love that shit. Why didn't you save this for me?"

Shelby frowned at the man, not understanding.

"Let it go," Mason murmured to him, but not taking his eyes off her.

"Dude, costumes don't work with bondage," the other man said, turning his gaze back to her.

"Go find Jedrek."

The other man huffed but started for the door. When he reached it, Shelby had to step aside to let him pass. Only he didn't. He stopped right in front of her. "I like French maids. You show up in that next week, and we'll pretend I've caught you stealing my silver." She flinched when his finger grazed her arm and trailed down it slowly. "After I've done a body cavity search, I'll whip you good."

"Emory!"

The man chuckled and looked over his shoulder. "Chill out, Mace." Then, as he walked out the door, he muttered, "I can't believe you're letting that uptight douche have all the fun."

He shut the door at his departure, and Shelby couldn't hide the shiver that ran through her at the realization she was now alone with Mason—the man who now seemed past his shock and was giving her a slow, sexy smile.

"Interesting clothes, pet." He started toward her. "I'm not sure if I should ask your reasoning or question you on the bag you're carrying first."

She licked her dry lips as she set it beside the door, making sure not to block it. "The answer is the same." She shrugged as she wrapped her arms around her middle.

"Is it now?" His smile brightened.

"Yes, Master." Mason's eyes heated at her address,

which gave a little bit of her confidence back. "You said to plan on staying the night. I wanted to be prepared."

"I would have seen to your needs," he chided softly.

"I..." She looked down. How was this man able to expose her with just a stare? She took a deep breath and focused on him again. "Thank you, Master. But my intention was to see to your comfort tonight. Should the scene go well, I mean."

"*My* comfort?" He seemed genuinely perplexed, and she found it adorable. *Adorable? He's a point of interest. Get it together, Shelby!*

"Granted, I don't wear this on my job, but I thought it'd be fun to be dressed naughty while I gave you a massage." Why was her throat so dry? She swallowed again and indicated her bag. "I brought some essential oils. For later, of course."

Now he seemed completely shocked. Her attire had made him temporarily speechless, but at the suggestion of her therapeutic offering, he seemed totally lost. "Why?" he finally breathed.

She lifted a lone shoulder. "You've been..." She stopped and shook her head. She was about to say that he'd been so helpful with her and her BDSM exploration, but suddenly, that felt too much like a lie. Even though it held more truth than anybody would understand. Instead, she kept her response simple. "Because I want to."

That look. Oh God, the look he just gave her would have melted her heart if she'd have let it. It held so much emotion, not the least of which was pride and something else she didn't understand. He took a step toward her, but the door opened, startling her.

"Sorry. Problem with a bouncer." The man shucked his jacket as he walked in and tossed it onto the couch. When

Shelby looked at Mason again, that warm expression was gone. In its place was cool indifference.

"It's fine," he said, darting his gaze at the man before finally walking to Shelby. He took her hands and guided her to the couch. The other man walked to the other side of the room, busying himself with what she could only assume had to do with their scene. "Pet, that's Jedrek." He tilted his head toward the other man's direction. Jedrek turned from what he was doing, gave her a short nod, and then twisted back toward his task.

Mason stared after him a few seconds more, but it was long enough for Shelby to question the type of friendship the two men had. He'd been so lighthearted with the other guy, but now that Jedrek was here, Mason's mood had instantly changed. She didn't know him very well, but with Rafe at the spanking scene, Mason had seemed at ease for the most part. Tonight with Emory, he'd been laughing even, but with Jedrek, he almost seemed on edge. Why? She made a mental note to look at his file again. Maybe there was more to this Jedrek man than they'd considered. She and her team knew it was a possibility that information could be garnered here at the club, but they hadn't considered some direct connection with F and B. From all accounts, the club and Mason's work with the firm were completely separate. Of course, she could be getting ahead of herself. Maybe the sudden stiffness in the air had nothing to do with her case. Regardless, she'd look into it.

Jedrek turned toward them. "Has he explained what we will be doing tonight?"

"Yes, Sir. I mean. I know you'll be tying me up."

"To some, bondage is just a form of restraint." The foreboding man wrapped a length of rope around his hand as he spoke. "There are some who'd rather use cuffs and be done with it. They don't understand the beauty, but I do. To me, bondage is an art. Come here."

The authority in his voice almost had her rising without question, but she glanced at Mason first. He nodded, and she stood, his permission all she needed to obey the other. She felt Mason walking behind her as she proceeded slowly toward Jedrek.

"Give me your hands."

Shelby trembled as she lifted them to him.

"What's your safe word?" Mason asked.

"Red," she whispered. Her insides were trembling and she hoped the shaking hadn't made its way outside her body.

He gripped her chin and forced her to look at him. "And if you just need a break?"

"Yellow."

"Good, girl. Tonight, pet, there are no other words that will stop this scene. Last week, you were given your safe word but also told you could tell us to stop with the reassurances we would. It was your first scene. You did well with it, so we are moving on to something harder. Do you understand?"

"Yes, Master."

"Are you ready to begin?" Jedrek asked.

She looked at him and nodded.

"Verbally," he said, biting.

"Uh, yes, Sir."

"Master," he corrected.

"*Sir*," Mason retorted.

Jedrek glanced at him. His neck stiffened, but that was the only sign he'd been unhappy with the little rule. "Seems you left more details out." He looked back at her. "Fine. Sir it is. Remove your dress."

Shelby trembled at the sound of Jedrek's voice. The man had an unwavering authority about him, but she still had to force her arms to lift to reach the zipper behind her.

Mason's gentle hands nudged hers away. "Allow me, pet," he murmured. She shouldn't feel safe with him, but she did. Damn it to hell, she did. He was the monster she knew. Not that she knew him well at all, but this Jedrek guy was scary. "Beautiful," Mason breathed when her dress hit the floor. His hands glided up and down her back before he stepped in front of her and stood by Jedrek. She had to admit her torturer tonight was attractive, but standing next to Mason, he paled in comparison. The cranky man was bald where Mason had beautiful brown hair, his eyes a steely gray to Mason's warm brown. The goatee added to Jedrek's hard persona.

"Hands," Mr. Mean barked.

She offered them without hesitation and watched as he skillfully wrapped her wrists damn near to her elbows. She stared at his work as he stepped to the side and grabbed another length of rope. Her arms felt okay. The binding wasn't too tight or even abrasive.

But the message was clear.

She felt more helpless now than she had last week when she was mounted to a spanking bench. Then, only cuffs had secured her wrists. This was completely different. Oh God, could she really do this? Her breathing spiked and her eyes darted to Mason.

"Eyes down," Jedrek ordered, and her gaze flew to the floor.

Mason's shoes came into view, but she still flinched when his hand rubbed her back again. "Good girl."

Her muscles relaxed at his praise. Her body liked pleasing him even if her mind struggled with it. She had many good reasons to struggle, but right now, she had to put them all aside. She took a deep breath, fortifying herself to her task. She could do this. When she got through the scene and she and Mason were alone, she'd pry him for information. Right now, she'd submit. Do what was needed.

Make Mason proud.

"Come," Jedrek said as he grasped her arm and tugged her to the middle of the room. He reached up and pulled down a ring, but realizing she should have her eyes downcast, she immediately dropped her gaze. She wanted to watch what he was doing to prepare herself. Something cool covered her eyes and she gasped.

"It's just a blindfold, pet."

Oh God, now she couldn't see! She swallowed through the need to hyperventilate, forcing the urge away.

"Say your safe word," Jedrek said calmly.

"Red."

"Do you want to use it?"

"N-no."

Lips touched her neck, and she flinched. Who was kissing her? She didn't want Jedrek to touch her like this. "Easy," Mason breathed against her, and she practically slumped against him. He clutched her waist and continued his glorious assault on her neck.

Shelby barely recognized her arms being lifted over her head.

Mason's hands trailed up her sides and cupped both of her breasts. Skillful fingers plucked at her greedy nipples, and she moaned as her head fell back onto his shoulder.

More rope found its way around her body—tummy, thighs, she didn't care. She was too focused on Mason's ministrations to give her attention to Jedrek's.

One of Mason's hands trailed down, and her hips thrust

to meet him. He ignored her silent plea, but she felt him squat behind her as his hands reached her thighs, trailing over the rope while he kissed his way down her back. She was suddenly lifted, suspended in the air. Her legs were moved into some position, she wasn't quite sure what, but the ease of it shocked her.

"Relax," Mason murmured. He was standing up with her, though she could tell he wasn't the driving force behind her change in elevation. His hands continued their soothing caresses.

Until he stepped away, and no one touched her.

No one made a sound.

She struggled, swinging slightly with her effort, but she was completely bound. Her hands did not budge, her feet, though moving, were not making any headway.

"Master Mason told you to relax." Jedrek didn't sound irritated, just stated it mater-of-factly.

"I'm trying, Sir." How the hell could someone relax where they were hogtied to the freaking ceiling? If this was supposed to be erotic, Shelby had totally missed the memo.

"No you're not," Mason said calmly. "You're too tense. Just let your body relax."

"Start with your feet," Jedrek said. She nodded and forced her legs to stop moving, allowing them to lay limp. "That's a girl, pet. Now your arms and chest."

It took her several seconds to ease her body into a calm state, but when she thought she'd finished, Mason was quick to correct her. "You're head."

"Huh?" She twisted it to the side as if she could see them.

"That's not how you address me, Shelby," Mason said sternly.

"I-I'm not sure what you mean, Master."

"Shelby," Jedrek started. "Your head is still up. You need to drop it. Relax completely for me."

Drop her head? How was she supposed to do that? She was suspended in air! Maybe he'd fashioned some rope-styled pillow for her? Slowly, she let it ease back, but jerked it up when she'd reached the end of her comfort zone and had not met any support. Now her body had tensed up again.

"C'mon, pet. You can do it," Mason encouraged. "Once you've let go, I'll show you how freeing it is to be so restricted."

How could she be free *and* confined? That didn't make any sense. With a steadying breath, she forced herself into relaxation. This time, she let her head hang.

She'd totally gone limp.

"Beautiful," Mason murmured.

"That she is."

She heard some mumbling between the two men, but she was too engrossed in this feeling of flying to care what they were talking about. The blood would've rushed to her head if she'd been at a different angle, but like this she felt amazing. When a door opened and closed in the background, she didn't bother asking if someone was leaving or coming in. She should care, but she didn't. Besides, she wasn't really given permission to speak, so she saw no reason to break this odd euphoria.

"It's just us, pet," Mason breathed right in her ear. And how did he get so close to her without her hearing him? That didn't matter either. She was naked and on display for him. Only him. And her body immediately electrified. His hand skimmed her inner thigh. "You're doing so well."

"Thank you, Master."

"Do you have any idea how beautiful you are?"

She wasn't sure if it was rhetorical or not, so she said nothing. She figured she was pretty enough, but she wasn't one to dwell on her looks. He pushed her legs open wider. Without warning, his tongue grazed her clit, and she gasped. "Such a good girl. I'm going to reward you now. If you want to stop, use your safe word, Shelby. Understood?"

"Yes, Master."

She'd barely gotten her reply out when he'd fastened his mouth upon her core. Any calmness her muscles had experienced left with the sudden tightening that engulfed her. She was so stiff that she'd swear no ropes held her, that she was floating of her own accord.

But that thought fled with the heat that consumed her, radiating from her as he feasted on her. She moaned, and he grabbed her rear to hold her steady and continued his assault. And it was amazing. Pure bliss. Her body hummed with so much energy she just knew she'd combust.

And come the fastest she had ever in her life.

*And* without any other foreplay.

"You can come as soon as you're ready, my beautiful pet." Mason shoved two fingers inside her and fucked her with them while he batted his tongue on her overly sensitized nub. Within seconds, she was screaming...maybe his name, maybe incoherent nonsense. She had no idea.

"Fuck. I'd planned on teasing you for hours. I can't. I need you. Now. So fucking bad."

She'd have screamed her agreement if she could be certain her sentences were back to being coherent. She was too eager to feel him, give him what he wanted, because it was what she wanted, too.

She heard a zipper, a packet being torn, and then he was pushing inside her.

"Oh God," she breathed. He felt huge, but she wanted it, wanted him. "Don't stop."

"Never." He pounded into her as if he was possessed. He'd grabbed her shoulders from underneath so she wasn't pushed away each time he entered her. His fingers dug into her so hard, she'd wear his bruises later, but it only heightened her ecstasy. She heard his belt buckle jingle as he moved, felt his sleeves on her thighs. He was fully clothed while she was naked. Naked, bound, tied, being controlled, yet she'd never felt freer in her life. It was so much to accept.

Too much to bear.

Stars exploded behind her blindfold as her body seized. If she screamed while she came, it was overshadowed by his shout.

Shelby wasn't sure how much time had passed as he hunched over her while her body tingled in the aftermath, but slowly he disentangled himself and moved away. She felt cold without him as she listened to him rummage around the room, but she wasn't alone long. He pulled her into his arms and she felt herself being lowered to the ground. A few tugs and snips and then she was free of everything except the blindfold. He pulled her into his lap before allowing her sight again, but with the first look in his eyes, she wished for the safety of the blindfold back. God, he looked so open. Emotions flew in his eyes as he searched hers. She felt a need to kiss him, but why she didn't know. Instead, she licked her lips and asked, "Did I pass?"

He blinked and the open window into is soul was shut again, but he smiled. "Yes, pet."

She missed the true openness as quickly as she'd feared its revelation, but she didn't have time to analyze that. This wasn't about her or him. Not really. It was about information. No matter how much her needs screamed otherwise, she knew her duty, and she would follow through. "And I'll be staying the night?" She knew that was what he'd wanted, but she wasn't going to assume that was still the case.

"Unless you safe word out." He stroked a piece of her hair behind her ear. "Although, I have to tell you, I'll do everything in my power to keep that from happening."

He didn't have to worry about that. Not yet anyway. "Good." She glanced at her bag of massage oils and then back at him, but she could tell his eyes never wavered from her face. "Then it's my turn to please you."

"It seems that requires minimal effort from you," he whispered so softly that she wasn't entirely sure it was meant for her ears. Though her heart pounded as if he'd shouted it from the rooftops.

This assignment scared her. She'd known that from the moment she'd agreed to it. But this was the first time she'd been really scared of what could happen with this man... and her feelings toward him.

# CHAPTER TEN

"Follow me," Mason said once Shelby was finished putting her sexy as hell dress back on. He still couldn't believe she'd thought ahead to wear something like that. No woman had ever grasped any foresight into what he'd like without being told first. It wasn't so much that he liked role playing, but the effort she'd put into pleasing him.

Besides the fact that, before Shelby, he wasn't one to be surprised. It was a development he rather liked...with a woman he was growing attached to. It wasn't smart, not with everything going on at the firm, but maybe spending some time with her would help keep his sanity. He'd do well not to overthink this. God knew his brain was already stretched to the max with other, less desirable thoughts.

"Where are we going?" she asked once they reached the stairway to the next floor.

He rubbed her back and kept his hand there to guide her up the stairs. "To the private rooms. We each have our own in case we don't want to drive home for whatever reason."

"Oh, that's good. I guess."

He didn't miss the shiver that danced along her back as he rubbed her there. She was so fucking responsive. If he wasn't careful, he could easily lose himself in her.

*What do you mean* could? *You've been panting over memories of her all week.* Wasn't that the damn truth. He'd laugh at himself if he could find the real humor in falling for a woman who wasn't in the lifestyle. Yes, she was submissive, but having those tendencies did not a willing sub make. He'd always known he needed to exert his dominance in the bedroom. He never cared for it outside. Everyone's needs were different, but his attachment to the life was purely sexual. A full-time sub was more work than he'd ever want to give. But with Shelby, he felt he was learning more about himself, too. With her, anything could be possible. There was so much to domination and submission that even with these four scenes, they wouldn't scratch the kinky surface.

And if she did go through with them all, then what? Would she walk away? Want more?

Would he?

She opened her mouth as if to ask something else, but shut it with a slight frown. Interesting. Why was she holding back her question? She obviously wondered about something. He hadn't told her she couldn't speak unless spoken to. Some Doms got off on that.

Mason didn't.

No, he rather liked it when a woman was free to express herself. Unless in the bedroom...then all bets were off. He needed total control in that area, couldn't afford to let that go.

*Then why are you letting other Master Doms conduct scenes with your sub?*

He knew why...because no matter how much a part of him wanted it—her—he knew she wasn't his. He was pursuing play, not courting a woman. He just hoped repeating it enough times to himself would drill that point home.

"What is it, pet?" he finally asked when it became apparent she wasn't going to speak without encouragement.

Her gaze danced around as they came to a stop at his door. "I thought we'd be going back to your place."

He chuckled when she shrugged delicately. She was trying to play coy, but he could see right through her. He opened the door and motioned for her to enter as he turned on the lights. "I think you'll like it."

She gasped and he smiled, though she didn't see it. She was too busy walking in and turning in circles, looking at the room. "Wow," she breathed.

Her bag fell to the floor.

He tossed his keys onto the side table. "My partners and I wanted comfortable rooms to stay in. No sleazy motel vibe."

She looked over her shoulder at him, blushing slightly. "I didn't mean... Well, I mean it's lovely," she said quickly as she turned back around, looking out the picture window to the grounds below.

"It's hardly a penthouse suite, but it'll do. There's a kitchen to your left and a bedroom suite to the right." They were standing in the living area, which made up the rest of his private room at the club. It was decorated in warm, neutral colors, but the features the space had were top of the line.

"This looks bigger than my apartment," she mumbled. He didn't think she was talking to him, so he didn't respond to her comment.

"Are you hungry?"

She seemed to pull herself out of her reverie when she

turned to face him. "No. I might want something to eat later, but for now, I'd like to give you a something special instead."

Mason's dick twitched. He couldn't remember the last time he'd been this turned on by a woman, but he willed it down. Shelby wanted to treat him to a massage, and he wasn't going to turn something she did for a living into a kinky game.

*But she wore a costume.*

He tamped that thought down, too. If Shelby wanted to turn this into something playful, then he was all for it, but he wouldn't go into this with the expectation. He'd let her define the boundaries because this wasn't a scene and he didn't have to control it.

But if she turned it into sex, then he'd master her.

"I didn't bring a table. We'll have to do this on your bed." The sly smile was very cute on her, and it immediately helped him relax the sudden and unfamiliar nerves. This was her show now, and he'd lie back and enjoy it.

"That works for me." He winked at her. "It's this way." He started for the bedroom and had to stop himself from taking her hand. He'd had massages before, so he'd give her the professional courtesy he had any other therapist he'd seen. But that didn't stop him from grabbing her bag and carrying it for her. After walking into the bedroom, he set the bag on the edge of the bed. Shelby clutched it and opened it.

"Why don't you tell me if you have pain anywhere specific," she said as she pulled out various bottles, focused on her task.

He chuckled and rubbed the back of his neck. "I don't usually get asked that. Normally, I take off my shirt and they just start rubbing."

She looked up then with a crooked smile. "But *I'm* asking you."

Dropping his hand, he said, "Fair enough. I guess my back is a little stiff." Another part of him was already trying to get that way as well with the knowledge her hands would soon be on his body. He cleared his throat. He was doing a piss poor job of not trashing her profession. She'd asked him a legitimate question, and he needed to answer it. Admitting to a few aches and pains didn't make him less of a man. "My thighs ache sometimes from sitting down so long at my office."

She squirted something onto her hands and rubbed them together as she nodded. "Okay, we'll start with you lying face down." She put a few select bottles on the nightstand and slipped her bag off the bed and onto the floor. "Take off your clothes."

He quirked an eyebrow at her as he started unbuttoning his shirt. "That sounded like an order, pet."

She blushed, glancing away. "Please," she whispered.

"I didn't mean to embarrass you, Shelby. You don't have to hide from me." He shucked his shirt and started on his pants. It didn't slip past him that he usually undressed without an audience before a massage, but this wasn't a typical session and he wasn't shy. He liked that she appeared to be, though.

"Would you like me to get you a towel to cover up?" she asked when he pushed his pants and underwear down.

"Not necessary." He climbed onto the bed face down as instructed. "Unless you'd feel more comfortable," he amended.

"Not necessary," she mocked playfully before crawling onto the bed beside him.

The moment her hands touched his back, he groaned. It

wasn't a timid touch of a shy woman. It was a skillful kneading of a person who knew exactly what she was doing. He was lost, transfixed as she worked knot after knot out of his back. Any remnant of sexual desire evaporated as he allowed himself to fully accept her handiwork.

"You're so tense."

His chuckle ended on a groan. "You're very good at this."

"When's the last time you visited a therapist?"

"Er, I don't know. A few months maybe."

She huffed. "You should see somebody regularly. At least once a month."

"Are you offering?" If she was the one tending to his screaming muscles, he'd make the effort to go.

She laughed. "Um, no. I'm booked the next two months. You need to see someone sooner. I can refer you if you don't have somebody else in mind."

"What if you were the only one I wanted?" Jesus, even saying those words on something unrelated to relationships made his heart race.

She paused, and he watched as she got more oil. He saw her nibble her lip before she was out of sight, tending to him again, and he wondered if it was a nervous reaction to the words he'd uttered. Still, he waited for her to reply. He was nothing if not patient.

"Why don't we table that until after you're through schooling me on the next two scenes? I don't want you to give me an unfair advantage because you're getting something in return."

"Pet, I am getting something in return already," he said softly.

Her hands stilled at the husky sound of his voice. He'd been doing really well not getting turned on, but talking of wanting her in any capacity fueled his lust. That's all it was. That was all it could be.

"So tell me about your family," she blurted as she moved up to his shoulders.

He'd let her diversion tactic fly and indulge her. Hell, he needed the distraction himself. "Not much to tell. Parents moved to Maine after my brother died in Afghanistan." He hadn't seen his parents very often since. They'd closed off after Caleb died, and he'd been too career-focused to make extra time for them.

"So you're not from the east coast?"

"No. Grew up in Louisiana." That seemed like a life-time ago. Hell, it was. He'd rather not delve too much into his past. Instead, he flipped the conversation to her. "What about you?"

"Darrell and Viola are like family." She stopped moving her hands but kept them there. He couldn't see her, but he got the feeling she'd revealed more than she wanted by how she'd stiffened.

"Who are they?"

Her hands started moving slowly. "Friends." She cleared her throat, and her attention to his back returned to the level she'd displayed before mentioning those people. "Um, I mean, I have family, but I don't see them much. I met Darrell shortly after graduating high school, and he took me under his wing. Viola is another massage therapist. We worked together at the same clinic last year."

It didn't escape him that she'd completely avoided the topic of family and mentioned friends instead. Although he didn't care for that, he especially didn't like the mention of this other man even more. "What's your relationship with Darrell?" he asked, hoping he hadn't barked the question at her.

"What do you mean?" She stilled again.

"Is he your lover?"

She gasped, and he wondered if he'd offended her, but then she guffawed, and he realized her gasp had been an inhale for her laughter. "God no. He's too old. And bossy as hell. He's more like a helpful uncle if anything."

Mason knew he was being possessive, but he couldn't help the emotions rushing through him. If she relied on someone for help, he wanted to be the one she turned to, not some other man.

It wasn't right. He was fully aware he could not be with her or any woman until the mess at F and B was handled. Knowing it, however, didn't stop him from having that carnal reaction to her.

"Okay, turn over and scoot down so I can sit behind your head. *Please*," she added softly.

"Good girl," he said, smiling as he rolled over and adjusted himself. He shoved all errant thoughts into the deepest recesses of his mind as she maneuvered into a new position. He had plenty of shit to fret about regarding work to have time to focus on anything else.

She dug her hands under his neck and rubbed. He liked this position much better because he could see her, watch her reaction as they talked. She touched a spot that was tender and he did his best not to grimace, but she frowned anyway. "Care to tell me what has you so stressed? I'm a good listener."

He half-smiled at her. "I'm not stressed."

"Your neck says otherwise." She dug into that spot harder, and he clenched his fists at the sudden pain. "Relax," she murmured.

Jesus, how could he relax when she was ripping his

head off? But as she continued, the pain lessened and the knot disappeared.

"Since you don't talk to your family and you're not married, I'm going to guess it has something to do with work."

He sighed. She wasn't completely wrong. "Yeah, but you don't want to know."

She licked her lips. "No," she said easily. "You will probably bore me to tears." Then she stopped and looked down at him. "And if you start talking about derivatives and shit, I'll know you're doing it just to be mean, so I'll have to squirt oil in your eyes as payback." He laughed, and her eyes twinkled back at him as she fought a smile. "But," she said as she continued rubbing his neck, "if something is bothering you, you should let it out. You'd be surprised how just talking about something can relieve tension."

"I think my boss is up to no good," he said, shutting his eyes as she went back to rubbing his neck. Apparently, releasing tension in his neck also loosened his tongue.

"Up to no good how?"

When he didn't reply immediately, she moved her hands from his neck to his chest, rubbing just above his pecs. He kept his eyes shut as she worked, but he wondered how much he could say without giving anything away. Too much was riding on him to take William down at all cost, now more than ever.

Fuck, he'd already said too much. If Shelby knew anything, someone could hurt her. Carl knew too much and had to be dealt with already. The thought of anybody hurting one hair on Shelby's head ignited fury. He couldn't chance it. He was in too deep and wouldn't tarnish any part of her with his dealings. He was getting close to her, and that was the problem. He had to put a stop to it, lock down his emotions.

Her hands traveled lower, caressing him on their path south. When she wrapped her oiled hands around his straining shaft, more tension flooded him, rather than leaving. He strained up into her grasp as she began to pump him because it had felt too good not to. He loved what she did to him, and he hated that. How could he push her away when he craved her so?

"Mason," she breathed, moaned, and his gaze flew up to her, yanking him out of his passionate haze with stark reality. He grabbed her hair, directing her to look at him.

"No," he bit out through gritted teeth. Her shocked expression tugged at his heart, which only spurred him on. "Don't call me that, Shelby. When it comes to sex, I am your Master." She let go of him, and he continued, "You're getting too close. This is not a relationship." His admonishment was as much for her as it was for himself. When she blinked a few times, he let go of her hair. Without looking at her, he rolled off the bed and stood. He needed distance right fucking now. "I think tonight was a mistake."

Her mouth dropped open, and her struggle for words was apparent as she quickly shook her head. "I'm sorry," she finally whispered, and looked down.

"We're done." He hated it, but pushing her away was his only choice. He reached for his pants and pulled them on. "I'll talk to my associates about finding you another Dom." He didn't like backing out of their arrangement. It went against his responsibilities as a Dom, but it couldn't be helped. Losing control was not a mistake he could afford to make.

"No." Her head snapped up. "You promised." Her

hands fisted beside her. The defiance she displayed toyed with his emotions on so many levels.

"You're in no position to fight me on this."

"I don't want to fight with you at all," she murmured as she relaxed her hands. "Please don't stop this. I trust you, and I want to keep going. I wouldn't be able to do this with anybody else. Not yet. I need you to help me, Master."

His eyes flared at her addressing him that way. He knew she did it because she was pleading, but he liked it all the same. He should stick to his guns and turn her away, knowing she could fall into the hands of an inexperienced Dom who could hurt her emotionally and physically. Or he could continue on with their scenes and risk being the Dom who would crush her in the end. He couldn't win either way.

No matter how much he wanted to stop this madness, he knew he couldn't, not completely, so he'd have to embrace another method.

If Shelby wanted to understand what being a real sub was all about, then it was time he damn well showed her... and hope she relented.

"Okay, Shelby. Be here at seven on Tuesday. Since you don't have an aversion to dressing up, wear a French maid costume like Emory suggested."

"Tuesday?" she asked, fidgeting with her hands. He could tell she saw where this conversation was going.

"Yes. The night we're open to everyone. If you want to continue with your training, the next scene will be public."

She swallowed, and he stood stock still, waiting, partly hoping she'd refuse, mostly hoping she wouldn't. Public scenes were common at clubs, and if she wanted to be in the lifestyle, she had to prepare for the possibility. Not that *that* was his motivation behind the reasoning. Oh no, he'd thrown a gauntlet in his frustration with her, frustration with their situation. Now, he waited.

"I'll be here Tuesday, Master."

Jesus. That was not what he wanted her to say. *Yes, it is, you prick.* "Goodnight, Shelby," he said, more clipped than necessary, and motioned toward the door. If she didn't get out now, he couldn't trust he wouldn't be groveling at her feet. For what, he wasn't entirely sure. He did know he'd always had precise control over his emotions and had never spoken to another woman like this. Sure, he punished subs when they were out of line, but this was different.

She picked up her bag and left without another word.

He heard the quiet click of the front door closing behind her, but felt it as if it was the door to his heart slamming shut.

As it should be.

He would do everything in his power to make sure it stayed that way.

## CHAPTER ELEVEN

In public.

That was what Shelby had thought about since last night, and it was all she could think about as she stared at whatever this file was on her desk.

"Normal people are happy on Fridays," Viola said as she popped over to Shelby's desk. Shelby glanced up, but was unable to muster a smile. Her coworker's face fell as she looked at her. "Did something happen last night?"

"Oh yeah." Boy did it ever. Before the realization her next scene would happen before everyone's eyes, she'd had amazing sex with Mason yet again. This time she'd planned on spending the night with him, only to be kicked out like a worthless slut. Then again, she was being paid to sleep with him, so if that was what he'd been going for, he'd nailed it.

"Uh-oh. Is that why Rick called the meeting this morning?" she asked, grabbing her arm. "Are you okay?"

Shelby was far from okay, but she couldn't go into it now. With the next scene being in public, she had an even bigger obstacle to clear. One she created herself, and one she had to fix immediately.

It was time to bring her team up to speed on everything. *Everything.* But she didn't have the strength to spew out all the sordid details more than once, so Viola would have to wait and hear it with everyone else. "Rick has new intel, and I told him I wanted to give an update since he was bringing everybody together." She picked up her cup and downed the last of its contents. "C'mon, I need more coffee for this."

Viola followed her to the break area and watched silently as she poured. "You don't look so good. Did he hurt you?" Her eyes narrowed, Shelby felt hers watering. She blinked a few times to hold off the tears. Yes, Mason had hurt her, but not physically. Threatening to end their association, telling her he was going to put her on display, and then kicking her out all because she'd called him by his name? Every bit of it bothered her. She didn't know what she expected, though. He wasn't her lover, not really. He was part of her job. She'd done this to herself. If she hadn't gotten too close to him, none of this would matter.

It did.

"I was bound last night. No lasting marks." On the outside. The inside was another matter, and one she wasn't ready to address. She headed to the conference room, and Viola followed silently beside her. When they got in, they sat beside each other and greeted the others as they came into the room. Shelby tried returning Darrell's smile, but it felt shaky. God, she wasn't looking forward to rehashing what had happened with Mason in front of Darrell.

The man frowned at her, obviously noticing something was off, but she quickly looked toward the door as Rick walked in.

"Thanks for getting here on short notice. I have an update, but first Shelby has a status on her investigation. We'll start with her."

Shelby's hands started sweating, and she looked down as she drew in a full breath, finding the strength to confess. When she looked up, all eyes were on her. She couldn't drag this out. The sooner she said the words, the faster this would be over with.

She looked directly at her boss because it made her feel more detached. "During my scene last night, I had sexual intercourse with Showalter." She didn't say she'd had sex with him during the first scene. She didn't want her ass chewed for keeping that a secret. The number of times it had happened wasn't relevant to the case. Although, if it had any importance at all, she'd lay it all out there.

Nobody made a sound, and Shelby was too nervous to look at their expressions. Rick didn't even flinch. She wasn't sure if that was good or bad.

"Were you forced?" he asked as he rubbed his chin.

"No, sir. I was a willing participant. I could have used my safe word to stop, but I didn't."

"Were you able to get anything out of him last night?"

"Not much." She swallowed, focusing her energy on the details and not the emotion involved. That was incredibly hard since sex on a normal day for her held a lot of emotion. Sex with Mason was off the charts in that department, in *every* department. But it was easier to stay detached if she relayed the specifics without the feelings. "He'd intended on me staying the night with him, but when I began asking questions, he ended our evening."

Rick's eyes darkened. "Were you made?"

"No," she said quickly. He had no idea she was an agent. "It took him a while, but he did say he thought his boss was up to no good, and he's stressed about it. I'm not sure if he would've said anymore last night because he's very closed off. I think he was surprised he said that much to me and used an excuse to put up a wall."

"What excuse?" Darrell asked, and Shelby wanted to groan at the sharpness of his tone.

She bit her lip and looked at him. "I called him by his first name."

"What do you normally call him?" Carson asked, perplexed.

"He's into BDSM," Viola said, and Shelby was relieved she'd come to her rescue. "What do you think?" she asked sarcastically. Shelby looked at her, and she was glaring at Carson. Then she looked at Shelby and gave her a short nod of encouragement.

"I call him Master during a scene. He and the other Doms that own the club are called Master by all the subs who are members."

Darrell mumbled something unintelligibly, and Shelby was smart enough not to ask him what he'd said. She was pretty sure she heard the words *kill* and *motherfucker*, though.

She swallowed before going on. "He's rattled. At one point, he was ready to call it quits with my training. Besides his boss, he mentioned details we already know—where he's from and his POW brother, Caleb, although he said he's deceased and not a prisoner. He eventually agreed to continue, but next time is not going to be easy." She took a deep breath and forged ahead to the other hard part of this conversation. "It's Tuesday night, and it'll be public."

"What the fuck," Darrell boomed, and a few others verbalized their concern and shock. Shelby shut her eyes and waited.

"Quiet!" Rick yelled, not willing to wait out the brief chaos. Once everyone hushed, he continued. "We knew this was a possibility." He looked at Shelby, and she nodded. He was right. This was a known complication. It was one thing to submit to a man in private. Knowing she had to do that had been hard to accept, but the possibility of being on display had lingered in the back of her mind where she refused to acknowledge it...until last night when Mason had told her it was happening.

"He's already fucked her," Darrell sneered. "He could take her right there in front of God and everybody. Tell me again how the hell this helps our case!"

"Because he's beginning to trust her." Viola said what they all knew. "And we need him to talk." There was no reason rehashing all the reasons why. Darrell was just angry, and although not helpful, Shelby appreciated his concern.

"I don't fucking like it," Darrell seethed.

"But Viola's right," Shelby said, and gave her arm a gently squeeze, thanking her for having her back. "He's not happy with me right now, but I also think he's not happy with himself."

"Which can make him dangerous," Carson said matter-of-factly.

Shelby glanced at him. "Yes, but I don't think he'd hurt me."

"Interesting choice of words," Rick said as he clasped his hands and leaned back into his chair. "The reason I called this meeting is because Carl O'Brian is missing. We have reason to believe he's dead, and one of the last known people to talk to him before he disappeared was Showalter."

Oh God. What was left of Shelby's tattered heart plummeted before taking off in a sprint. Had Mason been involved?

"That could be a coincidence," Viola said, waving her

hand dismissively while Shelby sat there mute. He couldn't be a killer, could he? That was crazy. So far beyond white collar crimes. Her thoughts continued to race as fast as the blood in her veins, but at every dark corner, she rejected the idea. Criminal? Maybe. Deadly? Not really. Not Mason.

"Or our Master could be a murderer," Darrell said, shaking his head. "Boss, we have pull Shelby from her assignment. It's too dangerous."

Shelby's gaze shot to Rick when he didn't immediately reject Darrell's suggestion. She understood their concern, but she hadn't considered they'd take her off the case. If she'd suspected this as a possibility, she sure as hell wouldn't have fought to keep her sessions with Mason. In some ways, this case was more hers than theirs, and it wasn't fair to remove her after all she'd been through. She could not let it all be for nothing.

Her boss regarded her as the silence stretched. "Is that what you want?" he finally asked.

"No." But that answer was laced with double meaning. No, she didn't want pulled from the case. No, she didn't want to stop seeing Mason. He might be through with her, and honestly, she was hurt and angry with him, but she wasn't ready to be done with him in any aspect. She couldn't wrap her head around the possibility he had something sinister to do with Carl O'Brian. It didn't add up to her. She wasn't sure how she'd get through Tuesday night at this point, but from the depths of her soul, she knew she had no other choice.

Rick nodded. "I want backup there that night."

Shelby gaped at him. "Why? I haven't had backup before."

"Because you've only been there on nights it's closed to the public. It would've been too obvious if a bunch of people showed up with you. We have an opportunity to get in and help you in the field, and we're going to take it."

It was bad enough strangers would see her naked—because she had no doubt that would happen—but her teammates seeing her was totally different. "It has taken him this long to talk to me. He's not going to start chatting with a stranger."

"Pull your head out of your ass, Landry. Someone else could snoop around while you're busy with Showalter. It's a public night and a chance we hadn't counted on. This is a good thing. We have a chance to blow this case wide open."

Oh God, she knew he was being logical, but if anybody showed up to investigate, they'd see her being whipped out in the open. Naked. Mason was pissed and closing himself off from her. There was no telling what he'd do to her. She had a feeling his decision to showcase her had been born out of anger, punishment for several reasons, not all she had any control over. Would he use their scene as further torment? Would he degrade and humiliate her in front of everybody? How could she look her coworkers in the eye after they witnessed something like that?

"I'll do it," Viola said, sitting straighter, and Shelby wanted to weep with relief. If anybody on this team had to watch her participate in an erotic scene, she'd pick Viola. "Carson would be too busy gawking at all the half-naked women to be of any help, and Darrell would get arrested for assaulting anybody who even looks at Shelby."

"I would not," Carson said, only slightly offended.

"Fuckin' A right," Darrell said at the same time as he crossed his arms and focused his glare on Shelby. Yeah, she knew there was no way in hell Darrell could sit idly by and watch.

Viola rolled her eyes and looked at Rick. "Dave and I

can go as a couple interested in the lifestyle. If we're asking a lot of questions, it won't seem suspicious." She looked at Shelby but kept talking to their boss. "And if anything goes wrong with her scene or my inquiry, I'm trained to handle it."

"Will your husband agree?" Rick asked.

Viola nodded. "I'm sure he'd like the idea of being there with me rather than me going by myself. If I show up alone, some other guy might hit on me and complicate my objective."

Shelby nodded and looked at Rick. "That could work. He knows I have a friend named Viola, and that she'd been worried about me before. I know the scene is going to be public, and a concerned friend might want to be there after finding out."

"The three of us could all go together—"

"No," Shelby said, cutting her off. "I don't know what will happen after. He could keep me well into the night. I don't want to be stranded there without transportation." She bit her lip as she thought. She liked the idea of not going in the club alone, but no way did she want to rely on Mason for transportation. Before last night, she might have felt differently, but he'd made it clear to her that they were not in a relationship. No matter how her chest hurt at his words. "I could follow you there in my car, arrive at the same time."

"Yes." Rick nodded. "That's cleaner than you going as a couple interested in the lifestyle. Dave might be immediately repulsed by what he sees, and I don't know how good of a poker face he has. If he becomes intrigued, then fine, you can work that angle into it, too. Either way, you could ask questions and see what you can find."

"Works for me," Viola said.

"Okay, people. Let's get back to work," Rick said as he stood, never one to mince words.

"Thanks," Shelby murmured to Viola as they both got up.

"Anytime." She smiled at her. "Let's go shopping tomorrow, so I can find the perfect outfit to wear."

Crap. Shelby needed to go shopping. She had a costume to purchase. Did stores even have French maid get-ups this time of year? "Sounds good."

Viola's face suddenly fell as she looked to the side, behind Shelby, and back at her. "We'll chat later." She flitted away before Shelby could ask what the rush was.

But when she felt a meaty hand on her shoulder, she knew the answer.

"Are you okay?"

She swallowed and faced Darrell. "Yeah, I'm fine."

He pulled her into a quick hug, which shocked her. Not that Darrell hadn't hugged her before, but he was usually all business at the office.

"I'm worried about you and this case."

She stepped away and sighed. "I know. But I'm doing okay. Two more weeks and it'll be over."

"Will it?" he asked, furrowing his brow. "Who says you don't get anything out of him during that time and you have to keep seeing him?"

She couldn't think about that right now. At the rate she was going, she wouldn't get anything out of Mason, but after last night, she was sure he would not be extending their arrangement past the initial four scenes. She had two weeks to get what she needed. Either way, her time was limited.

"If you need to talk, you know where I live. I don't care what time of day or night, little bit."

She smiled at him. "You worry too much."

"I have too much to worry about." He squared his shoulders, the business facade etching back into his features. "Now get back to work. We have a case to solve."

"Sir, yes sir." She smiled, and hoped it looked real. Talking to her team about what had happened and what was yet to come had been much easier than she'd anticipated, easier than what she'd gone through so far on this case, and a whole hell of a lot easier than what she would experience when Tuesday night got here. Her dread was multifaceted, but she would be lying to herself if she said she didn't feel any a spark of excitement. What did that say about her?

She didn't want to know.

## CHAPTER TWELVE

"I KNOW the perfect place where we should start. Punky's," Viola said excitedly as she navigated the treacherous traffic toward Main Street, lovingly called Pain Street by the locals. It had boutiques with the latest fashion trends housed in hundred-year-old buildings. Back then, there hadn't been a need for four-lane roads. Not that there was enough room, but the city had carved them in anyway. And parking? That was atrocious.

"There's a spot over there," Shelby said, pointing toward one of the few paid parking lots. Punky's was a good idea since it catered more to the party crowd and sometimes had some pretty eccentric clothing. Viola could find something cute to wear, and maybe Shelby would have some luck with the costume.

"Good eye." She whipped the car around, and Shelby grabbed the oh-shit handle.

"You're gonna get us killed," she groaned.

"Quit whining. Were you sick the day they taught defensive driving at Quantico?"

Shelby laughed. "It was more than one day, and I highly

doubt the bureau would be pleased you're using the skills you learned to chase down the bad guys to get a close parking spot for your Saturday shopping."

Viola smirked as she pulled the car into the spot in question and killed the engine. "Technically, this is bureau business, so we should've gone yesterday on the clock instead of on personal time. We should get overtime for this."

"Good luck with that." She'd rather get an all-expense paid trip to an island rather than time-and-a-half for her efforts. "We're duty bound. We're not in it for the money."

"Tell that to my husband."

They got out of the car and headed toward the shop Viola had mentioned. Because of Shelby's keen eye and Viola's mad driving skills, they were inside within minutes.

"Wow. I haven't ever been in here," Viola said, taking it all in.

"It's popular here during prom season. Gone are the days of traditional sequined gowns."

"Pfft. I wore silk to my prom."

When Viola picked up a red rubber-looking dress, Shelby shook her head. "I don't think a concerned friend would show up wearing that. In fact, you should probably wear something normal now that I think about it."

"Oh, hell no. I want to dress up. I need this." She went back to scraping the hangers across the rack as she analyzed each piece of trashy clothing. She seemed too intent, too focused, and Shelby got the feeling it wasn't because of their case.

"Hey," she said softly, drawing Viola's attention. "Is everything all right?"

"Yeah, why?"

But her eyes flicked to the side, a tale-tell sign of avoidance. Something was definitely off. "Are you and Dave having problems?" Shelby stepped closer to her. "Is that why you volunteered for this? To see if he'd be interested?"

Viola's shoulders slumped. "Kind of." She took a deep breath, but Shelby was already shaking her head. This was a bad idea. Viola needed to focus on the case and not some scheme involving her husband. "Just listen to me. Dave has been distant lately. I don't know what it is. He has to go out of town a lot, but he always has. It's not like either of us are working any more than before."

"Viola, I don't think this is going to be the time to light his fire. What if he doesn't like it?" Another thought slammed into her. "Is this something *you're* interested in?" she whispered.

Viola blushed. "I don't know. I've never thought about it before this case, but for the last few weeks I've been doing a lot of research. I'm intrigued. Like, maybe it could be something to try if Dave's game. No way would he go to a club like this without a reason, but if I can get him there for work and we both check it out then maybe he might open up to it."

"And what if you don't like it once you get there?"

She chewed her lip before finally saying, "Regardless, I think it's worth a shot."

"I don't know—"

"Look, Shelby. It's perfect. I'll be there working—and I *will* be working—and Dave gets exposed to something he otherwise wouldn't. If I approach him with the idea out of the blue, he'd think I was crazy...or worse, take offense. If I get him in the club and let him absorb it on his own, then maybe he'd be open to experiment a little."

Slowly, Shelby nodded. Viola had thought this through, and what she said made sense. Except for one detail. "And you're dressing up because?"

She flicked her blonde locks and turned back to the clothes. "Because I'm not stupid. If we go and Dave sees me wearing jeans, it'll be harder for him to fantasize about me. I need to look the part so his brain will be willing to cast me."

"What about Showalter?" Her throat tightened around his name. She hadn't said his first name aloud since he'd reprimanded her. She was torn between wanting to use it because of the closeness it represented and not wanting to use it because that was Mason's wish. Regardless of her verbalizing it, he'd still be Mason to her in her mind.

"What about him? He's your objective, not mine." She shrugged her shoulders and kept searching.

"True, but it doesn't make sense for my overprotective friend to show up dressed for sexing and not chaperoning."

Viola turned and put her hand on her hip. "I'm your friend. I'm not dead below the waist. It's completely plausible for me to dress up to come to this club. Hell, from what you said about the night you met him, you'd dressed like a Domme in your attempt to look the part of someone into the lifestyle. It's probably common practice for patrons to dress for the occasion. As your concerned friend, I'd be more worried about being kicked out because of some dress code violation if I show up in my sneakers. Your *friend* wants to blend in."

Though it wasn't as ideal, Shelby knew it had the potential to work. She'd told Mason at their first scene that Viola would come busting in if she didn't meet her afterward. As far as he knew, her friend was crazy enough to do it...and crazy enough to show up dressed in an outrageous outfit because she believed that was what people wore to clubs like his. "Okay, but maybe you should be one hundred percent the pissed off friend. If you talk to him or any of the partners, you could even complain about whatever you have on."

Viola wagged her eyebrows. "Does this mean I wear something really outlandish?"

"Whore it up, baby. Whore it up."

Viola squealed and rushed over to another section of clothing while Shelby hid her smile. They spent the next forty-five minutes rummaging around, looking for the perfect ensembles. She didn't have any luck finding an official French maid costume, but she did find a short *Alice in Wonderland* style dress that she could use. The right accessories and a feather duster, and no one would be expecting a White Rabbit to pop up anywhere around her.

But it was tame compared to what Viola had picked out. It looked as if it was made with belts and nothing else. Very bondage-inspired.

After they paid for the haul, the girls headed to Viola's car to drop off their goods before grabbing a bite to eat. Shelby felt her phone buzzing in her purse, but had her hands too full to fish it out. Once they got to the car, she felt it go off again, but this time, she heard the sound alerting her of the text message she'd received. She shoved her bags into the backseat, pulled out her phone, and gasped.

Mason had called.

Mason had sent the text.

"What is it?" Viola asked when she saw Shelby staring at her phone, not moving.

"Showalter."

Viola rushed around the car. "Let me see."

Shelby yanked the phone back out of her grasp. "I haven't even read it yet." She was almost too afraid to see what he had to say.

"What are you waiting for?"

She shook off her stupor and entered her password. As she read it, she frowned. "Just that he has a meeting Tuesday afternoon and might be late." She looked up at her friend. "He said to wait for him and not to leave."

"Okay. I guess it's good he gave you a heads up. Should you call him back?"

"No." She couldn't talk to him right now anyway. She didn't know what to expect when she saw he'd reached out to her. A little part of her had hoped he'd apologize for how things ended and maybe even make plans to see her outside the club. That same part of her that was being stupid because he'd done neither. To do so might encourage her to believe there was something more going on between them, and he'd made it clear that was not the case.

At least on his side.

The jury was still out on hers.

———

HE SHOULD'VE SENT her flowers.

Roses.

Yes, he should've sent her roses. Two dozen long-stemmed ones. That was what men did when they royally fucked up with their women. But Shelby wasn't his. She couldn't be his, not right now. He had too much shit going on at work to get carried away with her. He knew that. By God, he did, but it didn't make it easier.

Nor did it mean he couldn't explore something with her once he got William taken care of. But for that to happen, he needed to find a healthy balance between keeping her at a distance for now without her feeling completely dismissed by him. That felt too much like playing games, which he hated, but it was the best compromise he could come up with.

He'd realized this on Saturday, after the second night of no sleep and spending every daylight hour holed up in his office. If he couldn't be with her, he'd work, and he did, but his thoughts belonged to one long-haired brunette.

Mason had been so distracted by thoughts of Shelby he'd almost missed seeing William logging onto the system Saturday afternoon. What had made it stand out was William had connected from his office at the firm, not remotely from another location.

Why had his boss come to work on a Saturday? It hadn't made any sense. William spent as much time at the office as Mason did during the workweek, but the man never came in on the weekends.

Almost as quickly as William had logged in, he'd logged right back off. Although Mason had been exhausted from lack of sleep, he'd acted quickly, dragging his tired ass away from his desk to intercept his boss.

He'd succeeded in his efforts.

William hadn't been quick enough to hide his shock at seeing Mason at the office. That had told him William was doing something specific, possibly in a hurry, and hadn't been aware of anyone else being in the building or online. But what had been the strangest thing of all was William hadn't been alone.

Mason hadn't recognized the man with William, and his boss had fed him a line about leaving his access card to the country club in his office and needing it because they had a two o'clock tee time. Mason hadn't bothered asking him about accessing the computer network, rather, he'd made a mental note to check the logs for anything suspicious.

When William had asked why he wasn't out enjoying his Saturday, Mason had said he was looking for leads on the matter they'd discussed before. Mason didn't go into details in front of the stranger, but William understood he was talking about Carl. Before rushing out with his mystery guest, William mentioned he'd be scheduling a five o'clock conference call Tuesday afternoon with their Tokyo counterpart since it would be first thing in the morning their time.

Mason had much more important things to do that night, so he had fought down any immediate retort. That meeting was likely to last hours and would definitely interfere with his plans with Shelby.

No way was he canceling. He'd tried calling her to let her know he'd be late, but she hadn't answered. He'd immediately wondered if she was ignoring his calls, but didn't blame her if she was. He didn't like it, regardless, but everybody had a defense mechanism. He was sure hers had been activated.

Now it was Monday, and he still hadn't been sleeping worth shit. He hadn't found anything new on William or his involvement with the Culpepper Hedge Fund. From everything he could see, it all looked legit.

Too much so. Almost as if someone had made sure everything was in crisp order. That in and of itself had to be a red flag.

After seeing William at the office on Saturday, Mason had pulled out his special phone and relayed the details of his strange encounter to his silent partner. The man had been grateful for the information and was going to look into it immediately, but Mason hadn't heard back if they'd found anything viable. Unfortunately, that wasn't saying much. He was doing all the digging without much in return. It was as if he was on a need-to-know basis, and someone had decided he was on the ass end of that arrangement.

A meeting reminder popped up on his computer screen, and he rubbed his temple. He didn't have time to fret about any of this right now. He had work to do and a status report to give to one of his clients. So that's what he'd do. He would push the other stuff aside and give his all to his job. His *real* job here...making people money.

But the last thought he had as picked up his phone to make his scheduled call was that Jedrek had better be right about whoever this guy was helping him. His newest business partner was the one who'd suggested Mason contact him in the first place.

CHAPTER THIRTEEN

SHELBY WAS A NERVOUS WRECK! She'd taken the afternoon off to get her hair and nails done before her scene with Mason tonight, but instead of calming her, it made the night seem that much more ominous. Rather that enjoying her fresh look, she'd dwelled on the fact that yes, she'd be naked, but at least her hair would look good. As if anybody would be looking at her hair when her boobs were going to be the main event.

"You're late," Viola said once Shelby rolled down her window after pulling up beside her car at their rendezvous point down the road from the club. Dave sat quietly beside her. He didn't seem too thrilled at the moment, and Shelby really didn't have time to provide any reassurances.

"Yeah, yeah." She dug in her glove box for a napkin and shoved it into the collar of her dress to wipe away the sweat. As she stuffed the soiled napkins into the door's compartment, she said, "Let's go."

She pulled out, and they followed her to the club. Yes, she was running a few minutes late, but hopefully it wouldn't matter since Mason wasn't supposed to be on time. At least she hoped that hadn't changed because if he was there waiting on her, he might punish her for tardiness.

Then again, maybe he would stand her up, and she wouldn't have to go through with this. Frankly, she was okay with that idea at the moment.

They arrived at the club all too soon, and she got out of her car while she tugged her dress. The ruffled bloomers she had on left little to the imagination. The white collar and apron and bun would fuel any left, but the panties added a nice little touch to the costume.

Not that anybody at this club would be forced to guess what was under them. She shuddered at the thought. She'd put a lot of effort into dressing up tonight as requested, and she probably wouldn't be wearing it for long.

"You ready?" Viola asked.

"Oh crap." She dove into her backseat and grabbed the feather duster. "Am now."

Dave's eyes raked over her, but he didn't verbalize what he was thinking. He still didn't look happy, so she didn't feel the need to ask. What he thought of tonight didn't matter. He was here for show.

A nervous laugh escaped her. *She* was the one here for show tonight.

"Uh-oh. You should've had a few shots of to-kill-ya before coming here. You're shaking like a leaf."

"Tequila wouldn't help."

"It wouldn't hurt," Viola protested. "We'll both get drinks when we get in there."

"We're working," Shelby hissed. They both needed their wits about them tonight. Neither could afford to be in a drunken stupor.

"And we need it. If Showalter isn't here yet, then it'll

look odd if we're not drinking. It's a bar, for crying out loud."

"Yeah, okay." A drink sounded too good to pass up, so Shelby wasn't going to argue with her. She rubbed her hands on her short skirt and headed for the front door of the club.

They entered the club and paid the outrageous cover charge. Except for Shelby. She'd been informed she was on Mr. Showalter's guest list and didn't have to fork over the hundred bucks.

"Drink time," Viola said. "Grab us a table, babe. I'll get you a beer."

The area around the bartender was crowded, but that wasn't a deterrent for Viola. She grabbed Shelby's hand and yanked her along. She smiled and squeezed her way through the group to get to the counter. Shelby hunkered down behind her as she forged her path. Once they made it, Viola ordered several shots for the two of them and a light beer for Dave.

"There're a lot of people here." Way more than there usually was. Lord, she didn't know if she could let herself be on display.

"Just breathe. You'll feel better with a little liquid courage."

They watched as the bartender poured their shots and beer. Viola handed him her card, and Shelby clutched the tray of drinks. When she turned, though, she came face-to-face with someone she hadn't expected to see.

She blushed as Master Jedrek crossed his arms over his chest and stared down at her. Damn, he was intimidating.

"Hello, Sir."

"Shelby. Are those your drinks?" he asked, skipping the pleasantries.

"Their ours," Viola said, stepping up beside her as she tucked her card back into her minuscule purse.

Jedrek's nostrils flared, and his gaze heated when he looked at her partner in crime...and work, technically. That was more of a reaction than he'd ever shown Shelby. Jedrek gritted his teeth as he continued to look his fill. He wasn't being overtly obvious, but the time she'd been around him was enough for her to grasp that he wasn't one to express himself...at least not like this. It was too bad. He was barking up the wrong tree if he was interested in Viola. Thank God Dave wasn't standing here watching this man drink up his wife.

"And you are?" he asked, his voice dropping.

Viola didn't seem fazed by his response to her. Maybe being blissfully unaware was a side effect to marriage.

"I'm Shelby's friend, Viola."

"My *married* friend," Shelby specified. Viola looked puzzled, but the heat in Jedrek's expression slammed shut. Shelby swallowed. "Um, Viola, this is Master Jedrek. He's one of the owners of the club and a Master Dom here."

"Jedrek. What kind of name is that?"

His eyes narrowed infinitesimally, but Shelby noticed his agitation. The man was scary with a capital *scare*. Why was Viola being so blunt with him? Hell, Shelby knew Viola got flack for her name, so one would *think* the woman wouldn't comment on someone else's.

"A family one. Why are you here?"

"To support my friend. What's it to you?"

"Viola!" Shelby squeaked. She looked at Jedrek, but he was glaring at Viola still. "I'm sorry, Sir. She doesn't mean anything by that. She's just worried about me." She looked at Viola and whispered, "Knock it off."

"Why? I'm just being honest. It's one thing to engage in

kink in the privacy of your own room, but another to *make* someone do it in public."

Jedrek raised an eyebrow. "No one is making Shelby do anything. She's free to leave at any time."

"Yes," Shelby said. "And I don't want to." She looked at Viola, but her friend hadn't taken her eyes off Jedrek.

"Whatever you say, *Sir*." She sneered the title. Shelby blanched at the tick in Jedrek's jaw.

"It's Sir for her. *Master* for you."

"In your dreams, buddy."

Shelby had to defuse this situation before Jedrek snatched up her friend and hogtied her. He could do it. She knew first hand. "Viola, we should find Dave. Remember, *you* were the one who said maybe he will get inspired tonight," she said, trying a different tactic by mentioning her husband and the interest she had in the lifestyle.

It worked. She finally gave Shelby her attention. Shelby watched Jedrek, though, as he covertly scanned the crowd. Probably looking for Dave, but she wasn't sure if it was because he wanted to know where Shelby was headed since Mason wasn't here...or if he wanted to scope out Viola's husband. Not that it mattered if that was the case.

He looked at Shelby again, but she wasn't sure if he'd found his target. "Does Master Mason know you're drinking tonight?"

"No, Sir. Um, he didn't say I couldn't. He's going to be late, so I thought it'd be okay."

"And it's a free country," Viola said.

Jedrek growled. As in an *I wouldn't be surprised if he turned into a huge grizzly bear* sound. She was so going to hurt Viola for poking him. His gaze snapped to Shelby. "You can have two. No more."

Viola's jaw dropped and she started to protest as he

turned to leave, but Shelby grabbed her arm with her free hand and yanked her away. "Quit pissing off the big, bad Dom."

"What a dick!"

"Cool it."

They wound their way around the crowd to the table Dave had secured. He pocketed his phone and grabbed his beer as they sat.

"This was the best I could do," he said before taking a sip.

"It's fine, babe." She pushed a shot toward Shelby. "Here. Drink as much as you want. That guy isn't your boss."

Shelby picked up the shot glass and downed it, enjoying the burn. "I'm not disobeying him. That's one of Showalter's friends. Besides, he was the one who tied me up last week. I don't want on his bad side."

Viola's eyes grew wide, but Shelby shook her head, knowing where her thoughts were going. She knew Shelby had slept with Mason that night, but she'd never gone into any details with Viola or her team. "He wasn't there for the other stuff."

"Well, I still don't like him."

"Who?" Dave asked.

"Some jerk at the bar."

"Drop it, Viola. We're here to work, not bitch about the partners of Scene."

"Fine," she grumbled, picking up a shot glass. "I still say you should drink as much as you want."

"Not if she knows what's good for her," another man said from the side, and they all snapped their heads in his direction. She gaped at him, another man she recognized, but this one wasn't from a previous scene.

"Master Emory," she breathed. He was her tormentor for tonight.

"Emory Strom," he said, offering his hand to Dave. He looked at Shelby after shaking the man's hand. "Mason called. He said for us to get started."

She blinked, not understanding. "Huh?"

He smiled, and under different circumstances, she'd find him attractive in that pretty-boy kind of way. "He booked the main viewing room. If we start late, we might not finish before the next scheduled scene."

Uh-oh. "He wants me to start without him?" Saying the words aloud didn't help her grasp the concept. It was if she was talking about someone else, something totally different.

"Yes." His eyes never left hers as she absorbed this. He was serious. She and Mason had not planned on her doing any scenes without him. That hadn't been part of the deal. Could she do this? She looked at Viola who was watching the man acutely, taking him in and probably cataloging all his features. She was a hell of a field agent. Right. Because they were both here to do a job. *Hell, I don't have a choice.*

Then her heart fell. Was Mason making her do this without him as part of her punishment? To prove to her that he could still control the situation without actually participating? Was this another sign that he didn't want to have anything to do with her? How many times did he have to spell it out? If that was the reason, he was being loud and clear now.

"You'll be in good hands," Emory said softly. She got the feeling he was the one who coaxed the unwilling into the begging-for-more category. He was that convincing. She appreciated the sincerity since she had no other alternative but to follow through.

She slowly stood.

"You look lovely, by the way. Thank for you doing this for me." He cocked his head to the side and smiled as he took in her outfit.

She nodded without saying anything. She feared no words would actually come out.

"Here," Viola said, passing a shot of tequila to her. "For luck."

Shelby grabbed it and downed the precious liquid before giving her friend one last look.

Emory chuckled as they stepped away. "It might help your nerves, but it won't bring you the luck you need. There is no helping the pain from my whip."

The whip. She'd been so focused on being on display that she'd forgotten she was to be whipped tonight. Crap! How could she not remember something like that? It had taken her days to get over the spanking scene. This was sure to hurt a lot more.

Hmm...it was going to hurt again, no doubt, but maybe he'd go easy on her. Bondage had been difficult, but it showed her that BDSM was more about the mental and less about the physical. Pain wasn't a requirement.

And Emory seemed like an easygoing guy.

He picked up some kind of whipping tool and her jaw dropped. He swung it, and it snapped in the air, cracking the stillness like thunder. He smiled and crooked his finger at her to come closer. The smile on his face was anything but friendly. He seemed more than just willing to do this for Mason. He looked eager. It was then she realized he *wanted* to inflict pain on her. There was a word for Doms like that. Her eyelids fluttered shut as the term filtered through her mind.

He was a sadist. A *real* sadist.

The crack of the whip jolted her to open her eyes and stare at him.

"Now, Shelby," he said sternly, no longer wearing a smile.

*Oh, fuck.*

———

MASON HIT the alarm on his Porsche and strode to the back entrance of the club. The meeting with their Tokyo office hadn't lasted as long as he'd feared. In fact, it almost seemed pointless. The discussion of last month's quarterly earnings was old news, in his opinion, and the projections for this quarter weren't out yet. What was discussed could've been covered in an email or postponed until this quarter's predictions were finished. Time was money, and that meeting had been a waste of both.

Just another example of why William needed to be removed from his position, and Mason would be damn glad when that happened. Not that he'd gotten word yet from his silent helper. He didn't know how the man worked, and frankly, he didn't care. As long he got him something he could use.

The club was packed, but he knew it would be. In the years since they'd opened Scene, it had grown in regular membership at a steady pace, but it wasn't cheap. Not everybody had the cash or assets to join, so open night was always a success, regardless of the admission cost. But he wanted to consider a different business model, change the number of times they were open to the public from once a week to once a month. As long as memberships continued to increase based on previous trends, he figured they could do this next year.

Limiting the number of nights they were open to the public would increase demand, so they could charge a premium for the admission to offset the loss of income from the other nights.

A scream from around the corner jolted him out of his money-making thoughts. *Shelby.*

He checked his watch. He was only forty minutes later than he'd planned on being here originally. He'd called Emory after he left the office, so he could start the scene. He wanted to be here for it, but knew he'd only miss a few minutes, if any. Jackson had the room booked months ago for his anniversary, and Mason wasn't going to do anything to screw up his member's plans. It was either start Shelby's scene without him or reschedule. Ultimately, he knew he would be seeing her tonight anyway, and he didn't want to risk spending more time with her than he needed to. His instincts had screamed for him to not make the call to Emory, demanding that Mason be there for every second she was with another Dom.

So he did it anyway.

When he rounded the corner and came to the roped off area where the crowed had gathered, the air locked in his lungs. Emory had her strapped to a St. Andrews cross. The costume he'd instructed her to wear had been unzipped, the top half hanging over the skirt, but she still had on an apron. Her full breasts had engulfed the top of it. Seeing her partially clothed was sexier than if she'd been completely naked.

Her head hung down, hair covering her face.

Her welt-covered back exposed.

She was fucking beautiful.

Emory swung and tagged her again, and she screamed, her hands fisted, neck corded. The silver streaks lining her face sucker punched him.

"I-I can't," she sobbed.

He struck her again. "The only word out of your mouth should be your safe word." He whipped her again.

"Oh God," she screeched.

Mason shucked his jacket as he stormed over there and tossed it to the floor. He grabbed her chin and forced her to look at him. She needed grounding because when he'd seen her begging, she'd looked lost. This was what she needed *him* for. To help her accept the way of life, learn how beautiful it could be.

"M-Master," she sobbed.

His heart seized, and he stroked her hair. "You can do it, pet."

She shook her head. "It hurts. It hurts."

He looked to the side at Emory and lifted a finger for him to wait. The man nodded back at him.

Mason kissed her tears as she sobbed against him, and he kept kissing her cheeks and neck, trying to soothe her, until her crying finally eased. When she took in a stuttering breath, he moved his lips to hers and claimed her mouth. It was difficult to connect with her while she was strapped to the cross, but he needed to touch her, to comfort her. As she relaxed into him, he knew he'd gotten through her haze of pain and pulled away slowly to gaze into her wet eyes.

"Tell me why it hurts," he whispered.

Her breath stuttered as new tears formed, and he immediately knew he wouldn't like the answer. But, somehow, he already knew. It was why he'd asked *why* and not where.

"You weren't here," she whispered.

"Ahh, pet, I'm sorry." He kissed her cheek again. "I wanted to be."

"Really?" she asked, her eyes hopeful, and the pain in his chest shredded him. She was too vulnerable, too beautiful to play with like this. Pushing her away wasn't the right answer. He didn't know what was, but he knew he'd royally fucked up. Again.

"Yes, really. We're going to have a long discussion when this is through. I have much to apologize for," he murmured. Her smile was timid, and because he couldn't help himself, he kissed her again. "Are you ready to continue?" Her eyes grew, but he stroked her face to keep her from panicking. "I'm here now, pet. You have me to lean on."

She bit her lip and nodded.

"What's your safe word?"

"Red."

"Good girl." Mason glanced at Emory and gave him the go ahead to continue.

When the next lash came, he was right there with her, watching her, relishing her beauty, absorbing her pain. He held her face, refusing to break the eye contact he had with her, the view into her soul too precious to lose. He murmured words of encouragement, told her how wonderful she was. How perfect. Still he watched as tears streamed down her face, but no other reaction came from her. No more screaming. When her eyes glossed over, he knew she'd reached the sweetest nirvana reserved for subs, and she'd done so without one sexual touch from him. His chest expanded with pride for her because she'd let herself go and allowed it to happen...and for himself for being the reason she'd achieved it. Yes, Emory wielded the whip, but Mason mastered the girl.

One more strike, and he signaled his partner to halt. Any cheers and verbal encouragements the audience gave Shelby during her scene hushed to a quiet respect as they continued to regard her. He and Emory worked methodically to release her from the cross, and Mason wrapped her as if she was precious cargo before carting her toward the private room off the staged area. He needed his time with her, and her care wasn't for public display.

She remained dazed as he held her on his lap, and he simply caressed her tear-stained cheeks. She was a vision, and he'd be lying to himself if he pretended he wasn't turned on by her in this state. It was who he was. He loved a woman's complete submission, but something about her in this moment made it so much more....*more*. He didn't know what exactly. He was a sexual man, and he preferred the scenes he conducted to be physically gratifying in that respect. When a scene ended without that erotic connection, he didn't feel completely fulfilled. He would be pleased if the sub achieved her goals because it was his duty as a Dom to see to those needs first, but he would come away lacking that completeness too.

Until now.

This was the first time since he'd enjoyed play that he hadn't needed that physical release. The scene had been complete without it. She had been perfection. What did it say about him? What did any of his reactions to her say about him? He didn't know. God, he didn't fucking know. But they couldn't avoid what was happening anymore.

Before this night was through, they'd have that talk he mentioned. Maybe by then he'd know what he was going to tell her.

# CHAPTER FOURTEEN

A DULL ACHE roused Shelby from her trance. The mellow feeling that had engulfed her was quickly turning into a burning on her backside. She shifted and blinked, the room she'd been staring at coming into focus for the first time. Where was she?

And why had a swarm of bees attacked her back? Jesus, it was on fire. She hissed and turned to look over her shoulder. Her gaze immediately locked with Mason's concerned one.

Oh God, it all came rushing back to her. The whipping. The pain. She moved her hand to feel her back. Was she bleeding? It felt as if she'd been ripped to shreds.

"Don't, baby," he whispered, and she immediately stilled.

"It hurts."

"I need to put some ointment on it, but I didn't want to disturb you. C'mon. Let me get you upstairs." He rose and cradled her in his arms. "After I finish tending to you, we'll go to bed, and I'll hold you all night."

"Viola," she gasped. Where was her friend? Where was

Dave? Had they watched and wondered where she was now, or was her partner too busying snooping around? She couldn't concentrate on that right now, but she also couldn't leave without talking to Viola. "Where is she?"

"Who?" he asked, frowning at her. He put his hand on her forehead and rubbed. "You might still be out of it, baby. It's just us."

"No. I mean..." She shook her head to get the cobwebs out of it. She couldn't do anything about her dry mouth. "My friend Viola and her husband came with me tonight. She was worried about the public scene and wanted to be here for support. I can't leave without talking to her. She'll be worried."

He nodded slowly. "Okay, pet." He put her down, and she very gently settled onto the couch. "I'll find out who's working the front door and have him point them out to me. You stay here and rest. I'll bring them to you."

She swallowed, trying to get saliva to form in her mouth. He seemed to notice her need, bent over to retrieve a water bottle, and handed it to her. "Thanks," she whispered as she opened it. "Master Emory met them before the scene. You can ask him." That was all she could say before she guzzled a third of the bottle.

He stroked her hair until she pulled the bottle away from her lips. Without a word, he nodded at her and left.

She stared after him, wondering how long they'd been alone in this room. After looking around, she confirmed that she hadn't seen it before, so he must have brought her in here. She shifted and winced. Damn, but her flesh was screaming. That scene had been pure torture. She understood why Mason wanted her to experience it.

Because some people got off on pain, and she wouldn't know what she liked until she tried it. The spanking had been tolerable. Hell, it had been hot, but she doubted she'd like the whipping even if he'd been the one striking her.

In fact, she knew she wouldn't have.

With the first lash, she knew Hell had found her. There'd been no escape. No enjoyment, not even toleration.

Not until Mason had shown up. After he'd soothed her and touched her, she no longer had control of her body, her desires. She'd become his vessel of pleasure, and her instinct had been to satisfy his needs, regardless of what they were. She shivered as she accepted the fact that she would've had sex with him right there in front of everybody if he'd wanted it. Though sex wasn't what he'd sought.

She almost wished it had been. Him holding her, comforting her had touched her in a place she'd never felt before. It had felt completely foreign. And beautiful.

She blinked as she felt her eyes water. She couldn't fall in—*no*, she couldn't even think about feelings. Couldn't go there at all. To do so would force her to admit something she was too scared to.

The door opened, drawing her attention. Viola stared at her wide-eyed and slowly approached as if she was scared Shelby would be spooked by her presence and try to run.

"Hey," she said slowly.

"Hi." Shelby looked behind her, but didn't see anybody else come in. "Where's Dave?"

"He's outside with Showalter." She took her time moving toward Shelby and sat carefully. "How do you feel?"

She would've laughed without mirth if she could've mustered the strength. "That's the million dollar question now, isn't it?" She shrugged and seriously regretted the movement, but she tried to cover her grimace. "I don't know," she murmured. "Everything seems so... I don't know."

Viola reached over and took her hand. "That was intense. If Showalter hadn't shown up when he did, I was about to stop that shit myself. I don't know how. I think I started to on instinct because I'd stepped away from Dave all tense and caught that big bald guy watching me."

"Master Jedrek."

"Yeah, whatever. That dude has a serious attitude problem."

Shelby chuckled then. "I thought of him as Mr. Mean when I first saw him."

"It suits." Her smile was sad. "I couldn't find out anything. He watched me like a damn hawk. He didn't realize I noticed, but I sure as hell did. I had to play off the concerned friend, then the pissed friend when you were whisked away—emotions I did not have to fake, by the way. I even confronted Emory. He seemed cool and easygoing again. It was like he was a different person while he was whipping you. I demanded answers, but he gave placating ones. It was a total bust for me. I did have Dave hang out at the bar, though, to see if he could get some general information about the club. It's a long shot, but I didn't want to waste the resource."

"Smart."

"Maybe. I'll talk to him tonight to see if he picked up anything, but I'm not holding my breath."

"You did what you could. I don't know what Rick expected you to find."

"I think maybe he doesn't like you being here alone and wanted you to feel secure knowing you had backup this time."

"I get it, but the change of heart is too little too late."

Viola arched an eyebrow at her. "You know he's not leaving you alone here, right? Not really."

"I know protocol is to have a team in place in case something happens when one of us is out in the field, but this isn't a simple sting op. They'd have to have a team working twenty-four-seven since I never know when Showalter will call."

"True, but I heard him talking to Carson about taking the shift tonight. I asked Carson after Rick left, and he said they've had a surveillance team near the location whenever you're scheduled to be here. He didn't give specifics, and I got the feeling he'd been instructed to keep quiet about it."

Shelby's mouth dropped. "Why wouldn't he announce it in the meeting if he had someone watching the outside while I'm here?" That didn't make any sense. If their objective was to solve this case, then they should all be privy to everything.

"You know Rick doesn't believe in democracy. Not on his team. He's lord of his manner, and we all do what he says. I'm sure he has his reasons, and he'll align himself with them until the end."

Viola was right about that, but she had another nagging thought. "Then why didn't Darrell say anything? He's not one to keep secrets from me."

That earned her an eye roll. "Girl, I know you two are tight and all, but that man is so by the book the damn thing is fused to his hand. Maybe Rick didn't want you focusing your energy on anything other than getting close to Showalter. Who knows? If he told Darrell to leave you out of it, he would follow his orders."

Shelby nodded slowly. "Yeah, you're right." But as she looked at Viola, another thought came to her. "If I wasn't told because of some concern over my ability to maintain focus on my objective—"

"I didn't say that."

Shelby held up her hand to stop Viola's protest. "Anyway. Why weren't *you* told?"

She shrugged. "I don't know. It was just a theory. The guys are all single except for Rick. Maybe he didn't want me pulling all-nighters away from my husband unless it was necessary. Maybe he figured I'd be pulled in with you at some point for support since I'm the only other female on our team since Anna got reassigned. Who knows how that man's mind works."

"I'll talk to Darrell, see if he tells me anything since Carson didn't elaborate with you."

Viola shook her head and grabbed her arm. "Don't. If you tell Darrell, then Darrell will go to Rick and inform him you asked. It'll get back to him that Carson talked to me, and I don't want his ass chewed. No matter how much he deserves it for being such an irritating flirt." She let go and eased back. "At least now we both know what's going on, if not the details."

"We don't know anything other than they're out there somewhere."

The smile Viola gave her was calculating. "A few tracking devices and a nifty little app fixed that." She winked.

*Oh no.* "And you're worried about Carson getting in trouble? Have you lost your mind?" she whispered heatedly. "If Rick finds out—"

"He won't. I'm watching their backs, too. If the shit hits the fan, I'll be able to help."

Shelby's shoulders fell as realization dawned. "You tagged my car, too, didn't you?" she asked, deadpan.

Viola wiggled her phone and wagged her eyebrows.

She sighed. "Don't get caught." Using tools of the trade on suspects was one thing...turning them on fellow agents was completely another.

"You let me worry about that. I'm watching everybody." She checked her watch. "We should probably go. I'll drive your car, and Dave can follow me to your house. Unless you just want to come home with us." She frowned and made an attempt to look to Shelby's side for a glimpse of the marks she knew marred her back. "You shouldn't be alone. We have a guest room—"

"No."

"Okay. I'll stay with you. I brought a change of clothes since I wasn't sure how long I could stay in this getup, but it's surprisingly comfortable." She smirked and looked down at her outfit. "We can ride in together tomorrow, and Dave can pick me up from the office."

Shelby took a deep breath before clarifying. "I mean, no. I'm not going anywhere. Mason wants me to stay with him tonight."

If Viola's eyes opened any wider, they'd pop out. "I don't think that's a good idea."

The door opened then, and they both jumped. Shelby winced at the pain.

"I'm sorry to interrupt," Mason said, hanging onto the doorframe, not coming into the room. "But I really should get some medicine on your back, pet. Let me take care of that, and you can keep visiting with your friend."

"We're not visiting," Viola said, venom in her voice. "I was just telling her it was time to go. Dave can help her to my car."

Shelby glanced between the two of them. Viola looked pissed, but Mason didn't seem bothered by it. He slowly crossed his arms and leaned against the doorjamb. "I've asked her to stay."

"I don't care."

"Shelby?" Mason asked with a single raised eyebrow.

She licked her lips. There was no question where she'd be staying. She knew where she wanted to be. She looked at her endearing friend. "I'll be fine. We'll talk tomorrow."

Viola stared at her as if she was going to say something, or maybe communicate with her eyes. It didn't matter. Her reply would be the same no matter how Viola relayed her message. "All right." She leaned in and hugged her, careful not to touch her back.

When she stood, Shelby gave her a reassuring smile and watched as she walked away. By the slight smirk on Mason's face once she cleared the doorway, Shelby was sure her friend had given him the stink-eye on her way out.

He came toward her, and her body tried to come alive, which only intensified the pain. The blood rushing in her veins made her back throb something awful.

"Are you ready for me to take care of you, baby?" he said softly, and kissed her forehead.

He was so tender, and in that moment, all she could manage was a nod in response.

———

MASON WATCHED for any signs of discomfort as he placed Shelby on her feet by his bed. He would have lain her down if not for her clothes. He needed her bare to tend to her welts. Without outlining his intent, he pulled the blanket from her, tossed it to the edge of the bed, and proceeded to untie the apron from behind her neck, never taking his gaze off hers. He wondered if she realized she watched him so openly, but he worried she'd stop the moment he broke the silence.

So he didn't.

With her apron now puddled on the floor, her breasts were exposed. He dared not look.

Unzipping her short dress had been easy even without the benefit of watching what he was doing. Once it fell free, he clutched her hands and coaxed her to the side. She stepped out of it easily, and he squatted before her, looking up as she looked down at him, still locked in his gaze. He slid his hands up her legs and over her thighs to her panties to quickly divest her of them as well.

Now that she was completely naked, it was time to turn her away from him. He missed the connection before it was even broken.

"Lie down on your tummy," he softly ordered.

She turned and climbed onto the bed, her abraded back a glaring beacon, calling him to fix her. He wasn't a sadist, though he didn't judge those who were. He enjoyed some pain when mixed with pleasure, but his fascination with it wasn't to the extent of Emory's. His business partner thrived on the pain, but hadn't found anyone strong enough to endure what he needed to give. As long as Mason had known him, he'd always had to back off before he was ready. The man would never push a sub beyond her limit, would never take his skill too far with one, but that didn't mean he wasn't missing that feeling of completeness.

Though, right now, Mason had an insane urge to go downstairs and turn the whip on his friend. He pushed down that gut reaction as he walked to the bathroom to gather the necessary items. There was no need to avenge Shelby's whipping, no matter what part of him tried to demand it.

With a warm, wet cloth and medicine in hand, he returned to Shelby to find her in the exact same position as he'd left her.

"This may hurt, pet. I'll try to be gentle."

She moaned as he started to clean the sweat from her back, but he was careful not to irritate her skin too much.

"You did very well tonight, Shelby. I know I've already praised you, but it bears repeating."

"Thank you."

He tossed the washcloth to the side and hit the button on the ceiling fan remote to help dry her back before applying the ointment. She shivered lightly, and he caressed her arm as they waited. When her skin was no longer damp, he flicked the lid on the tube.

"You doing okay?"

"Yes, Master."

His chest tightened as he smeared the medicine on her marks. She'd wear them for several days, but Emory hadn't broken her skin. Good thing. If he'd made his Shelby bleed, Mason would have returned the favor.

*His* Shelby?

He swallowed and escaped that longing thought to focus on his task. When she was sufficiently covered, he wiped his fingers on the cloth and moved to the other side of the bed to turn down the covers. He stripped before scooting her to the exposed sheets and sliding into bed beside her, tucking them both in.

Because he couldn't help himself, he touched her cheek as she burrowed closer to him. "So beautiful," he whispered.

She kissed his neck and slid her leg over his hip. Lightning flashed in his groin when her knee grazed his dick, bringing it instantly to life. In her position, she was open to him, knowledge his body couldn't ignore. His hand found her hip and pulled her closer to him as his mouth descended to hers. She moaned, and he ate it up, possessing her mouth with a need so profound it rocked him to his core.

So he kissed her, massaged her tongue with his, inhaled her breaths, made love to her mouth while his hands swept over her body, discovering areas that were unorthodox erogenous zones. Beside her bellybutton, in the crook of her hip, along her waist, between her breasts. All the while he ravished her mouth, his kiss becoming impatient, which belied the gentleness of his exploration of her body.

When she groaned and thrust her hips toward him, he answered her call by rolling them until he loomed over her. He trailed kisses down her neck, and she clutched at his back. It had been a long time since he'd had sex with another woman, even longer since he'd done so without topping. His inner Dom usually demanded it, but right now, he just wanted to be with her. No restraints, no kink.

"Oh God," she breathed when he reached her breast and tongued her nipple. She arched into him, and he sucked it into his mouth. He devoured her offering, her whimpers and moans fueling him. When he released it, he dove for her other nipple, not letting her rest. Shelby fisted his hair as he worshiped her with his mouth. He shivered at the feel of her hands on him, a sensation he wasn't sure he'd ever experience without instinctively reacting.

"Shelby." He moved down, peppering kisses in his wake. The lower he went, the more her heady scent surrounded him. He could get drunk on her and love every second of it. He licked along the side of her labia, taking his time circling her pussy, inhaling her ambrosia. He knew when his tongue connected with her core he wouldn't be able to go slow. He was already about to lose his mind for wanting her.

"P-please."

That was all it took. He wanted to take his time with her, but her needs came first. She would never have to beg him to tend to her. Not ever. He licked up her center and growled and how good she tasted. The hands in his hair tightened, and yes, he ravished her. There had never been any doubt. He licked, nipped, stabbed his tongue inside of her while she became restless beneath him. He shoved her legs wider and pushed two fingers inside of her. He bent his fingers, rubbed the sweet spot vigorously, and sucked on her clit until her whimpers became screams.

"Fuck," he groaned, pulling away and fumbling in the nightstand drawer for a condom. He ripped it open and rolled in on before she came down from her high. He had to have her now. "I can't wait."

He thrust into her clenching pussy, and she gasped at the sudden intrusion. He didn't give her time to adjust. He pulled almost all the way out and forged in again, looking down, watching where their bodies were connected, the image too powerful to ignore.

"Maso—Master."

His gaze sought hers when she'd almost said his name. She'd corrected herself before finishing it, but he didn't know how he felt about that. He'd tossed her out the last time she'd called him by his name while being intimate. Now, he regretted her not saying it. Any Dom could be a Master. His business partners were all titled that at the club, but there was only one Mason in her life. It was another intimate level, another connection to make, one he was surprised he coveted.

He pushed those thoughts away and focused on the here and now. He held her to him, and she wrapped her arms around his back as he continued to take her. He tried controlling his thrusts, but it was so damn difficult with her breathing in his ear, clutching him like she couldn't get enough.

She hooked her leg on his hip, so he grabbed her knee and pushed her wider. He ground his pelvis into her, going deep, and she exploded. He roared as he came with her.

The sublime release.

A perfect woman.

He let go of her knee and collapsed onto her, barely remembering to catch his weight on his forearms. He kissed the tip of her nose. "How's your back, baby?"

Her face scrunched. "I hadn't noticed until you said something."

He eased back and stood beside the bed. "Roll to your side," he said before leaving to deal with the condom. When he returned, he smiled to see she'd done as he'd instructed. He loved it when a sub trusted him enough to do what he'd asked without question. It might seem barbaric to those on the outside, but he was man enough to admit how precious a gift that was.

How precious she was becoming to him.

As he watched her from a few feet away, he couldn't help how right this felt to him. How perfect she fit. He swallowed as his heart pounded while looking at her. The feeling in his chest was so strong it was getting difficult for him to breathe.

God, he was falling in love with her. He ran a hand through his hair, debating what he should do about that. Could he love her and not have her?

No. No, he couldn't, but that didn't change his circumstances.

His feet were cold by the time he crawled back into bed, so he was careful not to touch her with them. She turned to him, and he wrapped his arms around her. They still hadn't talked about things, but she was already breathing heavily, almost asleep. He couldn't put it off past tomorrow. The longer he waited, the harder it'd be. There was only one way he could ensure they cleared the air before he did any more damage to his heart.

"Spend tomorrow with me," he whispered into her hair.

She stirred and blinked up at him. "Don't you have to work?"

"You're more important."

She took longer than his comfort level preferred before responding. Then she smiled slowly. "Okay."

He stole a kiss because he couldn't help himself, relief and something else burrowing inside of him. Tomorrow, they would talk and make some decisions about what was happening between them.

Tonight, he would hold her.

# CHAPTER FIFTEEN

Shelby stretched sore muscles, a feeling of comfort and happiness blanketing her as she awoke.

Not in her bed.

She shot up and gaped at her surroundings, but it didn't take long before it all came flooding back, aided by the slight pain from last night's whipping. Nothing like a flash of reality to lift the sleepy fog from her brain.

Moving off the bed, she tested her muscles and her lightly aching back. *Hmmm...not too bad.* After what she'd gone through, she expected more stiffness or even down-right agony. The whipping had hurt like a mo-fo. There was no preparing for something like that. It had been blinding pain from the moment Emory had started...until Mason had shown up.

*Mason.*

She glanced around the room only to find that she was alone. It was dark, no light shining in from outside. The clock confirmed the insanely early hour. Where was Mason? Did he leave the bed after she'd fallen asleep? Had she slept alone all night?

Her heart fell as she accepted that possibility. She'd been too worn out and had literally crashed after he'd made love to her.

Made love? Oh crap. She couldn't think of it like that, no matter how caring he'd seemed last night.

And he had. God, he'd treated her with kid gloves. Not even that...he'd handled her as if she'd been precious to him. But she'd been through a difficult scene and needed tending to. Had it all been a reaction to some obligation he felt toward her, nothing more? If so, it made sense why he wouldn't sleep in the same bed as her. Besides, he didn't want a relationship. He'd made that perfectly clear, so why would he feel compelled to hold her all night?

But he'd asked her to spend the day with him. She felt so confused. Asking her to spend time with him had to mean something, right?

*It doesn't matter, dumb ass. He's a mark.* She shook her head to clear it as she looked for something to put on. She wasn't wearing the costume she'd worn last night. Hell no. She needed to get dressed in something more comfortable and call Viola. Mason wanted to spend the day with her—regardless of his reason—and she had to report in to let her team know she wouldn't be at the office. Viola was the only one she could risk contacting, and knowing her, she would track Shelby's every move today. She was a-okay with that. She was too conflicted to be left to her own devices.

Mason was an enigma. She couldn't begin to guess what he had planned for today. Knowing Viola had her back would make this easier. It would be even easier if she knew what *Mason* was thinking because she really had no idea.

*Maybe he's falling for me?* She cursed her speeding heart. She couldn't afford anything like that. She was already too connected to him, and this wasn't a normal situation. If he wanted her beyond their four scenes, she would have to...what? Hell, she didn't know, and that was the problem, one of many, actually. What she did know was that she liked him. A lot. Too much. Way too much. Then again, Rick would probably like it if Mason was enamored with her. Her boss didn't give a shit about her love life.

Love? Oh hell. This was all kinds of messed up... because she was well and truly falling in love with him. Mason, a man who'd stolen her heart faster than any other before him. A man who might be a murderer.

If her boss found out, he'd sack her. If her brother found out, he'd go AWOL just so he could toss her in a room and stand guard outside of it twenty-four-seven. If more powerful people found out, she'd be put under a microscope for sure with every decision she had ever made analyzed for anything illegal. She knew how it worked. Hell, she'd just worked on the case in Arkansas investigating the Bang Shift crew for that very reason.

She was so screwed no matter how she looked at it.

Shelby grabbed Mason's shirt from the floor and put it on. If she shut her eyes and inhaled his masculine scent, she pretended it never happened.

She tiptoed out of the bedroom in search of where he went. This place wasn't huge, so if he hadn't slept with her, he'd be on the couch. She didn't know what she expected to find or if she'd even do anything but watch him while he slept. God, she had it bad if she'd rather stay awake and be near him than go back to bed and sleep.

She froze when she heard muttering.

"I told you, I'd take care of it."

*Mason.* He sounded pissed.

Shelby took another step closer, but something inside told her not to make any noise. He was in living room, but definitely not asleep. Was someone in there with him? Who was he talking to at this hour?

"No," he said tersely. She hadn't heard any other voice, so she figured he was on the phone.

"Bullshit. I've gone over those numbers my goddamn self, Baxter."

Baxter? The *B* in F and B. There were several members of the Baxter family that worked for Fieldstein and Baxter. He could be talking to any one of them. He could be talking about anything. It could be nothing.

"I told you, I fucking took care of O'Brian."

Oh shit, shit, shit! He meant Carl O'Brian. She just knew it. Both Baxter or O'Brian being mentioned in the same conversation didn't leave any doubt. As far as the FBI knew, O'Brian could be dead, and some on her team liked Mason for the disappearance.

And he'd all but confirmed it. Her heart was breaking, and she knew right then that she wasn't just falling in love. She'd already taken the leap. She'd fallen in love with a criminal. If she could break down and cry and scream, she would, but she'd have to save that for later. She had a job to do, and now more than ever, she had to damn well do it.

Her hands shook as she took another step closer while her mind reeled with her options. She could pretend she hadn't known he was on the phone and just walk in, catch him off guard and see if he talked, or she could go back to the bedroom and wait for him to return to her.

"I hear you loud and clear, William."

William Baxter. President of capital management, and Mason's direct boss as of late. More confirmation the conversation was nothing short of damning.

Had Mason been promoted because he and William Baxter were in cahoots? That, she didn't know, but she had to figure out a way to get this intel to Viola without Mason knowing, so her team could investigate their connection more. This could be the break they were looking for.

"Well, then let me explain it to you. I know you skimmed money from that fund before you closed it. If I wanted the feds breathing down our necks, I'd have reported *you*. If I found it, I know others can. You're too fucking sloppy... Yes, I did just say that... Don't you fucking threaten me. I said I'd take care of it, but this is last fucking time I'm coming to your rescue. After this, you're on your own." He slammed the phone down. "Fuck!"

She jumped at his outburst and made a split-second decision. If he was emotional, maybe he'd let something slip while he was reeling with anger.

"Hey, what's wrong?" she asked as she stepped into the room.

He whirled, his hands fisting, breath sawing in and out, his naked chest heaving with effort. "My boss isn't qualified to be flipping burgers for a living. Wasting everybody's goddamn time with frivolous meetings. The only reason he's in his position is because he's family. But all he's doing is running the company into the ground." He grumbled a few more expletives toward the ceiling.

She licked her lips and moved closer. He was talking. This was good. *Isn't it? Because the more he says, the more he is sealing his fate and breaking your heart.* She took a deep breath, forcing her emotions away. She could not think about that right now.

"It's not what you know. It's who you know, right?"

He looked at her, his angry eyes turning sad, and her stomach dropped at the impossible look he gave her. "I don't think I can do this right now."

Shit. She was losing him. In more ways than one. What

was she supposed to say? The FBI never guided her on this. Hell, neither had her dad. He was both a man and a mark, and she literally had no idea what she was supposed to do.

He shoved his hand through his hair and blew out an obviously frustrated breath. "I care about you, Shelby. I didn't plan on that happening. I—*shit*." He dropped to the couch and let his head fall into his hands. "I can't get involved right now. Too much is at stake." He looked at her then. Were her eyes watering? She was blinking rapidly, and he was suspiciously blurry. "God, please don't cry," he said, pained.

The knot in her throat was sudden, confirming what was already obvious to him. She tried swallowing it down as she stepped closer. "I don't know how to wrap my head around—" She shook her head, trying to find words. She couldn't tell him anything, not really. It didn't matter that she was in love with him. They couldn't be together under these circumstances. They'd been doomed from the start.

"You're just infatuated with me because I'm your first Dom. It's natural to bond—"

Oh, she didn't want to hear any more of this placating B.S. She stormed closer, all other obstacles between them forgotten. "Don't you dare tell me how I feel, Mason. I mean *Master*."

He blinked at her, obviously stunned at her outburst, but then he shot to his feet, a new storm brewing in his gaze.

"What? We're not screwing right now. I can call you whatever the hell I want. If you're going to be a jackass, I'm going to call you out on it. So, tell me, are you going to tuck tail and hide behind your own goddamn insecurities for saying your name? Because it looks like you're about fucking to do that. But what the hell does it even matter if you're kicking me out anyway?"

In the back of her mind, a part of her was screaming out a warning that even if this man wasn't a murderer, he could still be dangerous, and she shouldn't provoke him. She really had no idea what he was capable of, but she was too consumed with the barrage of emotions coursing through her.

"Shelby," he growled, and came closer. "I don't know what you want from me."

"How about the truth, Mason." It was now or never. Only seconds ago, she'd considered fleeing, and now she was confronting him instead. If she didn't do it now, she may never get another chance. This was the moment she'd waited for...and one she'd slowly come to dread.

His eyes flashed right before he yanked her to him and she gasped at his sudden movement. "You want the truth? You can fucking have it." He crushed his mouth onto hers, and she tried pushing him away as she squirmed closer. She wanted him, but she knew she shouldn't. He was kissing her like a man starved, and what little battle she put up waned at his dominating seduction. This was crazy.

This was *need*. A desire so deep she didn't know how to control it. Not in this moment. Maybe never.

Her back slammed against a wall, and she gripped his shoulders to steady herself.

"Hands above your head," he barked.

She immediately obeyed.

The few buttons she'd fastened flew to the floor when he ripped open the shirt she had on. He pushed in closer, panting into her ear.

"You...only you can do this to me." He shoved at his shorts while her body shook with anticipation. He'd just told her he couldn't do this, but now neither of them could get close enough to the other fast enough.

He pushed into her without hesitation and fucked her hard, nothing like the tender loving he'd shown her last night. He was punishing her, punishing himself, and she loved every second of if.

"Mason," she breathed, and once she said it, she couldn't stop. She chanted his name over and over as he plowed into her. The freedom to say it during the height of pleasure too good to verbalize anything else. As if she even could.

"God, baby. You feel so good."

She locked her legs tighter around him and met his powerful thrusts as best she could. It was frenzied, and she didn't care. She wasn't going to last, and she wanted him owning her, owning this thing between them. He couldn't say the words, but his body was screaming them at her. He couldn't deny he felt something, and she knew it. If not before, she did now.

Her climax caught her off guard, her back bowing as she screamed.

He roared, not slowing as he joined her. Uninhibited.

Unprotected.

*Oh no.*

She was on birth control, so that wasn't the issue. And because of Mason's lifestyle and the possibility that they would have sex, the FBI had secured his medical records. She knew that even though it had been careless, she was still safe.

Yet, that didn't matter. Letting him come inside was giving him another part of her soul. She'd never had unprotected sex before. Ever.

"Shit," he breathed, and she figured he'd realized this little tidbit, too. "I'm sorry. I never lose control."

He stiffened against her before he eased her to her feet.

No, she figured he didn't like losing control at all. "It's okay. I'm on birth control and clean."

"I am, too." But he still didn't sound happy as he moved away from her, closing himself off. It hurt like hell that he was doing it so soon after taking her.

"Look, Mason—"

He laughed without humor, keeping his back to her. "How wrong is it that I like you saying my name?"

"It doesn't have to be."

His shoulders dropped, and he faced her. "Some things came up at work. I need to go in."

There went her heart again. He might as well punch a hole in her chest, rip it out, and be done with it already. "Are we just going to leave things like this?" she asked softly, not wanting to know the answer but unable to keep her mouth shut.

"I'll call you when I'm ready for our next scene." He turned to walk away, and dread like none she'd ever experienced before engulfed her. This all still felt very final. Sex hadn't changed anything. She was old enough to understand that, but it still hurt. "And after? What then, Mason?"

He turned to look at her, staring for several seconds before speaking. "I can't answer that, Shelby. Not yet."

She searched his eyes, but he was unmoving. "I don't know what's going on, but whatever it is, it's making you miserable."

"You don't *know* me."

If he'd slapped her, it would've hurt less. Because it was hateful and truthful all at the same time. She didn't know him. Nor did she know herself if she was capable of falling in love with a man who could kill someone for financial gain. Or could toss her feelings away as if they didn't even matter. The fact that the latter bothered her more was an unwelcome wakeup call. Unwelcome, but there all the same. "You're right," she said, resolve settling in. "I don't."

She turned to leave, but looked over her shoulder. "You don't know me either. It's better if it stays that way."

"Shelby."

She didn't wait around to hear what he had to say. It didn't matter. He thought he was teaching her to play, but in reality, she was playing him, working him on a case. If she stayed long enough, she might feel compelled to tell him everything, which would not only get her fired, but get her thrown in jail right alongside him. The government didn't look too kindly at obstruction of justice. No matter what her heart was telling her, her head would prevail. She had to get away from him. Now. And stay away.

Her purse had been dropped by the door, so she'd grabbed it before fleeing. She didn't care that she was half naked. She clutched the shirt closed and ran barefoot to her car. It still wasn't daybreak, so no one was around to see her leaving. No one except whoever watched the club while she was there.

Hopefully, the information she got from him today was enough to get a warrant, so the FBI could focus their investigation on him and William Baxter. If it was, the surveillance teams could disband because her involvement with Mason would be effectively over.

Her breath hitched as she started her car and pulled out onto the road.

*It can't be over if it never began.*

# CHAPTER SIXTEEN

Mason slammed his desk drawer and waited for his laptop to boot up, determined to focus on the new nightmare before him and not the one brewing in his personal life.

One minute he was pushing Shelby away, and the next he was trying to figure out how to keep her in his life...only to push her away again. Seeing the look of hurt on her face as she left gutted him. Because it held more than rejection. In its depths was understanding. It was as if she knew things could never really work between them, regardless of any feelings brewing.

Deep down, he knew it, too. Love would not be enough. He was strong enough to admit how he felt, and smart enough to put it aside. Frankly, he had no other choice now. The phone call he'd gotten from William this morning drilled that point home.

The only thing that man was good at was fucking things up and screwing people over. The son of a bitch had moved some money from one of the funds started by Fieldstein—a fund that Mason now managed—into a shell business. He purposely left a paper trail leading to Mason as the one behind the illegal activity. He didn't stop there either. William even posted some large unscheduled deposits into Mason's 401k and diverted more into an overseas bank account that had his fucking name all over it.

His boss was now blackmailing him.

He'd told Mason he was working something huge on the Culpepper Hedge Fund, confirming what Mason had learned from his source. Now, William needed him to move money out of it before the quarterly projections were finished, so it coincided with the earnings they would be showing to investors. It seemed the meeting with their Tokyo counterparts hadn't been as fruitless as Mason had believed. Because Mason had disposed of Carl, William believed he'd be willing to take the plunge to the dark side and join him in working the Ponzi scheme.

With a little coaxing.

If Mason agreed, William would fix the mess he caused, and Mason would go back to being as clean as a whistle—on paper.

If he didn't, then William would hang him out to dry. In an orange jumpsuit at a minimum-security prison.

As soon as Shelby had left, he'd called his silent partner on the untraceable phone and had relayed everything. Mason was ready to pull the plug on his plan and deal with William himself, but the man had talked him into playing along, convincing him this was a good thing. William was finally showing his hand, so it was only a matter of time before they'd get him. He'd assured Mason he would get his name off that money in the meantime and intercept the transaction William was forcing him to make. Mason had finally relented.

So, here he was, in his office at Fieldstein and Baxter,

logging into the firm's most prestigious hedge fund, and stealing money for William. If this didn't work, he was sealing his fate. He wouldn't have to worry about finding a new job when the shit hit the fan. He'd just have to worry about not dropping the soap. If he didn't believe his contact would pull through for him, no way would he do this, but he knew problems could always arise. The risk was still a major one.

It was surreal how quickly it took to steal millions of dollars. A few clicks, some highly secured passwords, and the deed was done. When he'd called William to update him, his boss had given him half-hearted praise and rushed off the phone. If the prick didn't fix the mess he'd caused, Mason would ensure it got done anyway.

At least he seriously hoped he'd be able to.

His assistant buzzed him, drawing him out of his frustrating thoughts. "Mr. Showalter?"

"Yes, Katie?"

"There's a David Lane here to see you. He doesn't have an appointment, but he says he knows you. Security won't let him up since his name isn't on your calendar."

Mason frowned, trying to remember someone by that name. He was good with them. In this business, he had to be. It wasn't ringing a bell, though, and he didn't have time to catch up with some guy who thought they were old college buddies or something. "I have a meeting with Joel Fieldstein in thirteen minutes. Go down and get his number. I'll give him a call."

"Yes, sir. I already told Jerry to tell him you were heading out soon, but he's insisting it'll only take a few minutes."

Mason rubbed his face and sat back in his chair. "Fine, send him up." Whoever it was, he'd get rid of him. Because of the crap with William, Mason hadn't had time to read over the agenda for his meeting with Joel.

When the man walked in, Mason stood. Ahh, Dave. The man who was at the club last night with Shelby. "Viola's husband," he muttered.

Dave nodded and walked toward his desk. Mason didn't like mixing his personal and professional lives, so he'd be ending this even sooner than he'd hoped. The guy was probably here to avenge Shelby on his wife's behalf. Whatever he had to say would be wasting precious breath. His private life might not get drawn into his professional one as a general rule, but Shelby was completely off fucking limits. Period.

"Whatever you're thinking, that's not it," he said, obviously reading the scowl on Mason's face. He stepped over to one of the chairs across from Mason and sat. Intrigued, Mason eased back down and stared across his desk at him.

"Mr. Showalter, I'm sorry to interrupt," Katie said, buzzing into his office again. "Mr. Baxter would like to see before your meeting."

"Tell him I'll be there as soon as I can." If Mason didn't get up to William's office, his boss would come down here. He looked at Dave. "What do you want then? I am extremely busy, and my attention is needed elsewhere."

Dave pulled out a manila envelope from inside his jacket. "A business deal. I have information I'd like to sell you."

Mason laughed without humor. "You've come to the Major Leagues with a tee-ball. I'm sure whatever it is, I'm not interested." He made as if to scoot back and rise. If he left now, he could be in William's office before the man had a chance to fume that he hadn't come running at his command. But Dave's next words stopped him.

"It's information on Shelby Landry."

Mason sat up straighter, pinning the man with his stare. "What the hell are you trying to pull?"

Dave's smile was sad. "It's simple. I made some bets I can't cover. My bookie will be here this weekend to collect. I tried putting him off, but he'll break bones this time, maybe even hurt my wife. I could borrow the money from her, but even she doesn't have this kind of cash available. If she found out about this, or what I'm offering, she'd leave me. Or worse. I can't help that. I'm in a corner, and I don't see any other way out."

Mason mulled that over. His interest was piqued at the mention of Shelby, but something else struck him. Dave was desperate, and a man led by that emotion did stupid things. Whatever he had on Shelby he was willing to sell. It probably wasn't much, but if Mason didn't bite, someone else could.

Someone like William. Dave was here at his office. William was expecting him. If he didn't show up soon, William would come down here and find him with Dave. So if Mason didn't give Dave want he wanted and get him the hell out of here, the man might come face-to-face with someone willing to gain any advantage over Mason. It was a stretch to even think that could happen, but when it came to Shelby, his instinct was to protect.

To anybody else, what Dave had wouldn't be worth as much, and if there hadn't been a serious risk of William finding out about Shelby and whatever Dave had on her, he'd throw this man out right now. He loosened his tie, preparing himself for the quick negotiation.

"What do you have?" he asked, indicating the package Dave carried.

"Do we have a deal?"

"I don't know what you want or if what you have is worth a fucking penny. Talk or get out. I really don't care." Mason waved him off, faking a nonchalance he'd perfected through years of business transactions.

Dave clutched the envelope tighter. "You'll want this, I promise. If you don't like what I have to show you, then don't pay. I'll let you judge for yourself if it's worth it."

He must think he had something really good on her to leave the deal open like that. "How much?"

"Forty thousand."

Mason half-smiled. That wasn't a small amount, but at least the guy wasn't trying to take him for millions. This, too, felt like blackmail, though, and he was sick and tired of people swindling him today. The sooner he got this over with, the sooner he could get back to work. "Fine. Show me what you have, and if I think it's worth the price, I'll have my assistant wire you the money."

Dave smiled and eagerly opened the envelope. He pulled out some papers, stared at them, glanced at Mason again as if he wasn't sure all of a sudden if he should do this. That only made Mason want to see them even more. Dave slowly offered the papers, and Mason snatched them out of his hands before the guy could change his mind.

*What the...*

Mason's vision turned red, fury boiling inside of him as he looked at the photos. "What the fuck is this?" he whispered heatedly. Though he knew. There was no doubt what the photos showed.

"Those are images someone on my wife's team took at various locations. There's one after a massage parlor bust last year and others at some office gatherings." He gritted his teeth. "I knew being married to an FBI agent was going to be hard, but when she went undercover as a masseur, I was ready to blow the operation just to get her off that case." He pointed to the picture. "That one is of them all celebrating the day they nabbed the criminals and closed the case. Viola is the one wearing yellow. The one next to her is—"

"I can see who it is," he said, cutting off the man as he continued to stare at the photograph.

Shelby. She was standing with her arm around a man who was faced away from the camera talking to somebody. She was smiling at Viola. They were all wearing gear emblazoned with FBI—hats, jackets, shirts. They were not hiding the fact they were all agents.

And Shelby was one of them. An FBI agent.

She had lied to him. Fucking *played* him.

"Yeah, well, I brought you the photographs so you would believe me when I told you Viola and I were at the club last night because it was part of her assignment. She didn't give me any details, but since Shelby is involved with you, I suspect they're investigating something you're involved in."

Oh, this just got fucking better.

"Mr. Showalter, I am so sorry to intrude again, but Amber called and said Mr. Baxter is on his way down," his assistant said.

"Thank you, Katie," he said numbly. When he leveled his stare on Dave, it took all he had not to kill the messenger. "You got your money. There's an extra ten grand in it if you keep this to yourself. You tell no one that you came to me or that you know what Shelby does for a living. I mean no one. You're going to walk out of here, tell my assistant how nice I am to donate to your cause, and you forget this conversation ever happened. If I find out you ratted out Shelby or your *wife* to anybody else, your bookie will be the least of your problems. Am I clear?"

"Crystal," the man said nervously.

"Get out."

He picked up the phone and gave Katie her instructions. Then he grabbed his other cell phone and those photos before marching right past Katie and Dave.

"Um, Mr. Baxter is on his way," she said, scrambling to stop his retreat.

He turned to face her. "Cancel my meetings this afternoon. Let Mr. Baxter know something has come up that needs my immediate attention. He'll understand."

He'd assume it had something to do with the Culpepper Fund, but it would buy Mason some time. As soon as he was out of the building and in his car, he hit the number of his own connection.

"Looks like William Baxter has already taken steps to fix the mess he made for you. See, told you you had nothing to worry about."

Fuck William. He didn't give a shit about him right now. He peeled out of the parking lot, no idea where he was going, but knowing he had to get away. "Find out everything you can about Shelby Landry." An agent. A goddamn FBI agent who was working him. And to think he'd fallen in love with her. He suppressed a roar. His heart was doing it already.

After several seconds of silence, the man asked, "Why?"

"Because I fucking said so! I want to know everything, and mean every-fucking-thing. I don't care how long it takes or if you have to stop working on William to do it. This is priority number one. I want to know all there is to know about her."

He sighed. "I won't have to stop working on anything to tell you about her. I already know all there is to know."

"Just what the hell does that mean, Parker?"

"Mason, you came to us because you found illegal activity and suspected William Baxter as the cause behind it. The SEC doesn't have the ability to conduct a full-on investigation like this, not when we realized the scope. We had to get help. She's one of the FBI agents assisting with the investigation, but I don't know the details of her involvement. She's a linguistics expert. I assume she's going over the foreign documentation to ensure it meshes with what Fieldstein and Baxter is reporting in the U.S."

His contact had assumed wrong.

It was clear to Mason just what her assignment had been.

"Mason, why are you asking about Landry? Fuck, is William on to the investigation? Talk to me, man. If she or any of her team's been made, I need to report it."

He gritted his teeth as he thought quickly. Mason had his secrets. Secrets he'd kept from Shelby, but the difference was he hadn't known his secrets had involved her. She'd been the one to break his trust, lie to him, play him for the fool. If they'd kept her real involvement a secret, then they had their reasons. If he let Parker tell Shelby and her team that he knew the truth, what then? She'd just get to walk away, knowing her behavior had been acceptable.

Hell no. If anybody was going to tell Shelby he knew the truth, it was going to be him.

"No." He forced a chuckle. "God, I'm losing my mind. She'd submitted a request for filings we made in Russia, and freaked the fuck out." He took a deep breath. "It's fine, man. But when this shit is over, I want an all-expense paid trip to a remote island somewhere. I need that vacation like yesterday."

Parker chuckled. "Good luck getting the government to

pay for that. You'll get a clap on the back for a job well done when William is exposed."

Mason laughed with him, though he felt little emotion inside. He did it to play along and get off the phone without causing any more damage. As soon as he was able, he'd be calling Shelby.

He had a little lesson to teach in double-crossing.

# CHAPTER SEVENTEEN

After showering and getting dressed for work, Shelby couldn't stall any longer. She'd cried in the shower until the water had turned cold, and no amount of makeup would conceal her puffy eyes even though she'd given it her best effort.

She drove to headquarters in a daze. Her mind replayed the events at Mason's apartment over and over, and no matter how she viewed everything, the various angles she attempted, the outcome was still the same. Mason was involved in criminal activity, and she was in love with him. Her breath hitched, and she swallowed down another sob. If she dwelled on this too much, she'd start crying again, and she couldn't afford that right now. She'd sent Rick a text informing him she had an update, and he wanted to see her immediately. He was already gathering the rest of the team, and they'd be there waiting on her.

The office was bustling around like usual. Cyber crime division was cracking down on fraud and identity theft. Terrorism worked both domestic and international threats. Organized and violent crimes had been major areas for the FBI for decades, focal points that many agents worked, regardless of specialty. Then there were counterintelligence and white-collar crimes...cases Shelby typically was assigned. It was business as usual here. Everywhere she looked, her colleagues were diligently working. Dedicated.

Unemotional.

She'd been that way once. Until she'd been assigned to work the Fieldstein and Baxter case. Her first major field assignment. The massage parlor bust hadn't required this level of involvement. She'd spent more time preparing than being on location, and she hadn't been working it alone. It hadn't been like this. If all of her major assignments were going to be like this, she wasn't sure how she'd find that disconnect again.

The conference room door was closed as she came to it, and she had a fleeting thought of just going, leaving, pretending her life wasn't where it was. She knew that wasn't possible, but the idea gave her the strength to push through and face her teammates.

"...We'll have to see about that. Oh hey, Landry," Rick said, waving her in. "We were just talking about pulling the finances at Showalter's club again and comparing them to any fluctuations in his personal accounts. Darrell seems to think if he's stealing from F and B, then maybe there's a trail with his club."

"I don't think he'd use his club to filter money," Viola said. "He's not the only owner. He'd have to get his partners in on the scheme if he's using the club. I don't see that happening. Four control freaks letting one man run the show? No way."

Shelby sat down and listened quietly, biding her time.

"It happens every day in the corporate world," Darrell

said. "I still say we yank it all. The club's accounts and their personal financial records."

"I agree with Lane," Carson said, shaking his head. "Scene is a privately held company. They're not subjected to the same disclosure laws. Even if we did find something questionable, a half-ass lawyer could have it explained away. It's a waste of time."

"It's not a waste of time if we're doing our jobs by investigating every angle," Darrell growled.

Rick lifted his hand. "Enough. Let's hear the latest from Landry, and then we can get back to deciding if we should delve deeper into the club." He turned to Shelby and asked, "Whatcha got?" before taking a sip of coffee. The man drank the stuff from morning 'till night.

She cleared her throat. "I overheard a telephone conversation between Showalter and William Baxter. He was enraged with his boss. It sounded as if Baxter was forcing Showalter's hand in something. He said he'd found proof of wrongdoing by Baxter and if he wanted the feds involved, he would have reported him. He then told Baxter not to threaten him and that he'd take care of whatever it was Baxter wanted him to do."

"It is William Baxter. I fucking knew it!" Carson said.

Darrell frowned at Shelby and turned to Rick. "It could be a setup. Maybe Mason made Shelby and is trying to make Baxter look guilty."

"He made himself look pretty damn guilty," Shelby said. "He also confirmed getting rid of Carl O'Brian."

"He said that?" Rick asked, squeezing his coffee cup to the point Shelby worried it'd bust.

"Yes. He told Baxter that this was the last time he was rescuing him. After this, he was done. I only heard one side of the conversation, but when he got off the phone, he was livid. He'd wanted to spend the day with me, but after that call, he said some things had come up at work." She didn't go into the fight they'd had. She hoped it wouldn't matter anyway. "I think this is enough to get a warrant for more information."

"You think he's guilty of the Ponzi scheme?" Viola asked, brow furrowed.

"He knows something. When he bitched about his boss, he acted as if the man was inept, that he was only in his position because he was family. If that's true, then Baxter isn't capable of pulling off something like this. Not on his own. If Baxter is part of this..." Shelby slowly inhaled, trying to calm her racing heart. "If William Baxter is involved, then Showalter is in on it with him. Baxter has no need to steal money. He's part of the family and grew up wealthy. His job was handed to him if Showalter is right. If I didn't hear that conversation myself, I wouldn't think Baxter was involved. What would his motive be? I still don't see it."

"We need more," Rick said, and Shelby gaped at him.

"What do you mean? He confessed to killing O'Brian in front of a federal agent. Start there," Shelby gritted. She could not keep seeing Mason to gain information. If she did, she couldn't trust herself to stay objective...assuming she was still.

"It's not enough. We need physical evidence. You did good, though, Landry. If William Baxter isn't involved, he at least knows something." He looked at Darrell. "Find out what you can on Baxter. If he's not directly involved but knows what's going on, maybe he'd be willing to cut a deal to save any embarrassment with his family's business. His testimony could put Showalter away."

"On it." Darrell stood. "I'll be at my desk if anything else comes up."

After he left, Viola looked at Rick. "I don't like it. Showalter was promoted long after the SEC started their investigation. Did he even have the means to do it before then? Seems too convenient."

"Agreed," Carson said.

Viola glanced at him. "That's twice now you've agreed with my assessment. You're kinda scaring me over there."

He chuckled. "I know greatness when I see it. Besides, I never argue with a beautiful woman."

"Annnd there you are." Viola rolled her eyes.

"Childers, you concentrate on all correspondence in the weeks leading up to Showalter's promotion—emails, texts, telegraphs, everything," Rick said as he stood.

Carson grabbed his stuff and pushed up from the table. "Do they even have those anymore?" He chuckled.

Rick looked at Shelby, who was now standing with Viola beside her. "Your assignment is still ongoing. Report back with any new findings."

"Yes, sir," she muttered to his retreated back.

"C'mon," Viola said. "You look like you could use a strawberry salad."

"If by salad you mean margarita, then yes, yes, I do."

"I won't tell if you won't."

———

SHELBY HAD BEEN LURED HERE under false pretenses. Strawberry salad hadn't been code for something else. It was actually a salad with strawberries. She had refrained from boozing it up on their lunch hour anyway, though the temptation to indulge had definitely been great.

"Okay, spill," Viola said around a mouthful of lettuce and berries.

"Er, there's so much, I wouldn't even know where to start." She could talk for hours and only be scratching the surface of her problems.

Viola stabbed her salad again. "Let's start with your puffy eyes and piss poor concealer job."

Shelby groaned. "I knew I should've forgone makeup today." Viola looked horrified at the thought of doing such a thing, and Shelby laughed at her comical expression. "Yeah, I know. Sacrilege and all that."

"No doubt." Then her smile fell. "How's your back?"

What back? The pain in her chest trumped everything else. "It's okay, I guess." She looked down and poked at her salad. Damn, she should've gotten a cheddar burger instead. With onion rings.

"Uh-huh. Now I know something is seriously wrong. You're wearing the aftereffects of a good cry, and you had to think about your back." She didn't push more, just ate her salad, probably letting Shelby ease into the conversation on her own.

"I think we broke up this morning."

Her head snapped up, and she chewed slower. "You think?"

Shelby groaned, dropping her fork. "I don't know. He's so closed off it's hard to get a read on him. He seems to want me one minute and then pushes me away the next. Last night he asked me to spend the day with him. He was going to take off work because he wanted to be with me. Then this morning he says he cares about me, but he can't do this. That I don't *know* him. I agreed and said he didn't know me either. He tried stopping me when I left, but only barely. It was a token effort, and I didn't stick around to hear anymore." Her laugh was nothing short of pathetic. "It's not even real. How messed up is that?"

"Is it real for you?"

Shelby stared at her for several seconds, weighing her options. The question was really the heart of the matter, why she'd been upset. But could she tell her friend, her *coworker* the extent of her involvement? She ultimately decided on the truth. It wouldn't change anything. "Yes."

"Oh, boy," Viola breathed, leaning back in her chair. "You can't compromise the case," she said slowly.

"I would never do that," Shelby said heatedly. She blinked slowly, letting her eyes stay shut as she gathered her strength for this confession. "But I want it over. I honestly believe we have enough to get the warrants and wire taps. When we get those, I don't have to do this anymore. I don't *want* to do this anymore."

"Are you trying to convince me or yourself?" she asked, arching a brow in question.

"Both."

Viola nodded. "But Rick thinks you still need to be on the inside."

"Doesn't matter if Mason doesn't want to see me anymore."

"So he's back to Mason now?" she asked with a smile. When Shelby narrowed her gaze at her, she raised her hands and said, "Sorry. Low blow."

"You understand my dilemma."

She cocked her head to the side. "And which one is that? The fact that you two have—for lack of a better phrase —broken up? Or that you're into a guy who you think is a criminal?"

"Take your pick," she muttered.

"C'mon, Shelby. You're doing your job. You haven't done anything wrong."

"Except fall in love with a man I'm lying to, and not telling my boss the extent of my involvement."

"You're in love with him?" she screeched.

"Oh God, I need something more than rabbit food if we're getting into all this." She waved at the waitress and ordered the onion rings she'd wanted. If Viola had looked horrified at the thought of going without makeup, she now looked ready to arrest Shelby for a capital offense. "It's a vegetable," she said in defense.

"Deep fried in fat."

"Vegetable oil." Shelby shrugged. Though it didn't matter if they were cooked in lard, she was going to savor every last one of them.

"You're in love with him?" Viola asked, shaking her head as if she was still trying to wrap it around the news and forget the artery-hardening snack on the way.

"Please don't lecture me," Shelby said, exasperated. "I don't think I can take it right now. I worked this case as assigned, and now it's personal. I didn't plan on that happening, but it did. I know there's no way this can work. Mason looks guilty as hell, and I will do what's necessary to bring him in because it is my job. If a judge and jury agree, he's going to jail. If by some miracle, he's innocent, I've used him to get information, lied to him about who I am. Believe me, I know how bad this is."

Viola smiled, and Shelby gawked at her. "You find this amusing?"

She bit her lips in a poor attempt to hide her grin. "No. Not that. I'm just wondering... I mean, you *like* the BDSM stuff, don't you?"

The tension she expected at the mention of that lifestyle didn't come. In fact, she had to fight her own smile. "Yeah. Weird, huh?"

Viola shrugged and focused on her salad again. "I don't know. I'm intrigued by it. Not that it matters now. Dave was disgusted with it. I guess I'll have to think of another way to rekindle the flame."

Shelby frowned at her. It hadn't been the first time Viola had suggested problems in her marriage. She felt like a selfish friend, always blabbing about her own problems and not listening to Viola's. "If you need to vent about Dave, you know you can talk to me, right?"

Viola waved a dismissive hand. "It's just a rough patch. Marriage isn't easy. I had the right idea to spice things up, but the club failed miserably. The whipping had been brutal, girl. If I wanted us to give it a serious go, we probably should've gone on a night when we weren't forced to watch someone we know being hurt like that."

Shelby didn't want to push the subject of Dave, so she picked up her fork, but dropped it when she saw the waitress coming with fried heaven.

"I admit it hurt like crazy before Mason got there. But once he was there to distract me, I was able to put the pain aside. I'm not saying I'd want to do it again, but it wasn't as bad as it had been at first." She thanked the waitress and nibbled on an onion ring. "Besides, there's so much more to it than pain. When Master Jedrek bound me, it was very freeing."

Viola rolled her eyes. "Don't call that prick Master. I like Mr. Mean better."

"He is that." Shelby chuckled. "But I think there are parts I could really get into. I've learned BDSM is what you make of it. I'd be lying if I said I didn't like how it made me feel. How Mason makes me feel when he tops me." A wave of sadness came over her.

"Are there parts you don't like? Besides being beaten, I mean?" Viola asked lightly as if she noticed the sudden change in Shelby and wanted to turn it back around.

She half-smiled and tamped down the sorrow to focus on the conversation, embracing detachment. "The rules seem silly."

"Figures. A bunch of egotistical men getting off on bossing women around," she scoffed.

"It's not like that. Not really. And there are Dommes, too. Submission isn't sexist. Nor is it limited to heterosexuals. When I was researching it, I found a lot of sites dedicated to gay and lesbian participants."

"Blah, blah, blah. Give me something good. You said silly rules. I want an example." She pushed her empty salad bowl away and crossed her arms.

Shelby giggled. "Okay, I've got something. When I was at the club, but not with Mason or one of the Master Doms, I was told if another Dom approached me, I had to tell him, 'My Master awaits.' It's code for *I'm not available*. It's so any man interested in me would leave me alone."

"Oh *hell* no. My Master awaits? How 'bout, 'Say hello to my little friend,' and pull your 9mm. I bet that'd make the pricks back off."

Shelby burst out laughing, but Viola's cold expression only made her laugh harder.

"I'm serious, girl."

"I know." She took a deep breath. "That's why it's so funny. God, I needed that."

"Then my work here is done." She winked.

The last onion ring was calling her, so she picked it up. "Sure you don't want one? Last chance," she taunted.

"Gross. I'll need to run an extra mile this afternoon just looking at those things."

She relished the yummy goodness as Viola dug in her purse. When Shelby's phone rang, she glanced at it half-heartedly until she saw the name.

Mason.

"Oh crap. It's him."

Viola needed no other explanation. "Answer it."

Shelby shook as she accepted the call and put the phone to her ear. "Hello."

"Wasn't sure if you'd answer," he said without anger or even humor. It was almost emotionless. She wasn't sure how to process his tone.

"Wasn't sure I was going to," she said, trying to inflect the same amount of indifference.

"I made you a promise, and I intend to follow through on my end. Couldn't have you going around calling me a liar." There was an edge to his voice now, and her nape prickled.

"I wouldn't do that."

"Of course you wouldn't," he said, back to no emotion. "I've cleared my schedule this afternoon. Meet me at my house in one hour, so we can finish your lessons."

Her mind was reeling. She wasn't ready to see him again. Her defenses weren't up. But according to Rick, she was still on this case, and had to use every opportunity afforded her. Still, she didn't want to give in too easily. This didn't feel right for some reason. She glanced at Viola, who was staring intently at her.

"I thought you had to work."

"I'm done. We'll do it now, or not at all. Something tells me you'll drop everything and come running, though."

"What the hell's wrong with you?" she snapped before she could stop herself.

"I've had a really shitty day, Shelby," he said, almost tired now. It made no sense.

And yet, it made perfect sense.

She had her own struggle to deal with. She didn't want to go, and yet, she did. She just wasn't sure her heart could take it. If she went, she would be that much more entwined with him.

She didn't have a choice. That fact should make this easier.

It didn't.

"Fine. I'll be at your place in an hour. The apartment, right?"

Viola's eyes popped, and she whipped out her phone, probably informing Rick of the new development.

"No, my house. I guess you need the address," he said with an edge of sarcasm she didn't understand before rattling off the location. "Shower before you come. No hairspray, no makeup, no perfume or body sprays. Nothing that could be flammable."

Fire. She shivered as she recalled what the scene would involve. "Fine."

He hung up without a goodbye, and she glanced at Viola.

"We're on it. Rick and Carson will be stationed outside his neighborhood. It's gated, so they can't get in without alerting him, but they'll be close in case something happens. Let's go. He wants you wired." Viola stood.

"What? I can't. I'll be naked, and I can't wear anything flammable. The glue on even a skin tag could ignite."

"It'll be in your purse. It's not as great of an option, but one we couldn't use in the club because of all the interference. His house wouldn't have music blaring like the club would and hopefully nothing that'd scramble the signal."

It was a weak attempt at best. She knew it, and so did Rick, which was why he hadn't tried this before. But she also knew this could be the last opportunity she had to get intel from Mason. He hadn't seemed excited about seeing her. More like resolved. Without any more scheduled visits, this could be the last time they saw each other. She was sure this was what motivated Rick to try wiring her.

"Let's stop by my house first," Shelby said, trying to find the mental strength she needed to get through this.

And by *this*, she didn't mean the scene itself.

# CHAPTER EIGHTEEN

Mason spent the next hour setting out the supplies he needed for the scene, while trying to keep his temper in check. He was furious, so much so that he knew it was a bad idea to play with Shelby today. He should wait until he calmed down before doing this.

But then he'd remember she'd been playing him all along, and he'd think *fuck it*. Rational thought had fled when understanding of her deceit had taken up residence. Though he wasn't doing this for her pleasure. Or for his. He was doing this to finish what they'd started with a little punishment thrown in. He wouldn't hurt her. Much.

Still, he'd never punished a sub when he was angry with her. He was too controlled to do otherwise.

Fuck control.

Shelby had used him, played him, insulted his intelligence, and crushed his heart. He couldn't be bothered with control right now.

Once everything was ready in his bedroom, he waited on the couch for her to arrive. If he had a dungeon, he'd have used it for practical matters, but once he'd opened the club with his partners, he no longer had a need for one in his home. He refused to do this at the club, so he should've at least set up in one of his guest rooms rather than his bedroom. But he had a bit of masochism in him. He knew every time he slept in his bed, he'd be reminded of her being in it, being punished, reminding himself to never get close to another woman again.

Before he'd met Shelby, he'd been in a relationship rut, not really connecting to a sub. He wanted to go back to that. What had been a rut before would be a haven now.

When the security guard altered him she'd arrived, he stood and faced the door, waiting for her. Her engine cut off and, moments later, his doorbell sounded. He crossed his arms and called out for her to come in. He wasn't opening the door for her. He'd let her come to him.

All the way.

Then he'd show her what Hell was really like.

The door opened, and his muscles flexed, instantly reacting to the need instilled in him to go to her. He fought the reaction, refusing to move. She shut the door and looked at him. She was even more beautiful than the day they'd met. He wondered if spiders thought that about black widows when they came for them, too.

"Lock it." She turned and did as he instructed without comment. When she turned around and took a step toward him, he lifted his hand. "Stop."

Her foot was in the air when she froze at his command, and she eased it back to the floor. Good. Though he wouldn't praise her for following orders. She didn't deserve it.

"Strip."

"Mason," she said, looking down.

"No!" Hell no. But he tamped down his anger for now.

If he pissed her off too soon, she might leave without her punishment. And he had no intention of ever seeing her again after today. "It's Master. You've gotten too lax on the rules, pet. That's my fault."

He watched her neck as she swallowed. "Something's wrong. I can see that, and it's not about what was said this morning. What happened at work?"

Yes, he bet she'd love to know that, and he'd tell her. Just not yet. "You're stalling. That's the only thing wrong with me right now. Take off your clothes, Shelby." He forced his arms to relax at his sides.

After standing there quietly for several seconds, she nodded slowly. He waited with baited breath as she removed her clothes, stripping down to her panties and bra before removing them, too. When she stood completely naked, head cast down to the floor, he took his time soaking in her beauty. Then he silently cursed his perusal. Of course she was beautiful. If the feds were playing him, they wouldn't send in an amateur. Then his stomach dropped as another thought occurred to him. Was Shelby already in the lifestyle? Had she played him so well that he'd been completely fooled by her feigned ignorance?

Didn't matter. This was a lesson he'd learned regardless of how skilled she'd been, and he would never be making this mistake again.

"Follow me." He turned to leave, but when she dipped to pick up her things, he stopped. "You won't need those." He glanced at the stuff in her hands and gazed at her again. "Put it all back on the floor."

She frowned at her things, but eventually eased every-thing back to where they'd been. New anger flashed through him when he thought about what might be hidden among her things. A gun, a recording device, mace, hand-cuffs. Any number of things she could use against him.

She wouldn't get the chance.

Once she stood empty-handed, he turned without issuing the order again, knowing she'd follow him. He made his way to the master bedroom with her in tow. He walked in and waited by the door.

"On the bed. Back on the fire board." He turned to lock the bedroom door and heard as she complied. When no more movement sounded, he rounded to face her, his back braced against the door. No matter how unemotional he stayed, the sight of her, naked, on his bed would be burned into his brain until the day he died.

He inhaled slowly, taking in her natural scent, noticing no chemicals altered it. Good, she'd obeyed him. Of course, she chose what she did and did not do on her own with no regard for him. She probably complied because of safety reasons and not because he'd ordered her to.

All of that was ending now.

"You will not speak unless spoken to. I don't want anything breaking my concentration. I would gag you, but I don't want anything unnecessary on your body. If I ask you a question, I expect a respectful answer. If it's not 'Yes, Master,' it better be something just as appropriate. If you don't comply, I will gag you anyway. Do you understand?"

She trembled. "Yes, Master."

He gave her a curt nod before stepping to the foot of the bed. He reached down and pulled up shackles that were connected to it and closed them around each of her ankles. Her legs shook as he spread them, using the chain as leverage until secured to the bed. Her thighs would not be able to close. She'd be completely exposed to him. Looking his fill before he chastised himself, he mentally ordered his body not to fall victim to her allure again. Next, he moved to her wrists and secured them above her head before sitting in the chair beside her.

"What we're about to engage in is fire fleshing. Technically, it's consider edge play because the flame can get out of hand, which makes this dangerous. But I believe it's pretty tame compared to other edgy style play. If using the proper precautions, then it's as safe as any other kink." He rattled off the description because it was the right thing to do. Even though they'd discussed this before, he was still her Dom in this scene, and he wanted her fully aware of what they'd be engaging in. "What's your safe word?"

"Red, Master."

His teeth snapped shut. He didn't like hearing her use that term with him. He'd demanded it because he wanted her kept at a distance, but once he'd accepted her calling him by his given name, he liked it so much more. To any sub at the club, he was Master. She was the only one to ever call him Mason.

"The only time you are allowed to speak to me without being prompted is if you have to use that word. No other."

He twisted, grabbed a fire wand, and lit it. The flame was high, and her tummy tensed as he neared her.

"Relax."

He swiped it across her skin and followed with his bare hand, soothing any sting. The fire barely made contact with her. It was just enough to shock and confuse the senses. He continued this pattern for several minutes, and she jumped a few times, but he knew any discomfort she felt was mild. As with much of BDSM, it was a mental game more than anything. After she was sufficiently primed, he snuffed the stick and retrieved a thin Kevlar tipped tool and the can of hair mousse from the side table. She'd done really well with bouncing. Now he was going to try streaking. He shook the can but stole a glance at her. She was frowning at what he had. He could explain to her the alcohol content in it was sufficient for his needs or that he liked the control it gave him when creating designs, but he chose to leave her wondering instead.

After double checking the bowl of ice water and towels beside him were in reach, he began to spray the mousse onto her abdomen. She flinched at the cool sensation, and his gut reaction had been to caress her, let her know she was doing a good job.

He didn't. Just the desire to do so infuriated him. He had her bound to his bed and her life literally in his hands. He spelled out *liar* on her flesh before he realized he'd done it, then he lit it and watched it flame. She gasped, and he wiped it away. He touched the wand to it a few more times in some of the places until the alcohol was completely gone. Then he spelled the same word out again with the mousse.

"Do you like what I'm doing to you?"

"Yes, Master."

He set the fire wand to the word and watched as it ignited. He snuffed out the remaining flame before spelling the same word again. He repeated this process a few more times in the same area, but not exactly over the same spot. The last time, she moaned a little and he dared a glance between her legs.

"You're wet, pet." He chose a different word to spell on the tender skin at the apex of her thighs. "Are you wet for me?"

"Yes, Master," she panted. Her hips lifted off the bed.

"Be still," he barked. She whimpered, but dropped back to the bed. "My name looks beautiful above your pussy." Then he lit it, and she wailed. When he rubbed his hand over the spot to soothe the burn, he let his fingers trail lower, massaging the skin, pulling it taut so it teased her clit. "You don't get to come, Shelby. Only good girls get to come."

He slapped her labia.

"Oh God," she groaned softly, and tossed her head back and forth.

"You'll be punished for speaking when I get done," he said calmly.

"But," she sputtered, and his glare flew up to her.

"Now you'll be spanked *and* have to see to my pleasure without getting to enjoy the same privilege. Keep it up, Shelby. I'll torture you all fucking day." Jesus, he'd had no intention of getting off on this, but watching her squirm around had made him harder than steel. He was holding back the desire to yank his pants off and fuck her where she lay.

She squeezed her lips into her mouth, so he took that as her understanding of how serious he was.

The next twenty minutes were hell. He'd burned the word liar all over her body, except the few places he'd inscribed "Mason's" at tender areas. At one point, he'd written "beautiful", and cursed himself when the words "Mason's beautiful liar" branded her chest. Because she was a beautiful liar, just not his.

He reached up, roughly unhooked one of her arms, and released the slack on the chain at her ankles. "Roll over," he said harshly.

He'd had enough of this. His frayed control was slipping, and he just might fuck her if he didn't stop now. His dick didn't care that she'd used him. He didn't feel vindicated. He was angry. Hurt. Turned on.

After she did as instructed, he pushed the fire equipment out of the way, locked her into place, and climbed onto the bed. He kneaded her bottom.

"Tell me what you're thinking, pet," he ordered softly.

"I-I don't know what's wrong."

His hand came down hard on her buttocks.

"You've been a bad girl, so I'm punishing you." He spanked her several more times on both cheeks, her ass a rosy bloom. "Say, 'thank you, Master, for spanking me'."

"Thank you, Master, for spanking me," she mumbled into the bedding.

"Do you want me to fuck you, Shelby?"

"Yes, Master."

His dick leapt inside his pants, and he squeezed her ass to keep his body still while he battled with reason. "Even if you don't get to come? You'd still let me have you?"

"Yes, Master."

"Goddamn it, Shelby. I want you to be truthful. Don't say what you think I want to hear. Tell me the truth."

"I'm telling you the truth." The truth? What did she know of it?

She let out a breathy moan and wiggled her bottom, but that only enraged him.

He swatted her again and again and again. He spanked her so many times that his hand burned and he had to switch to the other one. He was so absorbed in delivering her comeuppance that he barely held himself back. When he stopped and sucked in a breath, his dick throbbed with a want greater than he'd ever experienced before. Her legs trembled, ass in the air in a silent beg.

"God, baby, you're so wet." He unzipped his pants because he couldn't stand the pressure anymore. He could come just by watching her, looking at her like this, and still the anger inside him swelled. "Looks like you're telling me the truth, but I need more proof."

He spread her ass cheeks wide and spat onto her puckered hole. He rubbed his thumb all over it and pushed. "You ever been fucked here?"

"No, Master," she squeaked.

He spread her a little and spat again. He used another finger to push in and stretch her. The knowledge that he could take something no other man had experienced had his primal side roaring, but he did his best to ignore it. This was about punishment, not pleasure. If he touched her core, she'd come...and then he'd cave hearing the beautiful sounds she made. Playing with her like this would buy him some much needed time. If he gave in, he'd hate himself for falling victim to the allure of her body when he'd sworn to himself he would deny it.

"I'm inclined to believe you." He leaned over her, his cock poised at her anus, and gripped her hair so she'd be forced to look at him. "Though, I don't know why. All you've done is lie to me, *Agent* Landry."

Her eyes grew wide as she stared back at him, understanding dawning in her gaze as to why he was so pissed.

"What's your safe word?" he asked, deadly soft.

"Red," she whispered.

"Are you going to use it now?" he challenged. No matter how much he wanted to keep pushing her, *punishing* her, he would stop if she wanted him to.

"No, Mason," she whispered.

He growled at both her disobedience and his inability to just walk away. "Head down."

She immediately obeyed.

"You want me to fuck you like a dirty whore?" he asked

as he rubbed his cock along her cheeks. "You're getting paid to fuck me, aren't you?"

"Mason," she said, pleadingly, though she didn't deny it.

"That's not an answer."

"I-I'm sorry."

He did not want to hear that! She wasn't sorry, and he wasn't dishing out forgiveness. He reared up. He was too enraged now, his control a thing of the past. He fisted her hair so she partly faced him as he started jacking off. He wouldn't let himself fuck her, but if she got paid for being a whore, he'd fucking treat her like one by coming all over her face. She opened her mouth, though, willing to accept him, even now with everything that had happened...even now with the appallingly awful way he was treating her.

And he felt played all over again. He couldn't do anything right when it came to her.

Not. One. Fucking. Thing.

Instead of wanting to punish her more, he just wanted to get as far away from her as possible. He wanted to end this nightmare. He was so damn screwed because, deep down, he knew he'd never be rid of her. She was burned into his soul.

"Goddamn it!" he roared, letting go of his dick and unhooking her restraints. He worked quickly, not looking at her, not acknowledging her presence. Nor his raging hard-on. When she was free, he stomped toward his bathroom and yelled, "Get the fuck out," without sparing her a glance.

He slammed the bathroom door shut between them and banged his head against it once as he heaved in the air his lungs were starved for. He wasn't sure how long he stayed there, burning in the Hell of his own making.

When he heard her soft sobs, he still didn't come out.

# CHAPTER NINETEEN

Shelby had sent a text to Rick the moment she was out of Mason's house, informing him Mason knew she was an agent and requesting a few days off. She hadn't really *asked* for the time, but her boss hadn't argued with her on it either. Why would he? Her assignment was effectively over. She couldn't work undercover if her mark knew she was an agent.

She'd also fired off a message to Viola, so she wouldn't worry when Shelby didn't show up for work. Both texts had ignited a barrage of incoming calls by Viola and some of the others on their team. The constant soft buzzing of Shelby's phone had made her realize it'd only be a matter of time before they gave up on electronic means of communication and just showed up at her house. She wasn't ready for that. Without much internal debate, she quickly packed a bag and got in her car.

Shelby was in Mayflower, Arkansas by nightfall.

She'd considered renting a vehicle, using a fake name to book a hotel in some random town, and paying for everything in cash. As she ate up the miles, though, her desire for solitude slowly shifted and the thought of going to the small southern town gradually took over. Shelby didn't have many friends outside her close-knit team, but there *was* someone she could talk to there. Someone who knew what it meant to be on a difficult assignment involving a man she loved. Someone who'd been faced with the dilemma of professional life versus personal life. Her former teammate, Anna Sue Fisher.

Although Shelby and Anna no longer worked on the same team, they had worked on a major assignment together, the assignment that changed everything for Anna, forcing her to confront her feelings for Blade and altering the path of her career. Anna had been ordered to stick by Blade while Shelby had been stationed at the Bang shift Garage, digging into the guys who worked there. It had caused heartache and tested bonds, and frustratingly enough, that assignment was also all because of Mason Showalter.

Yeah. If anyone could relate to what Shelby was going through, it was Anna. Not that Shelby was sure she wanted to talk just yet.

When she pulled up to Blade and Anna's house, she killed the engine and stared at the front door. How was she even going to explain why she was here?

Taking a deep breath, Shelby got out.

"I wondered how long it was going to take you," Anna said from the porch. Shelby's gaze shot to her. The woman held up a bottle of wine and wiggled it enticingly. "Viola called."

"Of course she did," Shelby muttered. At least she didn't have to explain now.

"Get your bags. You're staying here." She'd planned on driving into Conway and getting a room there, so she opened her mouth to protest. Anna stopped her short. "Don't argue, girl. We're drinking, which means you driving anywhere else is out. C'mon. I'll open bottle number one."

Anna walked back into the house, and Shelby rolled her eyes, but got her stuff before following. She'd been questioning whether she was ready to talk, but wine sure did sound nice. She dropped everything just inside the door.

"In the kitchen," Anna called out.

Following the sound of Anna's voice, Shelby asked, "When did you get so bossy?"

"Oh, I'd say right around the time I got engaged." She pushed a full glass toward Shelby and looked at her. "Blade wants to get married in a barn just like Brody and Xan did. A *barn*."

Shelby chuckled, and it felt good to let go just a little. "It was beautiful, and you know it."

"Yeah, but that was before Roc started using it. I *refuse* to walk in horse shit."

"In heels, no less." Shelby laughed. "I'm surprised Blade's family doesn't want you guys to do it in Louisiana."

"Girl, I can't tell you how many times his mom has called me with locales down there, trying her best to talk me into it. When I told her I was planning an engagement party for up here, she about had a fit." Anna waved a dismissive hand before taking a sip, her huge engagement ring sparkling in the low light.

"I still think that's got to be the biggest diamond I've ever seen in real life."

Anna smiled down at it. "If I didn't know any better, I'd say Brax was overcompensating." She wagged her brows. "But I *do* know better."

"Lucky you," Shelby said, her humor fading a bit. Anna

was lucky. She'd come up against impossible odds and won. Both in life and love.

"I'm not gonna lie. It feels really good being on this side of the truth." She motioned for Shelby to follow and they went into the living room, glasses in hand.

Shelby made a noncommittal noise and took a sip of her wine. Then she took another, bigger drink. "It feels super awful being on this side."

"I know that, too." Anna's smile was sad. "But eventually, you'll feel better."

"Will I? No, I mean, really? 'Cause I gotta say, this sucks."

"Yeah. Granted, I knew Blade before that last case. Hell, we'd slept together." Anna took a sip.

Shelby grinned. "Can't believe you didn't share that info immediately."

"We all keep some secrets." Anna raised an eyebrow.

"I don't think I'm ready to go into all of that." Shelby took a big drink.

"Fine. We have all night. Just don't get too hungover because tomorrow, I'm sending you to the garage.

Shelby gaped at her. "What?"

"Girl, they are behind, and you could use a distraction. Besides, you're better than every one of them when it comes to cars. Well, except for Blade." She wiggled her ring finger. "I feel like I'm contractually obligated to be on his side on all things now."

She wasn't concerned with that. Shelby knew she was the shit when it came to auto repair, but she hadn't been back at the shop since everything went down on the last mission. There hadn't been time. She'd immediately been tasked to work the case in a different way.

"Are they mad?"

Anna tilted her head to the side as if she was thinking. "They were. Yes. I'd venture to guess they still don't trust the government."

"They're mercenaries. When did they ever trust us?"

Anna chuckled. "True. That's probably always been a touchy subject and will never change. *But* I think they know we were just doing our jobs."

"Knowing it and accepting it are two different things."

"Yep. I think you'll find they're not the type to hold grudges, though."

"Except for the mafia."

"Except for the mafia," Anna agreed.

"And people coming after their families."

"That too." Anna smiled, then stood and grabbed her cell phone off the counter. "Want some pizza?"

Shelby nodded. "And then what?" she asked, not talking about the food.

"We'll make ourselves sick on pepperoni," Anna replied anyway. She leveled a stare at her. "We'll worry about what happens next later."

Shelby could get on board with that.

———

WHAT WAS THAT OLD ADAGE? *Red sky at night, sailor's delight. Red sky in morning, sailor take warning.* Shelby wondered as she drove to the garage, the rising sun turning the sky a dark shade of blood.

She could call her brother, Axle, and ask him. He'd surely know how the saying went. The man wasn't just a sailor but a SEAL. She reached for her phone out of habit whenever she thought of him, but decided against calling him right now. She needed to be sure to talk to him while he was stateside, but she'd make it to the garage in a few minutes. Axle could wait. The Bang Shift guys couldn't.

Maybe that's why the sky looked so ominous. It was foretelling her future. Not just everything going down with Mason, but facing the men she worked beside not that long ago in an effect to gather intel for the government.

There was a disturbing pattern in all of this.

When she pulled into the parking lot and got out, she took one last look at the sky. Red...but beautiful. Dark, but somehow still light. Two contrasts competing for dominance and both winning.

The sound of an impact drill drew her attention to the shop. Someone was already here and working. She hoped it was Blade. He'd come in last night after she and Anna had been too tipsy to talk about anything important, but he'd at least been welcoming. She had no idea what faced her inside this morning. Gathering her strength, Shelby forged ahead. Voices echoed in the closed bay, signaling there was more than one of them in. She tested the front door, which was unlocked.

"...haven't even had a cup of coffee," Brody said.

"Quit your bellyachin'," Roc muttered from underneath an old Pontiac. "None of us wants to be here this fuckin' early."

"Roc," Bear said, exasperated. "Please."

"Just how the ladies sound," Roc said suggestively.

It reminded her of all the easy ribbing that had gone on while she'd been stationed here on assignment. Without any conscious effort, she jumped right in. "What?" Shelby quipped. "Full of disappointment?"

Tools dropped.

Roc rolled out into view.

Brody, Hunter, Gauge, and Bear stood from the various

cars they were working. Blade stared at her, too, as he wiped grease from his hands, but at least he was smiling. He was the only one sporting anything of the sort.

"Glade to see you finally got outta bed," Blade said.

"Wasn't easy," she muttered before rubbing her head. Looking to the side, she spotted the coffee pot, both a distraction and a blessing. "Feel like shit."

"You look it, too," Roc said as she made her way to the carafe. She smirked as she poured a cup.

"Dude," Gauge said. "Don't be an ass."

"Not a lie, though," Shelby said, and faced the men, cup in hand as a shield. She shrugged. "Too much to drink."

"And too much bullshit," Roc continued.

"Roc," Bear barked.

"Not a lie either." She sighed. "Look, I want to apologize for what happened—"

"Don't," Gauge said. "It was a job. Not a choice."

She looked at him for a long while. "Still doesn't feel right. None of this feels right."

"None of what?" Hunter asked, narrowing his gaze a little.

She took a sip of coffee while she contemplated her response. She could keep hiding behind her badge or she could come clean. She hadn't wanted to talk much last night, but now, with these men she'd worked so closely with, she felt an odd sense of acceptance no matter what she divulged.

"Working for an institution that makes me lie to people who matter."

"Even if it's for the greater good?" Gauge hedged.

"Who defines that?" She certainly wasn't qualified.

"The government," Brody said, crossing his arms.

"Even if you know it's wrong?"

"But do you know that?" Blade asked.

She shook her head. "I didn't believe for one second you guys were dirty."

Roc scoffed.

"Okay. You're shady as hell, but it still doesn't make what happened right. It was a major breach of trust, and for that I *am* sorry. The feds never should've sent me here on assignment. Or put Anna on Blade. It was wrong."

"I don't see it that way," Blade said. "It brought me and Anna together. I mean, as a shady-as-hell taxpayer, the folks could've spent my dollars a little bit more wisely, but that's on them."

Blade had a point. If it hadn't been for that assignment, he and Anna wouldn't be together now. He had a bright side to this mess. The other guys didn't have that perk.

"If we agreed with the feds' methodology on everything, we wouldn't be contractors. We'd be employees," Bear said.

She chuckled self-depreciatively. "Guess that means I should just come work for you guys. At least then I wouldn't be expected to fuck a suspect."

Bear gaped at her. Brody's gaze narrowed. Hunter stood taller. Gauge's smile flattened. Blade's mouth opened. Roc looked bored with this conversation already.

"Come again?" Bear asked.

"Oh, I *came* many times." She half-smiled. "I shouldn't be too surprised I also got emotionally attached." That was putting it lightly.

"You need to start from the beginning," Bear said.

"I don't know where the beginning is." She took another drink. "But it ends with Mason Showalter."

"Jesus," Blade said. "I don't think I want to know."

"Yeah. The SEC is still digging into his connections, and Rick is determined to see this assignment through no matter the cost. He sold Anna out to get to you. Then he tossed me right into the lion's den."

"He put you on Showalter," Brody said.

"He put me *under* Showalter." But she didn't go into how much she enjoyed that aspect of it. She focused on the facts. Mostly. "He's part owner of a sex club. The theory was I'd go in as a submissive, hoping he'd agree to introduce me to the lifestyle. Get what information I could on him. See if he was someone we could use as a source, or—"

"Someone to prosecute," Roc spat.

"Yep, and pimping me out worked. Until Showalter learned the truth. I'm sure Rick is pissed. I didn't stick around to find out just how irate he is. He's probably sifting through the remaining team members to decide who he'll offer up as collateral damage next. Good thing Viola went with me to the club one night, so he can't use her. Although, that means she's been made, too."

"What the fuck?" Gauge whispered heatedly. His neck slowly turned a shade of red not unlike the morning sky. She wasn't sure if it was because she'd just told him what she'd gone through...or if it was because she'd mentioned Viola. It was common knowledge the two of them had a history, but to what extent she wasn't sure.

She sure as hell wasn't asking him.

"So is he dirty?" Bear asked.

She opened her mouth to answer, but Roc snickered.

"I don't mean like that!" Bear glared at him.

"I don't know," she answered. "It doesn't look good. At all." She was *not* going to cry. She looked around the shop, took a drink of her coffee, set the empty cup down, and picked up a wrench, blinking a few times to keep the tears at bay.

"I'm calling Rick," Bear said.

She gasped and looked at him. Sure enough, he pulled out his cell phone. "Why? He knows where I'm at." There was no question about that. "And y'all aren't exactly on speaking terms right now."

"He needs to know if he doesn't give you time to decompress, he'll have us to answer to."

She opened her mouth to say something, doubting she'd be able to stop the waterworks with whatever she said, but he looked at Brody. "Get her suited up and started on Harvey's engine."

"C'mon. We got you something." Brody motioned for her to walk with him toward the shelves where extra gloves, coveralls, and other gear was stored. As she made her way over there, the other guys in the garage inched their way toward her. She glanced over her shoulder at them, but they gave nothing away.

"Here," Brody said, drawing her attention to him again. He pulled out a shirt like the ones they all had on. It had a patch on the side with the garage's logo on it just like theirs, but it also had something else.

Her name.

They had a shirt made just for her.

"Oh my gosh." She took it into her hands and caressed the stitching. "I don't know what to say."

"Just to be clear, we had that made *after* you left," Hunter said.

"We were going to give it to you at the engagement party Anna's planning," Blade said, and rocked on his heels. "But now we don't have to wait."

"You guys," she said, tears welling. The men all shuffled around, avoiding eye contact. It was almost comical how uncomfortable her emotions were making them. Rather than give in and boo-hoo, she decided to push it down and ease their discomfort. "But it doesn't match my shoes."

Roc chuckled and walked away.

The others smiled or shook their heads or rolled their eyes, all walking back to their respective bays.

And just like that, she'd been forgiven.

"So the government pimped you out, huh?" Blade asked as he loosened a lug nut. "How do we spread the word that we're now a brothel and car shop?" He looked up and winked at her.

Not skipping a beat, Shelby said, "Offer two for one rimjobs."

"Boom!" Hunter said. "Damn, it's good to have you back."

---

# CHAPTER TWENTY

Shelby's few days off turned into a week. Being with the Bang Shift crew helped her more than she'd ever anticipated. Hanging out at the shop, working on cars, worked so well to distract her during the day, and visiting with Anna, Xan, and Roxie in the evenings had been crucial. Maya and Heather even joined them a couple of times after they'd gotten back in town. They'd been gone the first weekend she got there. Something about a planned weekend with Heather's old friend, Caitlin Cooper. Shelby remembered the name since she'd seen some of Caitlin's news reports.

It was during those moments with them all that she'd slowly vented more and more about what she'd gone through. With the men, they'd comforted her with threats of bodily harm to Rick and Mason. With the women, they'd forged bonds of sisterhood-out-to-destroy-men. If it wasn't for all of them, she would've been holed up in a hotel room crying her eyes out.

Not that her time off changed anything. Mason had discovered she'd deceived him. How, she still didn't know. Bear had *reluctantly* kept in touch with Rick, but there hadn't been any new developments. Or so he'd said. What all he really knew she had no idea. She was just surprised she mattered enough to the guys for them to reach out to her boss.

Frankly, she hadn't been able to find the strength to care about the details. All she could manage was focusing on one moment after the next. If she looked at the big picture, grief would creep over her. So she'd hidden, and she'd worked.

But her heart was still broken.

At night, the pain had been strongest. Whenever she'd shut her eyes, all she saw was Mason's pain-ravaged face. She'd never forget the way he looked at her when he'd revealed he knew the truth. He'd been furious, but there had been more bleeding through, his soul open, and in that moment, she'd seen how much she'd truly hurt him. She would never forgive herself for destroying him like that. Her logical side tried to tell her she was just doing her job—just like everyone had told her over the last week—but her heart kept screaming in denial.

Being with them all had helped. Her pity-party was at a tolerable level now, but it was time to return and face the truth. She was nowhere near ready to see Mason again, wasn't sure what she'd do when she did, but she'd deal with that when the time came. For now, she was ready to be back home and talk to her team.

Starting with Viola.

She'd missed having her around the last week. They'd chatted some, but it had been brief. They had a lot of catching up to do, so when she reached town, she decided to head straight to Viola's house. It was Friday evening, so it was too late to go into the office anyway, and if she timed it like this on purpose, she wasn't going to admit that. She wanted to speak with Viola without the scrutiny of everyone else at the office. When she reached a stoplight, she fired off a text to Viola to let her know she was coming over.

Shelby rolled to a stop in Viola's driveway, immediately thrown off by what she saw. The front door was open, but Viola's car was not there. Frowning, she got out and walked slowly to the door, cursing when she instinctively reached for a weapon she didn't have. She didn't see anything suspicious except for the door being ajar. She hoped Dave was home and had left it open, and nothing serious had happened. When he came jogging out, she started.

"Jesus, you scared me," he said, surprised.

"Likewise." She chuckled nervously. "I was hoping to see Viola."

He shook his head. "She's working late on a case. I'm headed out of town. On business." His eyes darted, giving her the impression he wasn't being honest about something.

"Okay. I'll catch her at the office." But not tonight.

He turned and locked the door, not saying anything else. She guessed he was running late for a flight or something. Not wanting to delay him, she got in her car and headed to Darrell's house. If Viola was a long shot, Darrell probably was, too, but she was not going to the office. Not yet. If Darrell wasn't home, she could pat herself on the back for trying to reach out to not one but two people on her team, and then lock herself inside her apartment for the weekend.

It didn't take her long to get to Darrell's place. The bureau required they all live within a certain distance of their assigned office. She wasn't sure if she was pleased when she saw his SUV in his driveway or not. She'd already started liking the idea of going home. He walked out of his front door as soon as she pulled in, killing that possibility.

He knew she was here, and she'd have to at least visit for a little while before begging off. He crossed his arms and watched her as she parked her car and got out.

"'Bout fucking time you showed up, little bit."

"Good to see you, too," she muttered, walking up to him. He pulled her into a quick hug and stepped to the side, holding his screen door open for her. She walked in and sat on the old, comfy brown couch he had.

"Wanna beer?" he asked, trekking past her to the kitchen.

"No thanks."

"You missed some serious shit during your disappearing act. I'm going to let Rick know you're with me." He pulled out his phone and started clicking away on it. "He was getting a team together to come get you tonight."

"Um, why?"

"Because things changed about two hours ago."

Maybe she should've had the beer. "What?"

He pocketed his phone and sat on the coffee table facing her. "A body was found matching the description of Carl O'Brian."

She blinked. "And?" She knew there had to be more. A man matching the description of someone else was too vague. Hell, she matched the description of half the brunettes she passed on the street.

"He was found in a car registered to Carl O'Brian."

"Oh," she breathed. Her mind started was racing as Darrell continued.

"Yeah. He and the car were burned, so we couldn't do an immediate I.D. Medical examiner's pulling dental records as part of the autopsy." He clutched her hand in between his, his face solemn. "A package was delivered to headquarters earlier this afternoon with the coordinates to its location, along with video of Showalter and another man carrying something large and stuffing it into the truck of the same make and model vehicle. We're trying to identify the other man. It's not William Baxter, but it's definitely Showalter in the vid."

"Oh God." She was numb. She didn't think things could get any worse...until they did. There was no doubt now that Mason was who they were after.

"Carson intercepted a recent transaction where Showalter transferred large sums of money from an account we believe is linked to the Culpepper Hedge Fund to an overseas bank. Rick's worried he's going to jet." His thumb brushed over her hand. "That's not all," he said softly.

She yanked her hand away and steeled herself. How much more was there? The case being built against Mason was airtight. There was no way he wasn't involved. She couldn't even come up with a crazy scenario that'd explain his innocence.

"He's coming after you."

Shelby stood up. "What?"

"The package also had images from inside your apartment. One contained a note written on a pad and left by your key bowl that said, "I punish liars.""

She gasped, and Darrell ran a hand through his hair. "I'm sorry. We went to your apartment, but there was no sign of forced entry. No notepad. Does he have a key?"

She felt her head shaking no, but she wasn't sure if it had actually moved or not. Everything was so surreal.

"You're going to a safe house." Darrell started to leave the room, and she finally found her voice.

"What?" Everything was happening so fast. She shook her head, trying to process it all.

"I'll throw you over my shoulder if I have to. It's too

dangerous for you right now." He took a deep breath. "He could've killed you already. Jesus, you were alone with him. It could have been so easy. I just thank God he didn't." He walked down the hall and out of sight.

"I need to stop by my apartment for more clothes," she said a little louder, knowing she had no other choice but to comply.

He walked into the room carrying a duffle bag. "You'll buy some when we get there. C'mon. Viola is going to meet us since Dave is out of town on business. The others are staying back. As soon as the medical examiner confirms that's O'Brian's body we have, they're bringing in Showalter. If all goes well, he'll be in custody in a matter of days."

Shelby followed him outside, still trying to grasp what was happening. *Focus on the case, not on the man.*

It would take all her training to turn off her heart.

# CHAPTER TWENTY-ONE

"Open up! I know you're in there!" The shouting and pounding continued, pulling Mason out of sleep and into a massive hangover. The empty bottle of Macallan slipped from his grasp as he stood and grabbed his pounding head. Walking was tricky since each step magnified the pulsating sensation. He needed about a gallon of water and four aspirin.

He wrenched the door open and winced when something slammed into him.

The sun...shining in his face.

"Quit yelling," he groaned, and turned, leaving the door open for Jedrek and his cousin. They could find their own way in. He needed to make it back to the couch before he decided walking was too overrated and sat on the floor en route.

"Dude, you're a mess," Jedrek said, though whatever he was carrying was making so much noise he could barely hear his words.

Mason dropped his head into his hands when he made it back to the starting position. Small victory.

Jerome picked up the empty bottle and put it on the coffee table. "We brought you some food."

Mason opened one eye to look at the man. "Why are you here?" He could only image why his contact within the SEC had shown up at his home, and he didn't like any of the possibilities. He lifted his hand. "Never mind. I don't want to know." He glanced at Jedrek. "Can you get me some aspirin from the kitchen?"

Jedrek lifted a bottle and shook it. "Came prepared." He opened the medicine, poured out some pills, and handed them to Mason with a bottle of water. He downed them in one swallow while Jedrek opened the noisy paper sack. "Breakfast of champions," he said as he handed Mason some kind of sandwich. He didn't care what kind it was. His stomach growled at the smell, and he snatched it away.

"When's the last time you ate?" Jedrek asked as he sat in the chair across from him.

Mason shrugged, and said around the bite he took, "Don't know. What day is it?"

"Sunday."

Mason groaned. "Shit." He had to get over this hangover or tomorrow he'd be worthless at the office.

"Wanna tell me why you haven't been by the club or answered our calls in over a week? I haven't seen or heard from you since the scene Tuesday night."

Mason glanced at Jerome. "Ask your cousin."

Jerome frowned. "I don't know. I haven't heard from you since you called asking about Agent Landry."

Mason's stomach turned, so he dropped the half-eaten sandwich and fell back against the couch, rubbing his face. Shelby, God, he'd done nothing but think about her for days, and when he couldn't turn off his brain, he tried drowning it in liquor.

Yeah, he was paying for that now.

"Who?" Jedrek asked, stone-faced as usual.

"Don't, Parker," Mason bit out, glancing at Jerome, warning him not to say anything. "You shouldn't even be here."

Jerome sat on the couch, looking confused. "I have an update, but you wouldn't answer the phone I gave you. I called cuz here to let me in. You asked for my help, and—"

"I knew it was a fucking mistake, going to the feds," Mason snapped. He looked at Jedrek, and mimicked in a stoic voice, "My cousin works for the SEC. He can help you."

"I do not sound like that," Jedrek said, crossing his arms, brooding as usual.

"Yeah, you kinda do," Jerome said, smiling briefly before focusing on Mason. "You left your office on Wednesday and haven't been back. Why? Did something happen?"

Boy, did it ever. "Tell me something. How much control do you have over this investigation?"

Jerome frowned. "I'm not sure I'm following."

Mason licked his lips and narrowed his gaze. "I found discrepancies in William Baxter's accounts. I came to you to report him. I did it for selfish reasons, I admit. William is incompetent, and I want his job. When I found those reports, I saw an opportunity, and I took it."

"Yeah," Jerome said slowly. "I know."

Mason sat back and laced his hands together. The longer he was awake, the better he was feeling. It could've been the food or the medicine...or both, but he was starting to feel human again. His heart still ached, but he couldn't do anything about that now.

"Do you know everybody assigned to the case? What their *assignments* are?"

Jerome shook his head, looking confused still. "No. It's a joint effort between the SEC and the FBI. When you first came to us, we weren't sure the extent of Baxter's deceit. Once we realized the magnitude, our director pulled in the FBI. But you don't have to worry. I know a couple of those agents personally. Rick McMillian is team lead. He's a good guy. Viola Lane and I have worked together before, too."

Jedrek's head snapped up, and Mason's gaze slid to his. His partner's eyes narrowed, and Mason knew the guy remembered her from the other night. Too late to keep him out of the loop. If he hadn't put the pieces together yet, Mason was about to do it for him.

"And Agent Shelby Landry?" Mason asked Jerome.

"What the fuck?" Jedrek exploded.

Jerome jumped. "What?"

Mason looked at Jedrek and completely understood his rare display of emotion. "I found out Wednesday, which is why I haven't felt like taking any calls."

Jedrek's head whipped to Jerome. "Do you know about this?"

Jerome's eyes got bigger, and he looked completely lost. "No, he doesn't know," Mason answered for him, but looking at Jerome as he replied. "I called him Wednesday, and he told me she's a *linguistics* expert."

"I just fucking bet she is," Jedrek spat. Mason had to beat down the ridiculous urge to defend Shelby. His partner wasn't implying anything Mason hadn't outright accused her of himself.

"She is," Jerome said. "And she was able to bring something to the case no one else could."

A string of expletives flew from Jedrek's mouth.

"I'm fully aware what her skills are," Mason said, unable to stop the smile of sarcasm. "But do you know why *the fuck* the FBI is investigating *me* when I was the one who turned in Baxter?"

Jerome was struggling for words—that was clearly evident—and finally said, "What the hell are you talking about?"

"Shelby—excuse me, *Agent Landry*—came to the club a few weeks ago, claiming she wished to learn about the life-style and wanted me to be the one to teach her all about it."

"Maybe it's a coincidence," Jerome said, frowning. "Jed says all the time how there're all walks of life who enjoy kinky shit." But as he said it, Mason was sure the man was questioning the probability himself.

"She brought her *friend*, Viola, with her to the club."

"And she asked a lot a questions," Jedrek said, eyes turning dark again.

"Okay, it does look bad, but after studying your file and learning about your lifestyle, maybe she wanted to give it try?"

"She told me she was a massage therapist. She lied about her job," Mason challenged.

"Agents do that all the time. They don't share their career to just anyone. Hell, I lie about it all the time," Jerome said, shrugging. "I need more before I ask Rick about this. What if she approached you on her personal time and didn't want anybody to know?"

"Except Viola, another agent she works with?" Jedrek asked incredulously. "Bullshit. But hell, for sake of argu-ment, if she's working a case that involves Mason at all, why wouldn't she tell her boss she sought him out? That's a conflict of interest if it's not related to the case. Any idiot can see that." He shook his head. "You seriously expect him to believe two FBI agents assigned to investigate Fieldstein and Baxter Investments were at the club just for kicks?"

Mason was glad Jedrek understood right away. But he was a private man, too. He would not like anybody taking advantage of him.

"And speaking of Viola, her husband is a real piece of work." Mason stood and walked over to the package he got from Dave. He grabbed it and tossed it to Jerome. Jedrek loomed over his shoulder to look, too. "Everybody has a price, man. His was forty g's. If that isn't enough proof for you, I don't know what is."

Jerome opened it and pulled out the photos, his face darkening.

"He sold you that?" The question came from Jedrek. "He fucking sold out his own wife?"

Mason nodded. "He told me the FBI was investigating me and gave, er, sold me the photos to prove it."

Jerome grabbed his phone as he stood. "I'll get to the bottom of this." He was grumbling something as he made his call. "Rick, hey. Something's come to my attention, and I need some clarification on your team's assignment." He stepped into the hall as he listened. Mason watched until he heard some rustling and looked to his left. Jedrek had picked up the photos again and was scrutinizing them. He held the one that had Viola in the center of it. Mason couldn't be sure what was going through the man's mind, but his eyes stayed glued to the blonde.

"I'd heard about that," Jerome said, drawing his attention again. "We haven't discussed it yet." He glanced toward Mason as he said, "He's been out of pocket for a few days. We were just meeting, so I could bring him up to speed. He'd like to know why Agent Landry has been playing him, and frankly, so do I."

The mention of her deception burned deep within him.

"I don't blame you for getting drunk, man," Jedrek said.

"If it had been me, I'd have tied her up and whipped her ass."

He laughed without humor. "Oh, I did."

"What?" Jerome yelled, and Mason looked over, thinking the man was yelling at him for admitting that, but he was looking at a spot on the wall as he roared into the phone. "Why the hell wasn't I told about this..? No, this is bullshit... This was our damn case... Well, where is she..? Yeah, got it."

He hung up the phone and turned toward Mason, who was already staring, waiting for some answers. Jerome clicked on his phone as he walked back to the couch. He cussed and picked up the photos again, shuffling through them. He pulled out the photo with Shelby smiling and talking to Viola with another man in the background.

"Damn it," he breathed, and went back to scrolling on his phone.

"What's going on?" Mason asked, not liking the man's behavior.

"Got it." He held out his phone and showed Mason an image of a middle-aged man. "Have you ever seen this guy before?"

Mason took the phone and studied the picture. He got a flash of something, but it went away just as quickly. He frowned in concentration and then it came back to him. He had seen this man before, only his hair wasn't as short.

"Yeah." He tapped the phone, looking up at Jerome. "That's the dude that came to the office with William that Saturday and accessed the system. The one he was supposed to play golf with. I called you after they left and told you about it."

Jerome picked up one of the photos from the coffee table and handed it to Mason. "Look familiar?"

It was the one with Shelby partially hugging a man who wasn't facing the camera. The neck and profile were the same, though. She was hugging the man who had been with William that day. "Who the hell is that?"

"That's Darrell Tobin. He's one of the guys on her team."

Mason nodded slowly. "Darrell. She's talked about him before. Said something about him being like an uncle to her. What the hell was he doing with William? Is he working another angle on the investigation?" If they were trying to get close to William, it wouldn't work. Mason had known him for years, and his boss rarely let anybody into his inner circle.

Jerome fell to the couch beside him. "No." The look the man gave him had his heart pounding. "Darrell *is* their mark."

"English, Parker!"

"When you work for the government, your life is an open book. Somebody, somewhere caught wind of Darrell moving a large sum of money between accounts. Internal affairs got involved. They've been secretly investigating him and knew he had dealings with F and B. They weren't sure if his involvement was legit or not, but when you came to me and we started investigating the firm..." He trailed off, shaking his head.

"Somebody found the link."

"Yes. This joint task force wasn't created to crack down on F and B. That's solely the SEC's job. It was assembled to flush out Darrell."

Mason stood and paced as he let this settle in. She hadn't only deceived him, but she'd turned on her friend Darrell. He battled with reason and anger. If Darrell was a criminal, then it was her job to take him down. Did she care that a man she'd told Mason was one of her close friends was possibly dirty, or was she able to turn off her emotions so easily? "And she agreed to do this?" he said aloud, trying to make sense of it all.

"No," Jerome said softly.

Mason whirled. "No, what?"

"She doesn't know about Darrell. She was picked to seduce you because she's the closest one on the team to Darrell."

"She didn't seduce me," Mason growled.

Jerome sighed. "You know what I mean. She was picked because of her connection to Tobin. He's mentored her since she joined the bureau. William and Darrell apparently go way back, as in before college days. Rick said the director thinks Darrell has been helping William steal money and covering it up for years."

Mason mulled that over. "Okay, but why use Shelby?" It felt as if the feds were going about it in a manner that didn't seem functional to Mason's business sense. He was a straight shooter, and they were beating around the bush. The wrong bush at that.

"Think about it. If Darrell is in cahoots with William and knows the SEC suspects his dirty business partner, Darrell will be busy making sure nothing points to him. He needs a scapegoat to divert their attention, so the FBI gave him one. They want him thinking they believe you are the guilty one. You have means and opportunity. And I would bet a case of beer that Darrell was the force behind William blackmailing you to move that money. He's trying to frame you, steering the FBI's investigation in the direction he wants."

"But it's really a distraction," Mason said slowly. "Make

Darrell think one thing while they build their case against him."

"Exactly. And Darrell might get sloppy. Agent Landry knows him better than anybody else on the team. Putting her in the middle of this gives her the opportunity to stumble on something that might be overlooked by another investigator, allowing her to connect the dots for them."

"Because Mason's firm has a habit of leaving incriminating evidence lying around," Jedrek said sarcastically.

"So she has no idea," Mason said, feeling angry again, but for a completely different reason. "She's being played. Her own fucking boss is playing with her. They used her to get close to me, and they're using her friendship with Darrell to take him down."

"Pretty fucking shitty," Jedrek said, crossing his arms.

"Look, I'm not happy about this either. I should've been told about their plan. Hell, I've been trying to get in touch with you to tell you they were upping the ante, releasing doctored evidence that O'Brian was dead, hoping William would slip up. But I didn't know it wasn't only for William's benefit."

Mason's body grew cold. "Darrell. They want him to think they're closing in on William because, if he believed that, then he'd know it would only be a matter of time before his connection to him was discovered."

"Bingo."

"Fucking feds," Jedrek barked.

"Hey. I said I didn't know about it," Jerome said. He looked at Mason. "I would *not* have gone along with them using you. Or her, for that matter. I respect you coming to me and would've lobbied to keep the F and B investigation separate from Tobin."

"Which is why they didn't say a word to you about it,"

Mason said in resignation. Messed up didn't even begin to describe this situation. He was still mad that Shelby knowingly used him, but she was in deeper than she realized. If the feds weren't going to tell her, he would. She trusted Darrell, and that put her in a lot of danger. Mason could try calling her, but he didn't want to risk everybody on her team hearing what he had to say. He had no idea who all knew the extent of the investigation and who could be trusted. "Can you arrange a meeting with Shelby?"

Jerome swallowed. "You can't interfere with an ongoing investigation."

"Fuck that," Mason breathed. "You wouldn't have a goddamn investigation if I hadn't blown that whistle I found." He unclenched his fisted hands and took a deep breath. "You *will* get that meeting. If not, I'll go to the media and fuck everything up. I'll squeal like a goddamn pig about everything."

Jerome shot to his feet. "If you do that, they can throw your ass in jail."

"I don't care. Shelby needs to know the truth. She either finds out on the news once it's blasted everywhere, or I tell her in private. Your call."

"You realize since they staged Carl's death, she thinks you murdered him."

Mason shut his eyes, stifling a groan. He hadn't thought about it like that. If Jerome had done his job, it would look pretty damn convincing. And they wouldn't have told her the truth because they were using her to get to Darrell. Because her case hadn't been about Mason at all. "Yeah, that's a problem, but once I tell her everything, she'll understand."

"God, you're not going to let this go, are you?"

"No. Make it happen. I want to talk to her as soon as

possible." He just hoped he could stay detached when he saw her. Regardless of his need to inform her of what was really happening, it didn't change what had happened to them. What she had done to him.

Jerome cursed as he pulled out his phone. This time, he stomped out of sight. Mason didn't care. As long as the man got his meeting with Shelby, that was all that mattered to him.

When his contact walked back in, his face was pale, and he was moving too fast. Mason stood on instinct. "They don't know where she's at."

"What?" Mason asked, narrowing his eyes, his tone much calmer than he actually felt.

"She was pretty upset, so she took some time off." Mason swallowed the guilty lump that rose in his throat and forced himself not to defend any unspoken accusations. "She went to Arkansas and hung out with some people we've worked with. That's a long story, but she got back on Friday and was expected to be in the office tomorrow. When I told Rick you demanded she be brought in on everything, he put me on hold to call her. She didn't answer. He tried Viola, but the last word she got was a text on Friday saying she's back in town and was coming over, but she hasn't heard from her since. Darrell isn't answering his phone."

"Fuck, he's got her." Mason jogged to the door where he'd taken off his shoes and grabbed them.

"We don't know that."

Yes, they did, or Jerome wouldn't have looked panicked when he walked back in. Darrell had too much at stake, and if he thought Shelby was onto him, he'd take her out. Mason just knew it.

"You know where Viola lives?" Mason asked.

"I can find out."

"Do it."

"I'm coming, too," Jedrek said, standing. Mason didn't question if the motivation was to see Viola again or if he wanted to help find Shelby. Didn't matter.

"C'mon. I'll take all the help I can get."

———

SHELBY STARED out the window overlooking the beach. *Pretty swanky for a safe house.* The FBI had hideouts all over the place to stash witnesses, but she hadn't been to one this nice. Not that she got to enjoy it. Much like she'd been trapped here for her own protection, she'd been a prisoner of her mind, lost in thoughts of Mason's illegal actions.

And sensual touch.

Why did she have to love everything he did to her? Love the man himself? Was it possible to hate what he did and still feel this way about him? Yes, yes, it was. She couldn't explain it, but that didn't make it any less true.

She wished she had Viola to talk to. Shelby hadn't realized how much she'd relied on their friendship over the years, thinking they were close coworkers at best, until the last couple of cases they'd worked together. Viola would listen to her, even without having to hear the words first. Her friend would take one look at her, notice anything eating away at her sanity, and *make* her talk. If only Dave's trip hadn't been disguised as a romantic getaway for the two of them. Darrell had said that Viola would make Dave reschedule once she'd learned about his spontaneous plan, but her mentor had insisted he had everything under control. After hearing this, Shelby had agreed with Darrell. Viola and Dave had some marital issues to work on, and they needed a little alone time. Shelby wouldn't dream of condemning Viola to being locked up with her when she could be with her husband instead. Besides, it was just for the weekend. She would be here late tonight after her trip anyway, and Shelby could talk to her then.

Darrell usually was attuned to her and was pretty good at communication, but he was too focused on this case and her safety to notice how much she was hurting inside. Even if he hadn't taken her phone before they'd left to keep anybody from triangulating its signal, she didn't need to call anybody else.

She'd already had girl time with Anna and the ladies in Arkansas.

She'd hung out with the guys of the Bang Shift.

Her brother was in his SEALs rotation, not that she'd want to tell him—or her dad, for that matter—about any of this.

She sighed, stepping away from the window and rubbing her upper arms to comfort herself. She had many wonderful people in her life, but for some reason, she felt lost without Mason. That totally confused her. Was it need or want? She didn't know, but what she was slowly discovering was that the reason didn't matter. She loved him. It wasn't a healthy love because it was born out of lies, nor did she harbor any beliefs that her feelings were returned. It was best that they weren't. It didn't make any of this any easier to accept.

Darrell walked in the room, texting on his phone. He pocketed it when he looked up at her.

"Hungry?"

She shrugged. She hadn't had much of an appetite lately, so she defaulted to eating when Darrel ate.

"I have some stew and cornbread cooking now. It's not much, but I don't want to get out unless we have to."

"You told me that already," she said, smirking.

"Sorry, little bit. Been distracted since the shit hit the fan on Friday."

She smiled. "I know. It'll be okay, though. Viola will be here tonight and you can take a break."

He nodded slowly and opened his mouth to say something, but his phone rang. He pulled it out, glanced at the display, and silenced it. "I'll check on the stew."

He walked into the kitchen, looking at his phone.

Yes, the man was distracted, and she didn't blame him.

For the next fifteen minutes, she heard his phone go off a few more times while he was in the kitchen and she in the living room, scanning the television channels for a distraction to watch. When he came back into the room, he carried two bowls of stew and some grilled cheese sandwiches.

"Yum," she mumbled, taking the plate he offered. "This smells so good." She stirred the contents in the bowl and spread her sandwich apart so it could cool. She took a sip of the broth and hummed appreciatively. Since it was too hot to dig right in and eat, she picked up half of her sandwich. "Any news yet?" She hadn't kept track of the number of times she'd posed that question to him, but half the time it was out before she could stop herself from asking. She nibbled on the cheesy crust and looked at him expectantly.

"No news from Rick."

Darrell's phone rang again, and he silenced the call.

"Who keeps calling you?"

His head snapped up, and he stared at her two seconds longer than she felt comfortable. Did he think she was prying into his personal affairs? Was she? "I'm sorry. I just hoped it was related to the case."

He rubbed his face and grabbed his spoon. "Yeah, it's related to the case. I've put some feelers out on Showalter, but none of my contacts have come through yet." He took a few bites of the stew. "Don't worry. We'll catch him."

She wasn't worried about that, but she was starting to be concerned about Darrell. "You're working too hard on this."

He shook his head, a smile tugging on his lips as he took another bite. "Anything for you, little bit."

His phone rang again. This time, he accepted the call and left the room. Shelby pushed any worry for him from her mind and ate her stew. When he returned with some crackers, she'd already eaten most of her food.

He chuckled as he put the crackers on the table. "I guess you were hungry. Want more before I sit back down?"

She blushed, shaking her head. "No, you eat." She was full, but the food was there and comforting her.

"We have a bead on Showalter."

Shelby's heart started racing. "Yeah?"

Darrell nodded and took a bite of his stew. She pushed the last of hers away, not able to eat anymore, snuggled into the couch, and turned down the television before giving him her attention again. "Yeah. He's still in the state, but Rick wants me to bring you back now that they're watching him. They're not letting him out of their sight."

"When?" she asked, sitting up straighter.

"As soon as we're ready." He dropped his spoon into his bowl and began stacking their empty dishes.

"I'll pack the stuff I bought when we got here." She stood.

The room spun.

"Whoa." Darrell lunged for her and steadied her before she fell.

She rubbed her head. "I guess I stood up too fast." Did her words just slur?

Why was the room becoming fuzzy? She was being lowered to the couch, and Darrell sat beside her, stroking her hair. What was wrong? Was she having a stroke? Had the stress been too much for her body?

"You'll be okay," he said softly. "You're just taking a little nap."

Nap? She wasn't tired. She couldn't move her limbs. Those were completely different things. "What's hap-happening?" she asked slowly, trying with what little strength she could gather to get the words out.

"No time to explain. We have to go before they find us."

"Who?" she asked, frowning. Hadn't he said Mason wasn't anywhere around here? She heard a door open but couldn't see over the couch since she couldn't turn her head.

His smile was sad. "I really don't want to have to kill you, little bit. Be a good girl, and we might let you live."

Panic shot through her at his words, but the face that came into view chilled her to the bone.

William Baxter.

"You're in no position to make such a promise," the man she'd only seen before in photographs and video said. "Everything ready?"

"Yep. We'll be out of the country by this time tomorrow."

She looked at Darrell and opened her mouth to begin asking him all the questions that bubbled up in her hazy mind, but the blackness surrounding her vision closed in, carrying her into an even darker reality.

# CHAPTER TWENTY-TWO

MASON KILLED the engine to his car and bounded up the steps to Viola's house. Jedrek and Jerome Parker were behind him in Jerome's car, but he didn't wait on them. He pounded on the door three times before it was yanked opened. A tired-looking Viola stood in the doorway, gripping a gun.

When she saw who it was, she raised her weapon lightning fast.

His hands flew up. "Whoa."

"Viola, don't!" Jerome called out as he and Jedrek came running up the stairs. She glanced to the side, frowning at him.

"Parker? What the hell's going on?" she looked at Mason and sneered. "What are you doing with him?"

"It's a long story. Can we come inside? I'll explain as fast as I can."

She waved Mason in with her gun and kept it trained on him. He left his hands up for good measure, hoping it was proof she didn't have to worry, but if Shelby believed he was a killer, then Viola did, too. Unless she was in on the real reason for their involvement. The way she was glaring at him, hand at the trigger, led him to believe that wasn't the case. "You have two minutes."

Jerome gave her the super condensed version of the story, and Mason watched as her face changed from anger to confusion to rage. When she finally dropped the gun, he took a calming breath and let his hands fall to his sides.

"Darrell," she growled, and stomped to the couch where she opened her laptop. Mason and the guys huddled in and sat on the sparse furnishings. "Looks like he's in North Carolina."

"How do you know that?" Jedrek asked. Her head snapped toward him, seemingly just realizing the man was here.

"Tracking device." She shrugged. "Rick had me tag everybody on the team. He wanted cars, suitcases, brief-cases, jackets, anything that anybody might be traveling in or have on them. He wanted to know where everybody was when this mission started."

"So you know where Shelby is," Mason said, hope flaring in his chest.

She shook her head. "Not yet. I put one in her wallet behind an old prescription card. Nobody uses those things unless you need to scrape ice off your windshield. Give me a few seconds, and I'll see if she's carrying it."

A few seconds turned into minutes, and Mason started bouncing his knee. He didn't like sitting idle when he could be out looking for Shelby. Yes, he knew he'd have better luck using Viola's skills, but his analytical side was panick-ing, too.

"Hmmm." Viola frowned.

"What?" All three guys asked at the same time. Mason

glanced at them and noticed he wasn't the only one feeling on edge.

"She's in North Carolina, too."

"I knew he had her." Mason grabbed his phone and called the charter service his company used after selling their private jets several years ago to help their company image. After the housing market crashed and the economy tanked, corporate excesses had been frowned upon. Right now, he praised having that connection with the company. He could get there much faster with them than if he took a commercial flight. They answered on the third ring, and he rattled off instructions to get ready to fly out, and because they appreciated his business, they'd be ready in an hour.

"She's not with him, though," Viola said, frowning. "The signals are miles apart."

"Maybe he's stashed her somewhere. I don't give a shit about him. I'm going wherever she is." He stood and pocketed his phone. "You can come with me if you want. Plane will be ready soon."

"And what if she *is* with Darrell?" She pointed to her computer screen. "All this tells me is where her wallet is, and you can't go off half-cocked with just that. Besides, *you* are not law enforcement. I'll call Rick and have him notify the FBI office out there. Her signal isn't moving. His is. Those agents can get there before we can, and if she's there, they can retrieve her. If she's not, then that's one less place we have to look."

"Fuck," Mason breathed. He gritted his teeth as he stared at her. "Fine. Make the call."

"Wasn't asking for permission," she muttered as she whipped out her phone and called her boss. She relayed what Mason's intent was, and she seemed to be defending the need to go to Shelby...until she mentioned Shelby and

Darrell's locations in another state. The atmosphere changed at that moment. When Viola got off the phone, he knew their boss was playing ball.

"He's getting Carson and we're headed to North Carolina. You're not going."

"The hell I'm not—"

Viola held up her hand. "Listen. Rick will not allow you to travel with us. What you do on your own is your business. I can't keep you from showing up, even if I stepped out of the room and you happen to look at my computer to get the address."

Mason nodded, immediately understanding. Viola would go with her team, but he would still take the private jet. "Darrell is still moving, though." An address to his current location wouldn't help Mason when he landed in a few hours.

"Don't look a gift horse in the mouth." She shook her head. "Give me your number. When we touch down, I'll give you an update. Happy?"

Not yet, but he would be once he knew Shelby was safe. Thank God she had a friend like Viola. Then she asked the one thing he hadn't prepared for. "Mind telling me how you found out she was an agent? Parker seemed to skip that part of the explanation."

He shut his eyes and silently cursed her husband.

"I'll tell her," Jedrek said, and Mason's gaze went to him as he slowly stood, his chest expanding as if challenging Mason for the right. Jedrek was an oddly quiet man who didn't like to get in the middle of other people's shit, but he'd obviously taken a liking to Viola. If the big brute wanted to break the news to her that her husband was a worthless piece of shit, Mason would let him. He'd rather focus his energy on finding Shelby anyway.

So he nodded and turned away, concentrating on his own problems while Jedrek exposed Viola to one of her own.

When Mason found Shelby, he wasn't sure what he'd tell her. He loved her, so he'd stop at nothing to make sure she was safely away from Darrell Tobin, and they needed to clear the air between them. It would not change what happened or the lies she'd told him, nor would it change their relationship. Mason was a Dom at his core. He craved sexual obedience, but he demanded trust.

He no longer trusted her, and that was the core of the problem. He might never be able to again. He had to prepare himself for that. The thought also occurred to him that none of this would matter. He was, after all, just an assignment for her. He didn't know how intricate the web of lies was. She could have a boyfriend. He doubted it. He also completely rejected the possibility that she could be married. No way would a husband let his wife get close to another man like that. He'd seen it in the lifestyle—poly relationships—but those were molded out of communication and trust. Two things that he and Shelby sorely lacked.

"Why didn't you contact me?" Viola screeched, jerking Mason out of his reverie. He looked at her and Jedrek only to realize she'd directed her question at Mason. She stared daggers at him, her hands fisted in her lap.

"He's been in the middle of a pity party," Jedrek said softly, and Mason gaped at how tenderly he was looking at Viola, as if witnessing her pain was hurting him, too. Oh, hell. The man was clearly smitten. He didn't know much about him, had never seen him with a woman more than once, but the man couldn't take his eyes off her. It would never work, and Mason knew the man would never act on whatever attraction he felt. Jedrek didn't believe in relationships, and the woman was married. Her husband was worthless, but he was her husband nonetheless.

"Yes. Major pity party. I'm sorry. You deserved to know the truth right away," Mason said, trying to ease her.

"And you told Shelby?"

"Not about how I found out, but she knows I know the truth about the investigation, which, I apparently know a whole hell of a lot more than she does."

"Oh my God," Shelby breathed. "She was a mess when she left your place. You hurt her, you son of a bitch." She stood and Jedrek rose with her. Great. Just what he needed —a pissed off woman with a gun and a behemoth of a man ready to avenge her. "What did you do?" she asked slowly.

Jedrek crossed his arms, and Jerome came to stand beside Mason, looking a little nervous. "He just told her he knew the truth, right, Mason?"

He looked at Jedrek because the man would understand. "And then I spanked her ass her for lying to me."

Jerome groaned.

Jedrek actually cracked a smile.

Viola gasped. "Why you—" She stormed toward him, but Jedrek grabbed her arm. She whirled on the other man since he was the one actually restraining her. "I'm going to kick his ass," she yelled at Jedrek as she tried fruitlessly to yank her arm away.

"No, you won't. He was within his right to punish her."

She stilled. Mason wasn't one to be easily scared by a woman's wrath, but this was an exception. He preferred her screeched and jerking than standing dangerously still. "What does that mean?" she whispered.

"He's her Dom. She betrayed him." He glanced at Mason. "Did she use her safe word?"

"No."

Jedrek looked at Viola again. "See. If she didn't want him to punish her, she would have used it."

"She didn't want him to hurt her!"

"I didn't want her to hurt me," Mason roared, feelings of betrayal flooding him at the memory. Fuck, but her deception had cut him to the core.

Viola jumped at his outburst, and Jedrek let go of her. She looked at him warily for several seconds. He could see the wheels turning, her mulling over the truth. There was no way she could spin it to change what had happened. Finally, she said, "You're right. She did hurt you. She didn't have a choice, Mason. And I will say this, she wished more than anything that she didn't have to."

He snapped his mouth shut and turned away. He was not going to discuss this with her. He looked at his watch to gauge how much time he had left before he needed to leave. *Fuck it*. "I'm heading to the hangar." He leaned over, turned her laptop toward him, and pulled out his phone. He saved the two North Carolina addresses into his device. "What's your number?"

She rattled it off, and he stored it in his contacts. He hadn't missed Jedrek doing the same. Mason sent her a quick text, so she would also have his number.

"I need to go, too," Viola said as she reached for her gun. "I need to tell Rick about Dave before we head out." Her eyes fell, and he hated that she was hurting. Hated it because she was someone important to Shelby.

"Let me know as soon as you know something concrete," Mason said, and looked at Jedrek and Jerome. "Let's go."

He couldn't wait a second longer.

———

THE COOL SURFACE felt so good Shelby didn't want to get up. She didn't know why she was so tired, but lethargy wasn't a bad thing, she decided. Somewhere inside the haze, she knew there were things she didn't want to face, and sleep would protect her. The surface rocked, lulled her. No, she didn't want to wake up, not right now, even as the knowledge lingered that she didn't have a choice in the matter.

Sometime later, she stirred at the sound of voices. The cool surface now stuck to her sweaty cheek. She heard a click, and the voices stopped. Her barely awake mind tried to identify it. Maybe she'd fallen asleep watching television, and the autotimer had shut it off. But the sound had been louder, closer. She inhaled deeply and stilled any movement. The surface smelled rugged, like leather, which didn't make any sense. Her couch wasn't made of that.

She opened one eye first and blinked in confusion at a closed sunroof above her. She was in a car. She looked to the side and amended that—a limo. How could that be? The clicking sound was probably the door shutting with the voices belonging to...who? One was probably Darrell, she thought halfheartedly.

*Darrell.* Her memories assaulted her then, jolting her heart. God, he'd drugged her, kidnapped her. He was working with William. He was probably the other voice.

No. That couldn't be right. Darrell was a heck of an agent, always doing things by the book. He wouldn't turn on them like this. She rolled to her side, groaning with the effort it took to move her body. She felt as if she weighed a ton, the effects of the drugs still strong within her. She panted as she listened, but no longer heard muffled voices. Where were they?

Rick must have Darrell working on the inside, though

the thought of that angered her. Why would he divide the team like this and not tell everybody what each of their assignments were? Hell, she blushed, remembering how she'd found out her objective, and she'd been told in a roomful of people. Rick must have his reasons for keeping Darrell's assignment private, reasons that could've come from higher up. If Darrell was working a classified angle, no one would've been told, and he was too much by-the-book to let even Shelby in on his assignment.

His last words echoed in her mind, *"I really don't want to have to kill you, little bit. Be a good girl, and we might let you live."* He'd been convincing. She'd been scared in her confused state, but he'd had to make it realistic if William was to believe he would actually hurt her. If anybody could sympathize with Darrell and his need to play his role to his best ability, it was Shelby. She'd been given an impossible assignment, having no choice but to accept it. The same was true for Darrell. If the bureau needed him to be undercover, then she knew he'd accept whatever task that had been laid before him. How he was able to get in, she didn't know. Whatever key he used to unlock that steely door guarding the path to William's trust had worked. Hopefully, with what he had on William and the evidence they'd gathered on Mason, it would be enough to take the two down.

Though she didn't like Darrell incapacitating her like this. Why had he brought her here anyway? He knew Mason had found out she was an agent. It was too dangerous for her to be around William.

Oh crap. Had William ordered her dead? Was that why Darrell had to stage a kidnapping? No matter what the others said about Mason, she didn't think he had it in him to kill her. Carl? That was a different matter. But Shelby? No, he wouldn't kill her. He'd had the chance to execute her if that had been his wish. She'd been bound and at his mercy, all the while he'd known the truth about her. He'd been enraged. She'd seen the hurt in his eyes and had known how utterly devastated he'd been. If he hadn't killed her in his fury, he wouldn't order it after the fact.

Unless he'd had time to calm down and realized he'd screwed up by not killing her when he'd had the chance.

That thought hurt more than she liked to admit.

She jerked at a sudden shout, muffled by the car, but it was a panicked sound still. She hoisted herself up and glanced through the window. Where were they? If Darrell was in trouble, she should try to help. More importantly, if something happened and he was made, she didn't want to be waiting around for William to show up alone without Darrell around to protect her. She fisted her hands and rolled her neck, forcing away the numbness from the weaker parts of her body. She had feeling, but not one hundred percent. It would have to do. She couldn't sit here doing nothing.

And what if the shout had nothing to do with trouble? It would look as if she was trying to escape. Darrell might have to drug her again. No way did she want more of this crap in her system. It was a risk she had to take, so she'd have to be careful. She opened the door and slipped to the ground, staying low. She gently shut it and looked from left to right, searching for any sign of Darrell. She was in a shaded area, and when she looked up, she realized she was in a large building that was completely open on one end. She crawled to the side and hid behind some crates as she peered around the opening. She watched as a jet took off in the distance and then, much closer to her, a smaller plane's hatch opened, stairs distending.

An airport.

There was no movement. Things were almost too quiet considering her whereabouts. The scream she'd heard hadn't made any sense. Then again, maybe it hadn't been a scream at all. Now that she knew she was at an airport, it could've been a jet engine starting. For all she knew, Darrell and William were on the plane talking and there was no immediate danger.

Then she heard it again. Someone shouted...another voice yelled after that.

"You're surrounded. Come out with your hands up!"

Yes! Darrell must've called in backup. But where was he? If he was still with William, he would be vulnerable. The jackass could try to kill him if he discovered Darrell was playing him. She looked to the side and saw a sniper stationed on the opposite side of the runway. A glance to the right confirmed more guys closing in wearing SWAT uniforms. She didn't know these people, which meant they didn't know her and probably not Darrell. If he was on the plane with William, the jerk could push him out, instigating fire. If the men thought their lives were in danger, they'd shoot first and ask questions later. She had to warn them about Darrell possibly being trapped on that plane.

Shelby crouched over the crate and slid against the wall until she reached the opening. Staying low, she crawled out and to the side. The movement in her peripheral caught her.

"Childers?" she said, shocked. What was Carson doing here? Had her team been on location all weekend preparing to take down William and Mason?

Then she looked to the side and saw a furious-looking Mason closing in on Carson. Oh no! On instinct, she jumped from the side of the building and screamed a warning to Carson before Mason could take him out. She moved slower than she wanted, her body still not completely cooperating with her commands.

Someone fired.

Mason roared.

Shelby fell to the ground, fire lancing her back as gunshots erupted around her. She grabbed her chest as she wheezed for the air that had been knocked out of her upon impact.

Footsteps pounded toward her as she squeezed her eyes against the pain. She must've landed on a paver or something. She just hoped it was a cavalry coming to pull her out of harm's way and not the enemy.

Someone dropped beside her. "Look at me."

*Fuck.* She knew that voice.

She opened her eyes, though she knew it was Mason who'd gotten to her before her teammates. She had to have been still pretty drugged because he sounded too worried for her brain to understand. He should be furious and trying to get away, not running toward her.

"Hurry up!" he yelled above her and looked at her again. "Let's roll you to your side. I need to see how bad it is."

She took in a rattling breath as he rolled her and coughed, struggling to get in enough oxygen. She tasted copper and wiped her mouth, her hand coming way streaked with blood. "I'm hit," she tried saying. Her body began to shake as pain bloomed. She'd been shot.

"I know, baby. Help is coming. Hold on. Hold on. You're going to be okay."

"Why...you...here?" She tried asking why he was there with her and not on the plane trying to escape. She didn't want him fleeing justice, but she didn't understand why he hadn't tried getting away.

"I came for you, baby."

Another man dropped next to her with Carson and Viola taking up places around her. The guy ripped the back of her shirt and started doing something to her back, but she couldn't see. Mason had grabbed her hand and held it as he watched her intently. She gasped at the pain and coughed more blood when the sudden intake of air triggered it.

"Darrell...have to get him...on plane."

"Don't worry about Darrell. Rick has gone after him. He won't let him get away. Just focus on you," Viola said, squeezing her upper arm.

Shelby glanced at her and frowned at the words. They didn't make sense. "Get away?" she breathed.

Viola's gaze jerked to Carson. "Don't worry about that now, Landry," he said. "Just know that Showalter here isn't a criminal. He was the mole. He's been working with Jerome Parker to take down William Baxter."

"What?" she asked, looking at Mason again and hacking up more blood.

"We'll explain everything later. Right now, I want you to quit talking, breathe slowly, and relax," Mason said calmly.

"This will help," the man said behind her. Warmth spread throughout her body, deadening the pain, making her eyes heavy.

"No. He gave me something already." Though she wasn't sure if the words came out. She didn't want to pass out, medicated or otherwise. She wanted to ask questions, find out what the hell Viola meant about Darrell, and get clarification on what Carson said about Mason. She felt confused. Surely she hadn't heard them right. She jumbled their words round in her head, trying to find the correct order of them so she could comprehend what they'd tried telling her.

She shut her eyes on a sigh. Just thinking about everything was taking too much effort. The areas where hands touched her began to tingle and a sense of flying came over her.

The last thing she felt was Mason's lips against her ear as he said, "I've got you, baby."

Whether or not it was her confused mind still playing tricks on her, she knew how true those words really were.

If only he knew that.

# CHAPTER TWENTY-THREE

*"Carl O'Brian is alive."*

*"Mason Showalter is the whistleblower."*

*"Darrell Tobin is dead."*

Bits of conversations Shelby had heard while in her hospital bed after having surgery had flitted through her mind every day since. A lot of time had passed, but she still hadn't been able to accept the truths she'd learned that day. And after two weeks in the hospital and another three weeks at home, Shelby wasn't back to her old self physically either. Doctors had told her it'd take at least six weeks, possibly longer, to heal, but she didn't like those terms. She was going crazy being cooped up at home with her thoughts. Her memories.

*"Darrell Tobin is dead."*

*"Mason Showalter is the whistleblower."*

*"Dave sold you out."*

That last bit of information had come from Viola. She'd been fighting tears when she'd confessed this, and Shelby had known her friend had felt at fault. She wasn't. Shelby refused to accept that, but no matter how she'd tried telling

Viola this, she wouldn't listen. She would close up and change the subject. All Shelby had gotten from her were the facts. Dave had a gambling problem she hadn't known about. He'd gone to Mason and sold him the truth about their identities to pay a large gambling debt. Viola had wanted to pay Mason back the money Dave had extorted from him, but the man wouldn't hear of it. She loved him a little more for that, not that it helped Viola. The woman had gone through more these last five weeks than Shelby could even dream. Sure, she'd been shot and was healing, albeit slowly. Viola, on the other hand, was uprooting her life, getting divorced from the man she thought she knew, and living with Shelby temporarily. The F and B case had changed them both.

*"Darrell Tobin is dead."*

Her eyes watered at the reminder. She and Viola hadn't been the only ones affected by the case. The knowledge that Darrell was a traitor to the bureau hurt more than the physical pain she'd gone through. She hadn't believed it at first. The scenario she'd devised after waking in the limo had felt more believable. Her instincts couldn't have been that far off. When she'd voiced this to Rick, he'd gently but firmly stated that it was her sense of preservation that had concocted it. Her heart hadn't wanted to believe a man she trusted with her life would be so willing to throw hers away for money. He'd been right. She hadn't wanted to believe it.

In the end, the man Darrell had been working with was the man who shot him, though he was now in custody and wasn't talking. The hope was that Darrell had come to his senses in that dark hour, when they'd been surrounded, that he'd tried convincing William they should turn themselves in. It was a conversation that could've happened after Shelby had been shot. Ballistics matched the bullet in her lung to the gun found in William's possession. But that theory was just that—wishful thinking. William had lawyered up right away. Even if he had been the one to shoot her, any attorney worth a dime would pin it on Darrell. Yeah, Shelby and her team didn't know what really happened in Darrell's final moments, and they probably never would.

Shelby hadn't gone to her mentor's funeral. She'd still been in the hospital when he'd been laid to rest, but she still mourned him. No matter what kind of man he'd turned out to be, she still wept for him, for the loss of a friendship. A loss that would've happened whether he'd lived or died.

The fact that Carl O'Brian was alive made things easier. She was grateful he hadn't been killed and beyond relieved that Mason hadn't been behind any ill dealings surrounding the man.

*"Mason Showalter is the whistleblower."*

That revelation had stunned her. It explained why her teammates hadn't tackled him to the ground when he'd rushed toward her the day she'd been shot. But the knowledge made her feel even guiltier over using him on the case. She'd had a job to do. One she'd been thrust into without proper understanding, but she'd known full well she would be lying to the man. No matter how relieved she was at his innocence, it didn't erase the fact that she'd played him.

She had been played, too. Darrell had monopolized her friendship for financial gain. The FBI had used her and her relationship with her mentor to take him out.

Shelby couldn't put Mason in that same category, though, as those who'd played her. He'd had no idea of her true identity, so he'd had no need to inform her about anything. She'd been a stranger to him—at first. No man would relay that kind of information to someone he was just getting to know. He'd been a private man, not easily accepting of others, but she believed he would've told her about working with the SEC in his own time.

Because he had trusted her. She knew he had, but that acceptance had been built on a foundation of lies. It was a false connection, never real, and she couldn't fault him his anger. One day, he might learn to forgive her, but the damage was done. Regardless of what happened between them, one thing bothered her that she couldn't ignore. Something maybe her brother could help her with. It would be a long shot, and it wouldn't change anything, but—

"You should frame that," Viola said from behind her, drawing her out of her thoughts. Shelby looked over her shoulder at the woman. Her eyes were still haunted, her skin pale, her body thinner than it had been before she'd learned the truth about her husband. Things Shelby didn't point out. She knew Viola was aware, but she also knew her friend would bounce back. She was going through a different type of mourning—the death of her marriage—and when she reached that stage of grief where she learned to accept what was happening in her life, she'd grab it by the balls again and steer it in the direction she wanted. That was how Viola was.

Shelby looked at the get-well card she'd gotten while in the hospital. It had come with the roses Mason had sent her.

She still had those, too, couldn't bring herself to throw them out. They were over a month old, dead and brittle, a metaphor of their relationship. Still he'd given them to her. The card attached had simply stated, "Get well soon. Love, Mason." She'd traced over the L-word so many times the card was browning in that spot. It was a common salutation among people who were close. She knew better than to read anything into it. But logic didn't always dictate one's actions.

"Maybe I will," she said, tossing it onto the kitchen table. The flowers were in her room, hiding like she'd been doing.

Viola sat at the chair across from her. "I found an apartment."

Shelby sighed. "You know there's no rush. I might not show it very well, but I like the company."

She nodded. "I know, but it's time. The divorce papers were filed two weeks ago, and he's already filed his response, not contesting anything. He's agreed to refinance the house in his name and use the equity to pay off our bills."

"Are you sure you want to give up your house?"

"Yeah. Too many memories. I need a fresh start. Besides, the apartment doesn't allow pets, which will keep me from adopting a bunch of cats. I've been finding them too adorable lately, and if I kept the house, it'd be filled with them."

Shelby chuckled. "I wouldn't let you turn into a cat lady. I'd make you draw the line at two."

"A true friend." Viola's smile was short-lived, but it was a start.

She hadn't told Viola she liked her being here. She didn't want her to feel obligated to hang around longer than she wanted, but Shelby did like the company. After everything that happened, she felt confused, lost, and having someone around helped her from drowning in her sorrow. Okay, she'd been dog paddling in it for weeks, but she'd stayed afloat because Viola had been here.

"You know. You're my best friend," Shelby told her. Viola's eyes twinkled as she smiled again.

"Is that because your brother doesn't count?" she asked

with a smile, and Shelby noticed a subject-change when she saw it. "That hunk of a man can come visit you anytime he wants."

Axle had stayed with her the first few nights she was out of the hospital, but he'd gotten called in on assignment. If Viola hadn't been here to watch her, she was sure he'd defied orders to stay by her side.

"He's too bossy to count." Shelby shrugged and got back to what she'd been trying to say. "If you get this apartment you're looking at, I want to hang out more. I think I'm going to demand it, actually," she teased.

Viola snorted. "I might be able to accommodate you."

"No might about it, girl. If I have to lure you out under the pretense of adopting kittens, I will."

"Oh, that's evil." They both chuckled. "Does that mean you're not moving to Mayflower and starting a new life there?"

Shelby chewed her lip. The idea held more appeal than she wanted to admit. Her phone buzzing saved her from having to answer, though. "Ah, it's my brother." She'd already had a missed call from him earlier.

Viola smirked and got up.

"Hello?"

"It's about time you picked up."

"Hey, I tried calling you yesterday." She rolled her eyes and leaned back. "And I'm allowed to shower without taking my phone into the bathroom. How was your mission?"

He grunted. "I can't talk about that. What's the deal with Showalter?"

"I'm doing okay, by the way," she grumbled, since he hadn't started off by asking something related to her injury.

"Shelby, answer the question. What's going on with Showalter?"

"Um, what do you mean?" she hedged.

"Don't play coy with me. When I was there, the man lorded over you like a hired bodyguard, and you were too drugged up for me to get the story."

She hadn't seen Mason since the day she'd been shot. Viola later told her that he'd stayed at the hospital that first week, often sitting by her side when she'd been heavily medicated and sleeping, but once he was convinced she'd make a full recovery, he'd left. He hadn't tried contacting her either, and she knew better than to reach out to him.

"I'm still on medication." It was the truth, but she wasn't on an IV drip anymore. "And you expect me to believe you haven't already dug into him?"

"Your FBI team didn't tell me dick. Hid behind red tape."

"And of course you didn't try other avenues."

He sighed. "I spoke to Hunter Anderson, former mafia and current member of a mercenary group the feds had you infiltrate before putting you undercover at a sex club. Jesus Christ, Shelby."

She winced. "The mercenaries worked for the government. They're good guys—"

"Oh, I bet. It's why they hide behind a car shop."

She wasn't surprised he got the information from one of the guys from the garage, although why it was Hunter, she didn't know. She figured Bear would've been the one to update him. Not that it mattered. "Axle, I'm not going to dog those men. They're great guys. Hearts of gold. And loyal to a fault. That's more than I can say about everyone on my *other* team." Because she was part of the Bang Shift now. Maybe not on their payroll, but the bond was there.

"I'm sorry about your friend, Darrell, but if he wasn't already dead, he would be."

"I know. But you would've had to have gotten in line to take him out."

"That's cute you think so."

She scoffed, but she also knew he'd have done whatever necessary to keep her safe.

"He's not just an informant," Axle said, no longer talking about Darrell, and not really asking.

"No," she answered anyway. "But it's a mess, and I'm not ready to go into it all."

"Did he hurt you?" Axle asked in that deadly calm voice of his.

"It's the other way around. I'm still coming to terms with everything, and that includes what I did to Mason."

"Mason," he muttered.

"Yeah, Mason. In fact, he's the reason I called you last night."

"Why do I get the feeling I'm not going to like this?"

Instead of answering him, she said, "He has a brother. Name's Caleb Showalter. When I was, er, working on the case, he said his brother was dead, but our records indicated he's a POW. Now, we didn't talk about families back then, and I haven't talked to him since I was shot. He could've just said that so he didn't have to go into the long explanation. It could be nothing, but I'd like for you to see what you can find out."

"You're with the FBI, Shel. You have more clearance than I do."

"That's not true. You're much more important in the military than I am to the government. Besides, the military protects its own. If it's nothing, you'd be able to find that out much easier than I could. If there's a cover up or something,

I don't know, more to this…you'd be able to figure that out, too."

"Why?"

"Because I owe him."

"You don't owe him shit. You had a job to do."

"If I wanted to hear the same thing I've heard a hundred times already, I would've called my boss, not my brother."

"Do you think it'll make a difference? Whatever happened between you two, do you think it'll change anything?"

"No, and I wouldn't want it to." She sighed. "If his brother is still alive, I want him to know, but that doesn't mean I'd go running to tell him. I don't care how he learns the truth, just that he knows it. It's the least I can do." She took a deep breath to continue, but gasped at the pain.

"Damn it, Shelby." She wasn't sure if he was talking about her request or the sound she'd just made.

"Just look into it. That's all I'm asking." The doorbell rang then. "I gotta go."

"I'll get it," Viola called out. "Go back to guilt-tripping your brother while secretly mooning over your card."

She was going to kill her.

"What did she say?" he asked.

"Nothing. Love you, bub."

"Love you, too, sis."

Shelby hung up and yelled, "It better not be a kitty delivery. The pet deposit here is outrageous."

She heard Viola's giggle, and her heart felt lighter. Partly for Viola, since it seemed her friend may be testing that stage of acceptance already. The other part was probably because of her brother and his willingness to help with Mason. Axle hadn't said he'd do it, but she knew her brother.

Soft voices filtered into the kitchen, so Shelby got up, put her glass in the sink, and headed to the living room to see who was here.

She didn't make it past the doorway.

"Mason," she breathed. His gaze left Viola's to find hers.

He shoved his hands in his pockets and rocked back on his heels. "Hi, Shelby."

"I..." What was he doing here?

"I was just telling Viola to stop trying to find excuses as to why she should pay me back." He looked at Viola again. "It's not happening."

"Oh. You came to talk to her." Shelby's already pounding heart seized.

He cocked his head to the side. "No, I came to talk to you. This one here is just using the opportunity to convince me again."

"It's not right," Viola said, fisting her hands.

"No, it's not," Mason agreed. "It's not right what Dave put you through, and I have no intention of making you pay for his mistakes." He licked his lips and looked at Shelby again. "Can we talk?"

Viola sighed. "I was just going to the grocery store." She grabbed her purse and car keys and reached for the door.

Shelby couldn't resist one more barb. "Stay away from the cat food."

Viola laughed as she left.

"Do I want to know what that's about?" Mason asked with a crooked smile.

"Just doing my part to keep her from turning into the stereotypical spinster cat lady."

"Ahh." He nodded.

They stood there, looking at each other, the silence thickening.

Shelby cleared her throat. "Sorry. Would you like something to drink?" She motioned for the couch, feeling like a completely inept hostess, and an emotional hot mess.

"No, but thank you," he said, sitting on the couch. She still stood in the doorway of the kitchen, knees locked, unsure of what to do. He patted on the spot beside him, making the decision for her. "Come here, Shelby." The authority in his voice had her moving before he delivered the command to go to him.

Now seated beside him, she couldn't stop herself from mentally cataloging all his features again, the flecks of gold in his brown eyes, the sexy wave of his hair at his forehead, the intoxicating cologne he sometimes wore. She should ask him the brand, so she could buy a case of the stuff. It would help her remember him when he was gone.

He took her sweaty hand into his, his thumb caressing her skin. "How are you healing?"

She swallowed and wondered how to best answer that.

The truth. She doubted she'd see him very often, if at all, but she'd decided he'd always get the truth from her now.

"According to the doctors, I'm healing at the normal rate. I can take deep breaths without sharp pains now, but I still ache. They won't release me back to work until I've completely healed." She shrugged and looked away, emotions coming to the surface, feelings she'd kept from everybody since the shooting. "If I decide to go back," she whispered. She hadn't even told Viola her thoughts about quitting.

Mason touched her chin and guided her gaze back to his. "What do you mean?" he asked softly.

"I—" She blew out a calming breath to get a stranglehold on her emotions. The last thing she wanted to do was cry in front of him. "I'm not sure I want to be an agent anymore." It had been on the tip of her tongue to tell Viola that earlier when she'd asked about Mayflower.

"Why?"

Even though she was facing him, she couldn't look into his eyes. She focused on the ceiling instead. "I don't know about anything anymore. I trusted Darrell with my life and he—" She blinked several times, forcing the tears back. When she felt somewhat in control, she looked at Mason again. "I feel lost. I don't know any other way to explain it."

It wasn't just what Darrell had done to her. It was how the bureau used her—putting her into an impossible situation on one hand, and lying to her on the other. She also felt lost when it came to Mason, though she didn't want to go into those details.

"That's understandable. I think that's a normal reaction when someone you care about breaks your trust."

Her eyes shut, blocking out his pain, but a single tear escaped anyway. He swiped it away.

"I'm so sorry," she breathed. "I didn't...I mean..."

"Look at me." When she did, he put his hand back on her cheek and caressed her face. "I'm sorry, too. I confronted you out of anger, used the trust you had in me to exact punishment. That was uncalled for."

"Please don't take any blame for that. You were angry."

"I was fucking furious." He narrowed his eyes.

"As you should be," she whispered. He had every right to feel the way he did. She did not begrudge him that.

"I was, but I'm not now." She gaped at him. How could that be? Maybe he was at his own stage of acceptance like Viola was discovering. Shelby wasn't there yet. Her life was a mess, and she didn't have anyone to blame but herself... and depending on who she asked, she had no blame to harbor. She had a job to do, like her brother had just told her and like Rick had said several times, reminding her of the professional she was. "I've been thinking about a lot of things the last month, and what I keep coming back to is the fact I don't want to be angry anymore. I've taken the time I needed to accept what has happened."

She stared at him, dumbfounded.

"There are still some things I need to work out, but I'd like your help answering the questions that have been plaguing me."

"You can ask me anything you want." She knew she should show more discretion, but she didn't care.

"Have you ever been topped before?"

She blinked a few times, processing his question. This wasn't the direction she'd anticipated this conversation going. Slowly shaking her head, she said, "No. You were my first."

"Did you like it?"

"Yes." When she'd parsed out all the reasons why she'd been set on this path and all of the emotion that evolved, looking only at what she experienced sexually, she knew at the core it had been a freeing experience.

He seemed to mull that over. "Is it something you want to continue?"

With him? The thought slammed into her. This was a scenario she hadn't allowed herself to even think about. Was he specifically asking about the two of them or was this more of a hypothetical question? She couldn't be sure. She settled on the truth again without staking any claims. "I've thought a lot about it."

He smiled. "Avoiding the question, pet?"

Her heart skittered at the endearment. "No, Sir. It's one of the many things I've felt lost about."

"I see. Well, you were...*are*...a lovely submissive. As much as I've tried putting you out of my mind, I just can't. I find myself not wanting to try anymore. Where does that leave us?" he asked softly.

"I don't know." That response felt so inadequate.

"I guess what I need to know is if things were real for you. You know they were for me, Shelby. But I also know you were assigned to act a certain way. Was it all just a job for you? If I was, you can tell me. I think I'm ready to hear that answer."

She shook her head. "No, it wasn't just a job for me," she murmured.

The breath he let out was long. "Okay then. When you're ready, I'd like to start over."

"What does that mean?" she asked slowly. Was he offering to redo her scenes, letting her explore the lifestyle without the cloak of her job? Or was he suggesting they try a real relationship? She would not assume anything.

"It means," he said softly. "That I love you."

She gasped as the tears she'd been fighting since he'd arrived rushed out. He pulled her into his arms and stroked her back, carefully avoiding her healing wound. "I don't expect you to love me back. Not yet. Who knows, maybe too much as happened between us. All I'm saying is I want to try, see if we can make it work, starting with a new foundation."

Shelby pulled away. "I-I—"

"Shhh." He placed a finger over her lips. "Don't say anything. Take some time to think about it." He pulled away and fished in his pocket, retrieving a key. He placed it in her hand and closed her fingers around it. "I'm taking an extended vacation. I've decided I needed more relaxation and less time working in my life. I'll be back in a few weeks, but if you decide you need to get some fresh air, you can join me at any time. No pressure."

She was too shocked to say anything.

He chuckled. "I could always blackmail Viola into making you come to the island. I have a feeling she'd be willing to do anything I asked to square away the debt she believes she owes." His smile ended on a sigh, humor leaving. "But I don't want any more trickery around us. No matter how tempting the idea is to me."

"I'll think about it," she finally said. He nodded and leaned in. Her heart leapt when his face got closer to hers. When he kissed her forehead instead of her lips, another ache formed at how tender the gesture had been.

Mason stood, pulled out his wallet, and gave her a card with the address and details how to get there. "Just in case."

She watched him leave, the words she'd tried saying earlier whispering into the lonely air. "I love you, too."

# CHAPTER TWENTY-FOUR

MASON SIPPED his scotch as he took in the beauty of the turquoise ocean surrounding him, wondering why he hadn't taken the plunge to buy a property like this before now. It wasn't as if he didn't have the money. No, time had always been his inhibitor. He'd joked to Parker that he'd wanted the feds to send him on a nice vacation after his duty taking down William Baxter was over. Not that he'd honestly expected an all-expense paid trip, or the time to go on one, but deep down he knew he needed the serenity of palm trees and saltwater.

The events over the last several weeks spurred him into fulfilling that need.

Because of Viola's guilt over the money Mason had given Dave for information on Shelby, Jedrek had talked Jerome into getting the government to reimburse him. The excuse for the expense had officially been identified as necessary for the take down of William Baxter. Pretty vague, but they'd needed validation to get past the red tape for the reimbursement to be approved. Mason didn't need the money. He'd invested wisely over the years and had stashed millions in several *legal* accounts. But Viola had felt obligated to pay him back even though she didn't have that kind of money. It was her guilt that had propelled Jedrek into action. If the government paid Mason back, then he wasn't out the money, and Viola wouldn't have to feel bad about her soon-to-be ex using Mason the way he had.

Jedrek didn't do it for Mason. He did it for Viola. He knew what Jedrek's motivation had been. The man acted out of character when it came to that woman. Mason still didn't see anything coming of it. Viola wasn't into the lifestyle, and his business partner hadn't overcome his demons. She was a distraction for him. One he'd tire of like everything else in his life.

But what did Mason know about women?

He did thank Jedrek for helping him out with Viola. If Jerome hadn't sworn him to secrecy for now, Mason would've told Viola about it when he'd seen her at Shelby's apartment. The SEC agent wanted to wait until the media storm surrounding the firm died down before mentioning it to anyone.

And what a political nightmare the past month had been! If Fieldstein and Baxter survived without imploding in on itself, it'd be a fucking miracle. Accusations had been thrown around, lots of finger pointing commenced. William hadn't acted alone, and Mason was sure more indictments would follow. The frenzy wouldn't end anytime soon, so Mason would keep his side of the secrecy bargain. Besides, he figured Jedrek wanted to be the one to announce it to Viola. He wouldn't take away his friend's chance at being a hero in the eyes of a woman he was so obviously attracted to —no matter how doomed that attraction was.

Since Mason had been forty thousand dollars richer— he would eat the other ten grand since Dave hadn't asked for it—he'd decided to do something constructive with it rather than moving it back into an account and letting it sit there. His first thought had been to take a nice vacation, but an online search had pulled up an island property that was for sale, not for rent, and he'd fallen in love with the idea of owning a piece of paradise. He got in contact with a local real estate agent to gather some listings. The next week, he'd flown out to look at some and had made an offer on this place. It wasn't overly large, but it was private with a wall of glass that pushed open, extending the living area out into the open. The money he'd gotten from the government was obviously nowhere near enough to cover a fraction of the costs, but that didn't matter. It had been what pushed him into taking the plunge.

After visiting Shelby, he was positive he wanted to give their relationship a chance. He'd had to work hard to expel the bitter feelings of betrayal because, in the end, if it hadn't been for her assignment, he would have never met her. His heart had conceded it had been worth it. It had taken his ego longer to accept that fact. But he did, completely. When he'd been ready, he'd gone to her, and she'd been so beautiful. Hell, he couldn't remember if he'd told her that. Injured, without makeup, comfy clothes—she'd been a goddess to him. He had missed her terribly and hated the last image he had of her was that of her weakened body, sleeping in that damn hospital bed.

He was pretty sure he hadn't told her how pretty she was, but he did tell her that he loved her. Because he did, more than anything. He'd realized that before Dave divulged his info, and the knowledge hadn't quelled his feelings at all. If he hadn't loved her, he wouldn't have hurt as much when he had learned the truth.

Once he saw her, it was hard leaving things unresolved.

He'd tried enticing her to join him on his vacation, but after three weeks without any word from her, he wasn't holding out hope. That was okay. He didn't get where he was today by being impatient. In a week, he'd be back stateside, and he would decide how to proceed with her then. He wasn't ready to give her up, but he also knew she'd been through a lot, so much so that she'd contemplated changing her career. If she needed time, he'd give it to her. Three weeks ago, he'd been prepared to walk away if what had developed between them had been one-sided. Now he knew that wasn't the case, and he wasn't willing to walk anymore. Time, he could give her.

His glass of scotch almost empty, he hoisted himself up from the chaise lounge on the patio and turned.

The doorknob on the front door jiggled, and he froze in the opening, a fucking knot in his throat. There was only one person who knew about this place other than his agent.

She came. She fucking came to him.

He should go to her, but he was too stunned to move just yet. He stood there, watching as Shelby struggled with the door and her bags.

Once she was inside, he forced himself to move into the house from the outside. She dropped her things by the door and turned, gasping when she saw him.

"You scared me," she said, hand over her heart...*his* heart—or it would be one day.

He smiled at her when he leaned over and put his empty glass on the coffee table, not taking his eyes off her. When he stood at full height again, he cocked his head to the side. "This is a private residence, ma'am. If anyone should be surprised at the presence of another, I think that should be me."

She blinked, hesitating before propping a hand on her

hip. "Well, a friend of mine suggested I come." She smiled. "And a blonde demon of a friend threatened to adopt twelve kittens and stuff my pillows with catnip if I didn't partake in the offer."

"I think I like this blonde demon friend of yours."

"She has her moments." She winked and stepped closer to him, extending her hand. "Hi. We haven't met. My name is Shelby Landry. I work sixty hours a week as a linguistics expert for the FBI. I speak five languages and two dialects of Chinese, but not all fluently. I've been studying Middle Eastern languages for about three years now since there's a shortage in that area, and it would mean more money."

Hmmm...he liked this little playful side of her. "Wow, I know a little Japanese since we have an office in Japan, but that's it." He shook her hand and continued to hold it. "Any other specialties up your sleeve?"

Smiled. "I can lube your chassis better than anybody you know."

He barked out a laugh.

"And you are?" she asked with a sexy as hell inquisitive look.

"Oh, my apologies. My name is Mason Showalter. I'm an investment banker, hedge fund manager, finance geek, and part-time accountant. Though, I don't like adding that last title to my list of professional responsibilities."

"Well, it's a pleasure to meet you, Mason." She slid her hand away from his, but that coy little smile had his dick twitching...and his name on her lips? Damn, he fucking loved that.

"Pleasure's *my* specialty." He winked at her before walking away and snatching his glass from the table. "I'm not sure where your friend's at Shelby—can I call you Shelby?" She moved toward the couch.

"Please." She nodded and sat.

"Good. As I was saying, I'm not sure where your friend is, but you're more than welcome to stay here at my place. It came furnished, but I'll be replacing a lot of it."

Her playful facade fell briefly. "This is yours?" She glanced around, almost nervously.

"Mmm-hmm."

He was fairly certain she knew his net worth. That information had to have been in one of the government files she studied, but reading it on paper and seeing it in real life were two different things.

She seemed to compose herself and shrugged. "My family owned a garage, so it's sorta the same thing."

"Ah yes, I met Axle. Nice fellow." He took a sip of his drink, which was mainly water from the melted ice. "Told me how skilled he was at torture and hiding bodies."

"Oh, I'm sure he did." She rolled her eyes. "Although, he failed to tell me about that."

"He seems the type to have lots of secrets."

"He's a SEAL. Comes with the territory. Although, maybe that's just something that runs in the family," she said, trailing off as she glanced around the room again.

He knew what she was getting at, but old secrets needed to stay where they were. In the past.

Mason walked away, letting her look her fill and giving her a moment to take it all in. "Would you like a glass of Scotch? I'm sorry, I don't have any wine or beer," he asked over his shoulder before heading into the kitchen.

"I've never had Scotch, but I'll have one if you're having one. You can experience my first time."

He chuckled at her innuendo as he grabbed another glass, put ice in both, and poured two fingers in each. "I'm honored to be your first," he said as he walked back into the living room, stopping dead in his tracks.

Shelby stood by the couch minus her clothes. Completely naked.

"What if I want you to be my only?" she asked softly, humor gone. He swallowed passed the tightness in his throat and made his way back to her. He placed the glasses on the table and cupped her face with both of his hands.

"You have me, Shelby. You already have me." He kissed her then because her lips were too tempting not to.

She squirmed closer to him, rubbing her deliciously nude body against his, making him regret the barrier of clothing he still wore.

He'd soon fix that.

Mason bent and lifted her into his arms. They needed a bed, and he was grateful he hadn't purchased a mansion with a lot of stairs. The master bedroom was just down the hall, facing the ocean. His lips never left hers as he made his way to the bedroom while still holding her to his chest. He gently placed her on the bed and stood back, quickly shucking his clothes. When he'd finished, he crawled up beside her and rested his head in his hand while his free one explored her body. She trembled at his touch, and he loved that she was so responsive to him. It made him want to wring out other responses from her, too.

"Hands above your head," he softly ordered.

Her gaze darted to him before she complied.

He trailed the tip of a finger along the curve of her breast. She sucked in a breath, arching into the touch.

"I want to play with you, Shelby. Will you let me?"

He watched her swallow. "Yes, Maso—*Master*."

His hand stilled, and he looked at her. "No, Shelby," he gently corrected. "You were right the first time. I like hearing my name on your lips. I want you to say it freely in and out of the bedroom."

She frowned, and he resisted smoothing the wrinkle between her brows—just barely.

"I don't understand," she finally said.

He smiled ruefully at her. "Me either, pet. I've always expected the respect that title affords me, but you...you're different. I've never allowed another sub to call me by my first name, but you're not like anybody else."

She nodded slowly, but he saw the wheels turning as she thought it over. "But you call other subs *pet* and the other Masters at the club sometime called me that. Shouldn't I get a title from you that makes me stand out above the others?"

He leaned down and kissed her softly, thrilled with her train of thought. He'd love for her to be singled out among all the subs at the club. He just wasn't sure how she felt about all of that. Yes, she'd come to him, and she'd implied she only wanted him, but they had yet to talk about everything. He would have engaged in that much-needed conversation in the living room if she hadn't taken her clothes off first.

He'd just have to concentrate harder to get the details out now, he thought as he reluctantly ended their kiss.

"That depends on how much you want from me, Shelby," he said, and kissed the top of her head, unable to keep his lips off her. "I know you wouldn't be here if you didn't want me to a degree. I'm okay taking things as slow as necessary until you're—"

She reached up and silenced him with the tips of her fingers. "I love you, Mason. I have for a while. I would've told you that day you came to my apartment, but you told me to take some time to think. I've done what you've asked, and it doesn't change what's inside my heart."

"Shelby," he breathed, taking her mouth with the force of his emotions. He knew she cared, but he'd had no idea how much. God, she loved him. She *loved* him! His kiss was hard, punishing and rewarding...regret for the past and acceptance of the future. He kissed her until he had to pull away to take in air because, with his mouth on hers, breathing had become less of a priority.

"To be clear," she said breathlessly, rubbing his cheek. "I want you in my life as my lover *and* as my Dom. I might not want to try everything there is in the lifestyle, and I can't make any promises that I'll even like what we explore, but I want to experience that with you."

He stroked her cheek, her bottom lip.

"We will learn our limits together, Shelby. But tonight will be about healing. I don't want to erase what has happened because we wouldn't be here today without it, but I want to start fresh. What's done is done, and I have no desire to reenact the four scenes we did before just to replace those memories. In time, we may do some of that again, with me as your only Dom." He arched an eyebrow at her, giving her a few seconds to absorb that. Mason didn't like sharing subs he played with. No way was he sharing the other half of his soul. "Each touch from here on out will be out of love. Nothing else. Only the love we have for each other."

"Mason," she whispered, a tear leaking over.

He swiped it away before taking the hand on his cheek and placing it above her head with the other. "I said heads above your head. Don't make me punish you on our night of healing, Shelby," he said, catching himself from calling her pet. It would be hard to break that habit.

"I'm so sorry, Master," she said playfully as she complied once again.

Memories of the night he met her, how she'd stirred his body into approaching her, solidifying her presence in his life, came to the forefront of his mind. He had told her to call him Master that night. He'd also informed her she'd be called pet. He no longer wanted her calling him that, and her request for a unique pet name mixed in with his thoughts. He licked his lips and gazed into her eyes, knowing right away how he'd address her from here on out.

It was after all, a night of new beginnings.

"Remember, call me Mason," he said softly as he stroked her cheek. "And for the rest of our lives, I will call you love."

# EPILOGUE

## THREE MONTHS LATER

Caitlin Cooper sat nervously as she gazed over the crowd. There were more people here than she'd anticipated, though a Bronze Star Ceremony was sure to be the talk of the town and draw even those normally uninterested in current affairs out of the woodwork. An event such as this garnered national attention, so in addition to the community and local politicians, there were also members of congress and congressional committees in attendance. It was odd to see such a mixed crowd and recognize so many of the people—both personally and professionally—especially when she hadn't been back in years. Not that she'd planned it that way, but as a news correspondent covering the War on Terror, her assignments rarely kept her on U.S. soil, much less in her old stomping grounds.

Of course, she had cut her journalism teeth covering local news in Arkansas when she'd been fresh out of college. She'd covered all kinds of stories from festivals to police beat stuff to, eventually, local politics. The turning point in her career had been when she'd interviewed the former governor regarding his stance on capital punishment when a bill to repeal the death penalty had failed to get the support it needed to pass. Though the story itself hadn't been the defining moment. In fact, it had nothing to do with it. She shivered at the memory and chaffed her arms as she thought back to the night when she'd reported live from the governor's mansion, and the cameraman had left to load some of his gear. She'd been alone with the governor's then-aide—and the current lieutenant governor—when he made an unwelcome pass at her. He hadn't crossed any official lines, but he hadn't reacted pleasantly to her rejection. Relief had flooded her when her colleague returned for the last case, and she'd quickly fallen into step beside him as he exited the building. If she were ballsy, she would go over to the scumbag now and thank him for the encounter, which had given her a kick in the pants to leave the comfort of her home state and reach for her dreams. Of course, he wouldn't be able to see it for the sarcasm it was. But she figured if she was going to get hit on in her own backyard by questionable politicians, there was no reason to fear the news outside of Arkansas.

*WWCAD?* That had been her internal mantra whenever she felt at a crossroads. *What would Christiane Amanpour do?* The woman inspired her. She was the reason Caitlin wanted to go into journalism. Within a month of leaving home, Caitlin had landed the job of a lifetime as a correspondent with a major twenty-four-hour news station in Atlanta. She'd paid her dues covering stories on the war, even had been sent on location to the Middle East multiple times, though not right in the action. Always on the outskirts of any real danger, tucked neatly within the press corp.

When Caitlin's gaze landed on a group of tough-looking

men entering the room, she quickly dropped it to her note-book as heat tinged the tips of her ears.

One of those guys was Hunter Anderson. There had been a time in her life, whenever he walked into a room, she'd swear her heart was going to jump right out of her chest. She'd had it bad for him growing up and should laugh now over her awkward adolescence and silly crush. If only she could tell her fourteen-year-old self that one day Hunter would be in the same room as her and *not* be the one making her heart pound like crazy. She was certain if she could actually go back in time and tell herself this, her *mini-me* would totally ignore her. Caitlin had spent an embarrassing amount of time in her bedroom listening to love songs on her iPod while staring at his picture in the yearbook...and that was when she hadn't gotten to spend the night with her best friend and Hunter's sister, Heather, sleeping under the same roof as him.

Oh how times had changed. She wasn't a little girl pining for a boy. The sight of Hunter did nothing to her anymore. Her racing heart and sweaty palms were because of the man standing next to him.

*Axle.*

Axle Landry. She knew there was no avoiding him today. Hell, he was the reason she was even here. Her starving gaze wouldn't be denied either, breaking her mental command not to stare at the man who'd stolen her heart in the desert. God, he still looked perfect, even though he walked with a cane now. His arms rippled as he leaned slightly into it as he moved. She remembered just how strong he was when he lifted her in the heat of passion just a few months ago, and she'd bet her life his battle injury wouldn't slow him down for a second. She had firsthand knowledge just how determined that man could be when he set his sights on something he wanted.

Several people in the crowd near him came over, shook his hand, and clapped him on the back, probably thanking him for his service to our country. She forced herself to look away, to look back down at her notepad. *Where's my pen?* Oh, the irony. She glanced around the floor beside her to check if it had fallen once she'd been seated. It wasn't there, and she huffed as she grabbed her bag to dig for a new one. She'd bought a new box of them when she'd gotten back to the States and had made a point to shove several in all of her cases and in her car, determined to never need to borrow another pen ever again. Instinctively, she looked up, knowing her hand would land on one without much effort.

As if he was her beacon, she looked to Axle. And froze.

He stared right at her.

Caitlin swallowed, locked in his hot gaze, instantly taken back to their time in the desert. She couldn't look away now even if she wanted to, and she didn't. She'd missed him so much since the last day she saw him...the day everything went to shit, and they'd been ripped apart by circumstance.

He took a step, then another, slowly making his way to the stage without breaking eye contact just yet. She wanted to run to him and help him walk, but she knew beyond any doubt he'd hate her even more if she offered him any assistance. He was a strong man.

He was a proud man.

And now, he was a disabled man. A former SEAL injured in the prime of his life. The career he carefully nurtured for so many years completely obliterated.

All because of her.

She should look away, make this easier on him, but she

couldn't. Not yet. Because she knew once this ceremony was over, that would be it. All hope would be lost.

She would never see Axle Landry again.

———

WANT MORE? **Axle,** the next book in The Bang Shift Series, is live!

———

HEY, y'all!

Thank you for reading my book. :) If you enjoyed it, I'd be very grateful for a review. If you didn't like it, then share that, too... as long as your review is honest, that's all that matters.

And ice cream. Ice cream matters, too.

Want the latest scoop? Be sure to sign up for my Newsletter! I mean, it's not as yummy as ice cream, but nothing ever is.


XOXO,
Mandy

# ALSO BY MANDY HARBIN

The Bang Shift Series

Brody

Hunter

Blade

Shelby

*Paranormal Romance*

Surrounded by Woods

Surrounded by Pleasure

Surrounded by Temptation

Surrounded by Secrets

*Young Adult written as M.W. Muse*

Goddess Legacy

Goddess Secret

Goddess Sacrifice

Goddess Revenge

Goddess Bared

Goddess Bound

# ABOUT THE AUTHOR

Mandy Harbin is a *USA Today* Best-selling author who loves creating stories that explore the complexities of everyday relationships...with some kissing thrown in. She is a Superstar Award recipient, Reader's Crown and Passionate Plume finalist, and has achieved Night Owl Reviews Top Pick distinction many times. She also writes young adult romance as M.W. Muse because teens like kissing, too.

After graduating college and working many years in technology, she threw caution to the wind and began studying writing at the UALR. Years of trashed manuscripts and rejections eventually led to contracts and representation. With over thirty books published, she now serves on the board of her local writing chapter.

Mandy lives in a small, Arkansas town with her husband and their bossy dog, enjoying her own happily ever after...with some kissing thrown in.

mandyharbin.com/newsletter
facebook.com/Author.MandyHarbin
instagram.com/mandy_harbin
bookbub.com/authors/mandy-harbin